*Will she say
"I do"
to the most
irresistible
passion...?*

The Bride Says Maybe

Prologue

Annefield
The Tay Valley
Scotland
February 8, 1807

When one is twelve, the whole sum of the world is captured in what can be seen and touched—and a word like "love" means nothing.

Lady Tara Davidson had not realized that someday her half sister Lady Aileen would wish to leave Annefield. It was their home—and a good one to Tara's way of thinking.

But Aileen had left. She was off to London with

their father to be presented in Court and to make her way into society.

She was off to find love because it is what Aileen said she wanted . . . and Tara was left behind.

Her sister was the only family that cared for her. She had the servants. Mrs. Watson and Ingold always kept an eye on her, and there were her tutors, but Aileen had been blood.

And now, what was Tara to do?

There would be no more evenings spent reading Shakespeare's plays aloud. No more sharing of secrets or receiving advice from the older sister she so adored.

"It may seem overwhelming now, but one day, you will want to do what I'm doing," Aileen had promised her. "Even if it means leaving people you care about."

Tara didn't believe that could be true. She'd never leave someone who idolized her as much as she did Aileen.

Aileen had hugged Tara close. "Please look after Folly for me."

"I'll ride that silly mare every day."

"Thank you. And, Tara, we shall see each other soon." With those words, Aileen gave Tara's shoulders one last squeeze and rushed from the room.

Tara had watched the coach pull away. She was accustomed to seeing her father drive off. He could barely stand staying four days in a row at Annefield.

He preferred his London friends to his daughters. His neglect had never hurt until the moment when he'd taken the only person Tara had trusted with him.

Loneliness filled her. She moped for days, praying Aileen would have a change of mind and return. She didn't.

Finally, she decided to go out to the stables and comfort the one other creature at Annefield who must miss Aileen as much as she did—Folly the mare. She had promised to ride the horse every day, and so she would.

Old Dickie, the head groom, greeted her. He'd been speaking to a young boy of about her age. He must be a new stable lad.

"Going for a ride, my lady?" Old Dickie asked.

"My sister wishes for me to keep Folly in good shape for when she returns."

"That's a good plan. Here now is a new stable lad. Ruary, meet your youngest mistress, Lady Tara Davidson."

The boy was shy. He pulled his hat off his head.

His mop of hair was the color of a crow's wind. Keeping his attention on the ground, he gave a quick bow.

"Where do you plan on riding, my lady?" Old Dickie asked.

"Over by the river," she answered.

"Aye, then Ruary, saddle that mare Folly in the first stall for my lady, then saddle Jester for yourself. You ride out with Lady Tara. Keep an eye on her and keep your distance."

"Yes, sir." The boy did his bidding, and soon Tara was in Folly's saddle and riding out of the yard. The boy on Jester kept a respectful length away from her.

Tara usually had someone accompanying her when she rode. Often it had been Aileen, but now it would probably be this lad. She didn't know what to make of him. He didn't look at her. She kicked Folly into a trot heading down Annefield's front drive. The lad followed.

Once they were out of sight of the house, Tara turned to him. "Do you want to race?"

Now she had his attention.

He looked up in surprise, and she was taken aback by his features. He had strong brows over sharp blue eyes. He would be tall. His arms and legs were too long right now, but she understood someday, he would fill out—just as people promised her that she would take on curves and the attributes to be desired. But right now she was thin and happiest on a horse than any place else in the world.

"I don't know that we should, my lady," he said. "That might not be wise."

"Oh, poo," Tara retorted, and set her heels to horse.

Folly bounded forward. She must have been in the need of the exercise because she did not hold back.

Tara heard a sound beside her and looked over to see Jester racing beside her. Ruary was laughing. He enjoyed this as much as she did.

Together, they bounded over several stone dykes and galloped across fields until, tired, they slowed to a walk—and Tara realized she had forgotten her troubles.

Furthermore, Ruary was not like the other stable lads. He was intelligent and quick-witted. That afternoon, the first of many, Tara found a friend.

And as so often happens, friendship grows into love.

In spite of their class differences, Ruary became very important to her. He filled the void Aileen's departure and subsequent marriage to some man in faraway London created. Tara could not imagine herself with any other man.

And then one day Tara's father sent for her to be presented in London.

She made a choice that day. Like her sister before her, she chose to leave the Highlands of her home for the unknown, sophisticated world of London. It was curiosity that made the decision, that and the hunger of youth to see what lies beyond.

She never forgot Ruary. She couldn't, but by the time she realized she should never have turned her back on love—it was too late.

And the cost was her very soul.

Chapter One

Annefield
The Tay Valley
Scotland
October, 1816

*Love was a mystery that Lady Tara Davidson was
certain she would never understand . . .*

Men wanted her. She'd been gifted by dint
of her birth with looks that appealed to them.
Indeed, gentlemen's circles had christened her
"the Helen of London" because of her beauty.
Many had declared themselves to her. These
men had claimed they loved her and yet, instinc-

tively, she'd known what they had really meant is that they lusted for her.

There was a difference.

She knew because she had once experienced love from the *only* man who had ever truly cared for her—Ruary Jamerson, her father's horse master.

And, in spite of his being beneath her station, she had loved him—

No, she corrected herself, I *love him*.

Currently. In the present. In spite of all that had happened between them. He was the person with whom she had been completely herself, and she rued the day she'd walked away from him.

In her defense, back in those days, some three years ago, she'd been too young to realize how rare a love like Ruary's was. He had begged her not to leave Annefield and this precious piece of Scotland that was her home, but even the dove must spread her wings.

Besides, Tara had been born to be presented to society. It was her destiny, and she'd excelled. She'd been introduced to the Court, feted, lauded, and even accepted a marriage offer from a very wealthy man who would have given her a life of untold luxury—until she realized in a moment of insight exactly what Ruary had meant to her.

Days before her marriage, Tara had done something no honorable young woman who wished society's acceptance would have thought of doing—she'd bolted. Knowing that her father would never let her cry off, she'd disguised herself in boy's clothing and run back to Annefield and Ruary as fast as she could travel. She had been willing to sacrifice everything for him.

But she'd returned too late. Ruary had chosen another. He'd fallen in love with someone else.

And the man she would have married? *That man* married her *sister* Aileen.

Humiliation is a bitter medicine . . . but a broken heart is devastating, especially once Tara realized this meant she was entirely alone. Furthermore, her former betrothed's father, the powerful duke of Penevey, was so angry at her for jilting his son, he was in the process of seeing that all doors in London were closed against her.

However, being ostracized by society was not Tara's worry. No . . . her fear was that all the joy, all the anticipation in her life was over. She'd always had that fear. Once a debutante chose her husband and married, it seemed as if she dropped off the face of the earth.

It was important to Tara to be relevant. She needed to matter. She did not like being ignored.

During Tara's second season, one in which she'd been busily toying with the affections of no fewer than six different men, a matron at a ball had warned Tara she was in danger of searching for the wrong thing in life.

"And what should I search for?" Tara had asked.

"A happy marriage," the matron had confided. "Be careful. In this world, we have one life; one love. Don't waste yourself on the trivial."

At the time, Tara had been insulted by the advice.

However, now those words rang prophetic.

One life; one love.

And she had lost hers when Ruary chose to marry Jane Sawyer. She would never love another man the way she did Ruary. Never.

If nunneries had still existed, Tara would have gone off to join one.

Instead, she found herself sitting in her bedroom, as when she was twelve, with nothing to entertain her other than the contemplation of the sameness of her days. What few friends she had were in London. She would remain here, unloved, until she was placed in her grave.

Tara could picture herself becoming an aged crone, an oddity in the valley's society. Children would wonder at her story, and their mothers would whisper her cautionary tale lest their own broods be as proud as Tara had once been. She was a female Icarus who had flown too close to the sun.

Yes, it was a very sad picture indeed—and not how she'd once imagined her life . . . *if* she'd stopped to think at all.

In fact, one of the challenges of the last few weeks was that she had been afforded too much time to consider all things. She now saw her defects of character and her shallowness, but how did one change? Especially if she was a woman with a bit too much spirit—?

A knock on the bedroom door interrupted her solitude.

Tara turned in her seat by the window. "Yes?"

"My lady," Mrs. Watson, the housekeeper's voice said from the other side, "your father wishes you to join him in the library."

Tara frowned but was not alarmed. "I'll be right down." Tara was glad she hadn't yet dressed for bed. Her father rarely spoke to her since the scandal, and perhaps this request was a sign his temper was cooling. She checked her reflection in the mirror, decided she appeared presentable enough and went downstairs. She rapped on the closed library door.

"Come in," was the abrupt order.

Tara turned the handle and entered the room.

Her sire sat at his desk, mounds of ledgers spread out before him. She rarely saw him attending his business. Aileen had been the one to keep the books and accounts in order.

A lamp had been lit, and its yellow light highlighted the sheen of sweat on the earl's pale complexion. He did not wear a jacket and had loosened his neckcloth.

The library's ever-present whisky decanter was no longer on the liquor cabinet but was on his desk, close at hand.

"You sent for me, Father?"

"I did. Sit."

She took one of the upholstered chairs around the small table in front of the hearth. A small coal fire burned in it. He came around from his desk, shut the door, and faced her, placing his hands behind his back.

He had once been an elegant man. He was tall, thin and had been known for his charm although his dissolute habits had caught up to him. He had a decided paunch, and his red hair had long ago turned to a mousy gray. Deep circles underlined his eyes.

For a long moment he stood, staring at her, his lips pressed together sternly.

Tara tried to sit still, to wait. At last, she could stand the silence no longer. "If you are going to berate me, start on it. I'm tired and ready for my bed—"

"We are done up," he interrupted.

"Done up?"

"Broke, gone, bankrupt."

The air seemed to leave the room. Tara forced herself to be calm. "How can that be? Didn't Mr. Stephens pay a marriage portion even though I was not the one he married?"

Her father's scowl deepened. "I spent it."

"*All* of it?"

He snorted his amusement. "It was gone before we left London. I'm damned fortunate he married one of my daughters, or my reckoning would be much worse than it is."

Tara grabbed the arms of the chair as if they were lifelines. "You spent *all* of it already?" she repeated in amazement. That had been a sizeable amount of money.

He nodded and sank into the chair opposite hers. "There were a couple of fights, and I wagered on the wrong men. Then there was that night I went out with Crewing. That night didn't end for two days." He gave an impatient wave of his hand as if he was done explaining and hopped up to cross to the desk and pour another whisky into a well-used glass. "I thought I could earn it all back. With luck, I would have."

"Oh, Father," Tara said, her stomach sinking.

"I have a bit of blunt. Stephens bought that mare from me. He overpaid, but the mare didn't bring in much." He drank deep, emptied the glass, and drew a breath before admitting, "And then it becomes worse."

"Worse? I don't think I can properly appreciate worse right now."

"You have to know," he said. His expression had softened into one of deep remorse, and she couldn't help but feel a bit sorry for him. Aileen had always been harder on him than she was. Aileen didn't trust him.

But Tara felt she must depend upon him, even for all of his notable faults. After all, he was her father.

"What is it I must know?" she asked.

"Someone has purchased my paper. He owns it all."

"Your paper?" Tara repeated.

"You can't gamble without money," he said as if stating the obvious. "I had to reclaim what I'd lost from bad wagers, so I borrowed from the money changers and a banker here and there. The man who now owns my debts came to me yesterday afternoon. He expects me to pay. He wants his money now."

"Can you speak to Blake?" she suggested, referring to her new brother-in-marriage.

Her father's laugh was angry. "No, there will be no money from that quarter. He told me he would not cover my debts. He said he'd see that food was on my table, but my losses were my concern."

Tara could not blame Blake. She forced herself to take a breath. "What of Annefield?"

His manner lightened. "It's entailed. There is no fear there. It will go to my heirs. I haven't lost that yet."

"But what have you lost?"

"It's what I *could* lose that matters. What I will lose."

"And what is that, Father?"

"My horses. I built my reputation on them.

They are my pride," he added. "It shames a man to know he could be so foolish."

"Is there anything else?"

"Aye, the land around Annefield."

"*What?*" Tara came to her feet. "Did you not say it was entailed?"

"The house is entailed, the rest is gone unless I can meet my obligations."

"Then we shall meet them." Here was something she could sink her teeth into. The case of blue devils that had been following her gave way to generations of pride. "We shall not lose the land. It is ours. Tell me all, Father. Between the two of us, we can create a plan. Who is this man who has purchased your paper?"

"Breccan Campbell."

It took a moment for Tara to overcome her shock. "The Black Campbell? The Beast of Aberfeldy? He has that much money?"

"He may be a giant oaf of a man, but he has a shrewd mind. He showed me the vouchers. They have my signature."

Tara found her temper. "I have *never* liked that man. I saw him not too long ago, and I thought him a brute. He was so rude."

"Rude?"

"Aye, of the boldest nature. I tell you *I welcome* this fight. So he thinks he can best us. Well, he is wrong."

"You are right, daughter," the earl said. "Although he did offer me a solution and one that I have accepted."

"What solution is that, Father?"

The earl sank onto the chair beside hers. He set his glass on the table. "Perhaps you made a better impression on him than he did on you?" His tone had grown hopeful.

"I don't care what he thinks of me. I don't like him. In fact, I detest him. Yes, that is how I feel. I have no desire to set eyes on him ever again." It felt good to be her old self.

The earl lifted his glass to his lips and started to drink before he realized it was empty. He lowered the glass, sighed heavily, and said, "That is unfortunate, my girl. Because the terms of receiving all my paper back is that you marry him."

"*Marry* him? *Me and the Beast of Aberfeldy*? Oh, no, that will not happen—"

"As a matter of fact it *will* happen, and it will be done in one hour's time. I've sent for the Reverend Kinnion. Campbell has secured a special license. You'd best go don your prettiest dress, daughter, you are about to become a bride. The groom will be arriving at any moment."

Tara sat dumbstruck. Pride now warred with hurt.

Did her father believe he could dismiss her so easily. That she would willingly allow him to *sell* her to a Campbell, and the Black one no less?

That was not going to happen.

She would show him. She would show all of them, including the duke of Penevey. She would return to London and make her own way. There was more to her than just a pretty face. It had taken intelligence to rule London the way she had, and she could do it again.

But she kept her thoughts hidden. She smiled at her father, and said, "Then please, excuse me, I need to change."

"That's my girl," her father said approvingly. "This will be a good marriage. You'll see. Aye, yes, you will be a Campbell, and it won't be bad. Well, maybe you won't be marrying into the 'respectable' branch of the clan, but you are a survivor, Tara. You will make them dance to your tune."

She smiled her answer, her thoughts filled with the image of picking up the whisky decanter and smashing it over his head.

Instead, she rushed up to her room. From the back of her wardrobe, she pulled out the boy's clothing that had enabled her to run away from London.

Now it would be disguise to return.

She would not marry a Campbell. Not now, not ever.

"Let my father marry him," she muttered to herself as she dressed. She wound her braid around her head and hid her vivid coloring under a wide-brimmed hat.

With more confidence and spirit than she'd shown for weeks, she opened her bedroom door and stole down the back stairs, heading for the stables and freedom.

Chapter Two

They rode through the mist with a purpose, three grim-faced men set on a mission, their hats pulled low over their brows against the weather.

In three hours, it would be darkest night.

In three hours, the tallest of them, Breccan Campbell, laird of the Black Campbells, would have a wife.

They reached the crossroad that would take them to Annefield, ancestral home of the Davidsons. Breccan started to turn his horse Jupiter up the road, but his uncle Jonas reined short. He was a spry man for his age and half Breccan's height.

"There is time to turn back, nephew," Jonas said.

"Turn back?" Breccan asked. "And do what?"

"Have a nice dinner and keg of ale," Jonas answered stoutly, "in front of a roaring *hot* fire." He
smacked his lips in appreciation. Ahead of them,
Breccan's other uncle, Lachlan, turned his horse
around to join them.

"And what of my word to the Davidson?" Breccan wondered. The Davidson was known as the
earl of Tay. Breccan held to the old ways. Breccan
himself would be considered an earl, but he was
proud to be laird. Laird Breccan they called him
to single him out from the other Campbells. He
knew the title was not always a sign of respect.
There were those who feared him and his kin,
and with good cause.

"Burn his chits and let him be damned," Jonas
said, referring to Davidson's debt vouchers Breccan now held in his possession. It had not taken
him long to collect them. None of Davidson's
creditors had thought he would honor his debts
and they'd been happy to sell them to Breccan
for mere shillings on the pound. "There are other
things you could have done with that money than
to buy yourself a bride," Jonas assured him. "Besides, *you* can have almost any other lass for free,
and she would be more robust and bonnie. The
Davidson lass is a whey-faced thing."

Yes, Breccan was buying a wife, but he did not agree with Jonas's description of Tara Davidson. She was no ordinary woman. 'Twas said that men in London lined the walk in front of her house for just one glimpse of her shining red hair and blue eyes. Breccan understood why. From the moment she had ridden onto his property, demanding to speak to his horse master with all the high-handedness of a queen, he'd been smitten.

He'd always thought tales of sirens claiming a man's soul or bawdy women leading men to destruction to be nonsense. Men were created of sturdier stuff than that—and then he'd met Lady Tara.

She'd barely spared him a glance that day, but her presence had moved something deep in his soul, something he would have denied existed if he'd been asked.

Breccan wanted many things in life. He wasn't afraid of hard work or making sacrifices, but in that moment of meeting, he'd never wanted anything more than he had her. He was obsessed with her. He'd even gone to the kirk so he could have another look at her. *Him!* A man who had always claimed the kirk walls would come tumbling down around him if he'd ever stepped foot in a sanctuary. But he had done so . . . for her.

And he knew himself well enough to realize he'd have no peace until he had her. Then, perhaps, he would be more himself again. Then he could pay attention to his accounts and his work and not lose hours in the day and night trying to recall the exact shade of blue in her eyes.

But Jonas and Lachlan did not know any of this. Indeed, he'd not mentioned her name until an hour ago when he'd announced he would marry.

Davidson had readily agreed to the marriage when Breccan had proposed the arrangement to him. Indeed, he'd happily sold his daughter if it meant Breccan wouldn't throw him into a debtor's prison. This far from London, the drunkard didn't have any of his English friends to protect him. And here, in Scotland, a man paid his debts, or it was taken out of his hide.

Breccan looked to his younger uncle. "What do you think, Lachlan? Do you agree with Jonas?"

Lachlan shifted uncomfortably in his saddle. "Does it make a difference what I think, Breccan? You've already made up your mind."

Because of Lachlan's years with the navy, his accent was not as thick as Breccan's and Jonas's . . . something that never seemed to bother Jonas but of which Breccan was painfully aware. Lady Tara had English manners, and her voice had just the melody of Scotland to it without the harshness.

"I would hear what you have to say," Breccan said. "Let us clear the air."

"Then before we ride up that hill to take your wife, I would ask what your reasons are, lad?" Lachlan said. "You've not shown a particular preference for any one woman before—"

"Because he behaves like a monk," Jonas interjected. "Which is a waste of a God-given gift. If I had what you had, Breccan, I'd be forking them all. The ladies would love me. Aye, that they would."

Breccan could feel the heat rise to his skin, and he was grateful for the wool muffler around his neck. Jonas might think a man's balls something to brag about, but Breccan felt anything but pride. He was painfully aware of his great size, and not just of his privates. He always stood a head taller than other men in the room. There was no way he could hide his presence or appear to be "amongst" the company instead of head and shoulders over it. His hands were the size of bear paws, and the cobbler always complained that his shoes required twice the amount of leather as a normal man.

A normal man.

A graceful one. A genteel one like his cousin Owen Campbell or any of the other of that side of the family. They all compared Breccan to a great ox and considered him as dumb as one. It was a grand joke amongst them. He would never be thought of as a gentleman or expected to cut a fine figure on the dance floor the way they did.

In truth, he was bloody tired of being mocked for his size. Aye, his great strength was good for chopping wood or for working his lands. There were few chores he could not do. Even the blacksmith would ask him to lift his anvil for him. But Breccan also had to watch his every move. If he was not mindful of his actions, he would swing his arm and put a dent in a plaster wall or knock over his chair if he moved too quickly.

And the worst was people's believing he lacked intelligence. They talked to him as if he were slow.

But their opinions would change when they saw him with Lady Tara on his arm. A man was not only respected if he had a beautiful wife, people were jealous of him.

There was also another reason he wanted to marry her—the Black Campbells were not a handsome lot.

Breccan's own mother had been a good woman but a homely one. And, for all his blather, Jonas didn't have a lady. Lachlan had been married once, but he was alone now. The Black Campbells were harsh-looking men. They had strong noses and jaws that were too square. While the other side of the Campbells were fair of hair and skin, Breccan and his kin were swarthy, with the look of the Romany, an unfavorable comparison if ever there was one.

Lady Tara would change that. She would give Breccan's children the fairness he lacked. His sons and daughters would be accepted. All doors would be open to them.

But these reasons were not ones Breccan wished to share with his uncles.

"I want her because I want her," he replied to Lachlan.

His uncle gazed up the mist-covered road a moment before saying, "A wife is not like owning a dog, Breccan. They have a will of their own."

"Aye, women can be pesky," Jonas agreed. "Your mother was a saint, bless her soul, but she was the exception. Lasses like her are rare. Women, as a rule, are demanding. They can make a man's life hell."

"If that was the case, why do so many men marry?" Breccan returned.

"That's a question every man has asked himself *after* the wedding," Lachlan assured him in jest. Jonas laughed his agreement.

Breccan straightened his shoulders and lifted his reins. "I must marry to keep the line alive, or would you rather have Wolfstone fall into the hands of Breadalbane to be turned over to one such as Owen Campbell?"

"Of course you must marry," Jonas said. "But not this woman." He kicked his horse forward as if to block Breccan's way. "I've seen her. She's a lovely morsel, but a pasty thing. There are kelpies bigger than her. You would split her in half, lad. You need a woman with some meat on her bones. One with breasts the size of melons." His eyes brightened with appreciation for the image he was conjuring.

Breccan didn't share his joy. Once again, his size was mentioned; however, for a second, his certitude wavered. *Could* he hurt Lady Tara? He wanted bairns off of her, but he didn't want to physically harm her to beget them.

Lachlan seemed to sense his indecision although he might not know its cause. "It's your choice whether we go up that road or not, Laird," he said quietly. "We'll follow, Jonas complaining as we go. You know how he is."

"I'm not complaining," Jonas shot back. "I'm being sensible. You want a wife, we'll find you one, Breccan. But this Davidson lass is not the one. Besides, nothing good comes of any Davidson. Do you not remember the tale of how Darius Davidson cheated our grandfather out of ten head of cattle—

He broke off at the sound of pounding hooves coming in their direction. All three men looked up the road to Annefield.

A bay snorting fire charged out of the mist. Whoever the rider was, he was riding as if the devil were on his heels. The horse started to slow at the sight of the three Campbells, but then the man on his back kicked him hard and sent the horse flying past them, mud splattering up from his heels.

Breccan recognized the horse immediately. "That's one of Davidson's prime studs." The Davidson racehorses were to be envied. Breccan didn't just covet Lady Tara, he was well on his way to creating a stable to rival the earl of Tay's. He knew those horses. He'd studied them with the goal of beating them.

"Who was on his back?" Lachlan asked.

"I don't know," Jonas said. "But that animal can run. I barely had a glimpse of the rider."

"And there is no reason for the horse to be out on this road in the evening," Breccan said. "Someone is stealing that stud."

He didn't wait for his uncles' responses but set his own heels to Jupiter. The stallion bounded forward, anxious to prove his own mettle. He was young, strong and ambitious, much like Breccan himself. Given his head, he charged forward, gaining on the other horse in spite of Breccan's weight on his back. All Breccan had to do was hold on.

Meanwhile, the other rider was having difficulty. Davidson's horse knew something was wrong and didn't want to leave his home. The horse tried to pull up, tossing his head and throwing off his stride. This gave Breccan the opportunity to catch them.

However, just as Jupiter approached, the stud decided to go flying again, giving a buck or two for his balance. His rider appeared to be no more than a lad in a filthy coat and a wide-brimmed hat. Those bucks proved to be too much for him. With a shout, he went tumbling off into the ditch on the side of the road. In a blink of an eye, the horse raced back to the safety of its stable, cutting across the road and disappearing into the forest.

The lad climbed out of the ditch on shaky feet. He looked up, saw Breccan, and decided to run, but Breccan was not going to let a thief escape.

He was a horse owner. He was outraged that the lad would help himself to horses, even if they were Davidson's. He leaned in the saddle, scooped the lad up off the ground by the collar of his jacket and threw him across his pommel, knocking the wind out of him—

An unexpected softness brushed Breccan's thigh.

Furthermore, the lad had a well-rounded and enticing bum.

For a second, Breccan was so startled by his reaction to the boy, he was tempted to dump him to the ground. He wasn't one for lads.

But then the curve of the thief's legs caught his notice. The boy wore boots that were too tall for him, but these were not the gangly legs of a young man.

Lachlan and Jonas rode up to join him. "You caught him," Lachlan said. "Now, what shall you do with him?"

"Hang him," Jonas said. "That's what I say. Hang him now."

Instead, Breccan lifted the lad by the scruff of the neck and held him out so that he could have a good look at him.

The boy was not happy. He flailed his arms, struggling to be free.

"Hold off," Breccan barked . . . but all other words died in his throat as the lad's hat fell off his head to release a braid of shining copper red hair. Large blue eyes, the color of the summer sky, turned their fury on him.

It was Jonas who summed up the situation with his usual aplomb. "You have caught yourself a wench, Breccan."

"This is no wench," Breccan said, speaking past a throat that had gone suddenly dry with desire. Now he understood the softness that had rested against his thigh. It had been the feel of firm and full breasts. "This is Lady Tara Davidson."

Oh, yes, it was the beautiful Tara herself . . . dressed in lad's clothes. Who could have known her legs were so long? Or so shapely?

What hot-blooded man wouldn't find himself speechless at the sight? Breccan certainly was. Indeed, he couldn't breathe.

He wasn't the only one.

"God's balls," Jonas said with a whispered admiration.

"Aye," Lachlan solemnly agreed.

For a second, Lady Tara hung helpless by Breccan's hold on the back of her coat. She looked wild, adventurous, bold.

And then she surprised them all by doubling her fist and punching Breccan right in the nose. "Let go of me," she commanded.

Lady Tara had a bit of strength in her arm. Her blow hurt. It was as if she'd discovered the one weak spot on his body.

Oh yes, the attack made him angry, along with the understanding that Tara Davidson was running away . . . and there was only one person from whom she could be fleeing—him.

She was attempting to escape marrying him. He'd heard rumors that she'd run from the last man she had promised to marry. And now she thought she could treat him with such disregard?

Breccan did as she bid. He let go.

Chapter Three

*I*t was one thing to be tossed by a galloping horse but a completely different matter to be dropped— even when Tara had ordered the brute to do so.

On the horse, she had realized she was falling. She'd had trouble controlling the animal from the moment she'd climbed on his back. Choosing to steal her father's prize stud for her escape had not been a wise choice. The beast was obviously better for breeding than riding, but Tara had been angry and wished to strike out at her father any way she could. She'd had a vague plan to sell the horse at some point, so that she could arrive in London with a certain amount of style. And then after that—?

Well, she would improvise something. She was very good at thinking quickly.

However, once she'd realized the horse was the most obstinate animal she'd ever ridden, and she had a very good seat, she knew she would have to bail.

When the stud had started bucking, she'd been able to swing herself down and had landed with some grace in the tall grass beside the road.

However, there was no time to be graceful with Laird Breccan. His was a commanding presence, an intimidating one. He held her as if she weighed nothing. She had struck out at him out of alarm and a need to gather her courage. It had been a reaction on her part and not a deliberate action.

But she hadn't expected him to comply with her order to release her with such immediacy.

Tara's bum hit the mud of the road with a thud.

For a second, she sat in surprise, her very brains feeling jarred and her bottom growing wet from the ground.

She wasn't the only one shocked. "*Och*, Breccan, you dropped her," one rider whispered. "You just dropped her."

The other released his breath before saying in awed tones, "You have nerve, nevvy."

"I was honoring my lady's request," was the deep, rumbling reply—and her temper took hold.

She jumped to her feet, proving no real damage had been done although she would be verily bruised in unmentionable places on the morrow. "How dare you treat me in such a rude, insulting manner." Her words fairly sizzled out of her mouth.

His hat was pulled low over his brow. She could not make out his expression beyond the grim set of his unshaven jaw. He obviously did not like being spoken to in this manner. Good! She'd do more of it. He was a huge, brawny man on a horse that would tower over any in her father's stables, but Tara had spirit. Her temper was usually slow to ignite, but when it did, she had the fearlessness of a dozen men his size, and she did not hold back on opinions.

"The idea that I would ever marry someone with your boorish manners is so beyond reason it is laughable," she said, each word a whiplash. She'd reduced men to tears with fewer and gentler words than she now used on him. "I'll *not* marry a Black Campbell. Not ever, do you hear me? No, no, and *no*."

The men with him literally gasped aloud. She

didn't care. These were the sort who would agree to anything the Black Campbell said. Besides, it was medieval to have retainers to do one's bidding. She wanted to scoff at him for riding around the countryside like some Highland chieftain of old.

However, instead of blustering or spouting out in pride, Laird Breccan lifted his reins and turned his horse around. With a tilt of his head, he indicated his men should follow, and he set off down the road—leaving her behind.

Tara stared in incomprehension.

He couldn't be leaving her. Why, she was several miles from Annefield and all alone.

Furthermore, he'd dropped her in the mud. Did he really think she could walk back? Wasn't he at least a bit concerned?

He kept riding.

"You are *no* gentleman, Campbell," she shouted at him.

He stopped, kicked his horse round to face her although he kept his distance. "Aye, you are right, *Davidson*."

Tara frowned. He didn't act like most men did around her. He was far from fawning or compliant. She should let him keep riding . . .

"I thought you wished to marry me," she heard herself say, sounding like a petulant child even to her own ears.

His horse pawed the ground, a sign he was anxious to be going. Laird Breccan held him quiet. "I had thought to do so. I've changed my mind."

"Because I wish to run away?" she challenged. "To stand up for myself?"

"Because you have no honor."

His words hit her with a force she'd not known before. "I have honor," Tara said.

"Do you now?" He let his horse come forward, walking toward her. When they were within six feet of each other, he stopped. "Is it honorable to run away from your father's promise?"

"It is *his* promise, not mine."

"Are you not a Davidson daughter? Is his word not your own?"

Tara frowned. She wished he'd remove his hat so she could see his eyes. She knew what they looked like. They were gray, the color of ice on Loch Tay on a winter's day. "I make my own promises," she declared.

He considered that for a moment, shrugged his shoulders as if giving her the benefit of a doubt. "Be that as it may, you are willing to see your father thrown into a debtor's gaol instead of honoring his word."

Her father was penniless, as she was herself now. "I choose not to be sold into marriage."

The lines of his mouth hardened. "Is your heart fixed upon another?"

Yes, she could say, *she loved Ruary Jamerson,* then they'd be done with each other. She sensed it. She knew men; she understood them. Breccan Campbell was not one to share anything, especially a woman. It would not matter to him that Ruary no longer loved her. Campbell was telling her that he would expect her complete allegiance. What he claimed, he kept.

Instead of answering him, she said, "You could have set me on the ground. You didn't need to drop me."

"I was obeying my lady's command."

"You say 'my lady' as if it leaves a sour taste in your mouth."

His horse stepped restlessly. Laird Breccan had straightened at her soft accusation. "I don't stand on ceremony."

"Oh, I believe you do, Laird. You accuse me of having no pride, but perhaps you have too much of the same quality?"

"I spoke of honor, my lady. There is a difference," he returned.

Tara had met many men whose opinions of themselves were overinflated. Laird Breccan was not one of their number. He was no braggart. "Tell me," she ordered quietly, speaking to him as if they were equals, "you pay off my father's debts leaving him free to squander what money he has to his name again, but what is in this marriage for me? Why should *I* agree to this match?"

"Other than the dignity of being my wife?" His voice was laced with unpretentious irony.

"I could be the wife to at least a hundred different men," she answered.

"You think highly of yourself, my lady."

Tara shook her head. "I understand the vanity of your sex. It is my looks that have attracted you, Laird, plain and simple. You know nothing of me. We've only spoken once, and it was not a memorable conversation. At least, not of the sort that would indicate a man was interested in a woman. I was surprised when I learned you'd offered for me . . . and had gone to considerable trouble to do so." She knew she was tweaking the bear's nose. She had everything to lose if he walked away. Her father's foolishness would be exposed. He would be ruined, and her humiliation would be complete.

Still, that realization didn't stop her from adding, "So now who is the one who thinks highly of himself?"

The grim line of his lips tightened.

Tara was not one to be rude if she could save herself from it. However, something about this man challenged her. She remembered first meeting him, remembered being aware of his presence.

He was very still a moment, then he swung down from his horse. His men now started to ride up. They had kept their distance while she and the laird had been throwing words back and forth to each other.

Laird Breccan held up his hand, a silent command for them to stay back. They obeyed immediately.

He towered over Tara. It took all her courage to stand in her place. He believed she had no Davidson pride? She wanted to prove him wrong, and yet the urge to run was very strong inside her.

"You have a sharp tongue, my lady."

"I do," Tara admitted. "There is more to me than just my looks. I've a mind as well." She'd never said such a thing before. In fact, she'd once believed that all she had to offer was the arrangement of two eyes, a nose and a mouth.

But suddenly she wanted someone, anyone to realize there was more to her. There had to be. There must be.

"What if all I want is your looks?" he asked, his voice so low only she could hear him.

"Then I would think you as shallow as all the others. And you would be doomed to disappointment. Looks do not last forever. Even a rose loses its beauty to age and time. Are you certain you wish to marry me?"

She could see his eyes now. She'd expected them to be hard, sharp, and there was a touch of anger in his curt answer. "Yes."

To her surprise, her body reacted to that one word. Something deep in her very core tightened, and she found herself starting to lean forward.

She held herself back, startled by such a strange fancy. Tara might have been desired by many men, but other than Ruary, whom she loved passionately, no others had moved her.

Yet here it was, a twinge of yearning. And the focus of her desire? The laird of the Black Campbells.

He did not seem to notice the turmoil inside her. He stood as if he could have been carved from stone. "And what of you?" he challenged, his voice still quietly low. "What is it you want?"

No one had ever asked her that question before.

For a moment, she had no answer. She'd been taught her job was to please. Be pretty and pleasing, the watchword of every debutante presented in society.

And yet, she realized she was haunted by just that question. What *did* she want?

Why had she been running?

"I want to return to London," she answered.

"London?" He snorted his opinion.

"Have you been there?"

"I don't need to go. Everything I could ever want is here."

"And how do you know? Have you never gone to Town?"

"I dinna wish to go," he answered, his accent thicker, a sign she had touched a nerve.

But a new thought had crossed Tara's mind. She took a step toward him, no longer intimated. "You asked me what I wanted. I told you. If I marry you, can you help me? Will you?"

He frowned as if she spoke gibberish, but she

was seeing her way clear now. At last she realized here was her chance to make a bid for her own life.

She did not wish to rusticate in the wilds of Scotland. During her three years in London, she'd learned she had a taste for the sophisticated life of the city. She'd been happy to shed the Highlands from her voice and from her person. And she wanted to return to that life. She understood it, found it safe. A woman had more opportunity in London.

"A man's wife should be by his side," Laird Breccan said.

"That is not true. There are many couples, well-respected ones, who live separate lives. They are honest with themselves." Yes, she could see that now. What had once seemed puzzling to her young mind, the idea that a man and woman could be married and rarely speak to each other, now appeared honest. "We are not a love match. We don't know each other, and, truly, we are from two different worlds. You don't even want *me*. You want my body."

There it was, the basic negotiation between a man and a woman.

He released his breath with one long sound as

if he didn't know how to respond to her declaration.

The air between them seemed to crackle with unspoken words. She sensed he wanted to deny her logic . . . but couldn't. He did want her.

And he didn't just dismiss her outright. He appeared to consider her words.

Few people did that. Most treated her lightly, as if she were a bauble without a thought in her head. As time had passed, she'd found it easier to be what they assumed—except for now. She wanted Laird Breccan to understand she had a will of her own.

"I want bairns," he said at last.

Bairns. Children. "How many?"

He pulled his hat off his head and raked gloved fingers through black hair that was overlong although clean. A haircut and a shave would do him a world of good. He was not as old as people supposed. Perhaps ten years or so older than her own one-and-twenty.

"I can't believe I'm having this conversation," he muttered.

"Why? You talked to my father about money. Can you not do the same with me? After all, this arrangement involves my life. We should speak plainly between ourselves." Aileen would be impressed. Aileen prided herself on her forthrightness and had criticized Tara for the lack of it. "So, how many children must I give you?"

"As many as I can have."

"That is an unacceptable answer. I'll never have the opportunity to return to London if that was the case." She thought a moment. "One."

"One? Are you daft?"

"No, sensible," she replied a bit offended. "And watch your tongue. No one has ever accused me of loose brains before."

"They must not have known you."

His murmured comment almost startled a laugh out of her. "You are right. Few know me." But they would in the future. She promised herself that. She pressed on. "One child. That is fair."

He did not like the offer. For a moment, he stared off into the distance but then turned to her, a canny Scotsman ready to strike a deal. She braced herself.

"Aye, one child," he surprised her by saying. "But he stays here with me. You'll not be taking my bairn to London."

Tara considered his counter. Leave the child here. The thought did not disturb her. She'd grown up without a mother, and most women she admired left their children in the care of nannies.

"What of funds for my London house?" she asked. "And I'll expect a handsome allowance."

"You are not concerned about leaving your child?" There was disapproval in his voice.

"Do you intend to be a good father?"

"Aye, the best."

"Then our child shall have more than what I had."

His brows came together. He had shapely brows. They were not shaggy and bold like her father's and other men's. Indeed, if he shaved and cut his hair, he might be rather handsome instead appearing so forbidding.

She'd heard that children were afraid of him and many adults as well. There were dark stories told about the Black Campbells.

But she didn't have any fear.

"Very well," he said, again surprising her with his easy agreement. "A house, an allowance, a son."

"Or daughter," Tara was quick to add. She didn't want to be forced to tarry wanting to bear another child.

"Want a male bairn," he said.

"And I want to go to London." She wanted to be reasonable. "May I have the second child there?"

"Without me?"

"You want to see your children born?" She appraised the big man with new eyes. She hadn't really considered that any man had a care for babies. Her father hadn't.

"Aye. And they need to be born at Wolfstone. That is their home."

Wolfstone. She'd heard of it but had never seen it. The house was centuries old, and people said it had never been improved upon. She imagined a stone fortress, an inhospitable place for birthing babies . . . but then, her freedom was at stake.

"One child, then we shall discuss the second," she countered. She wanted to be reasonable. They were making a bargain between them, one that had many advantages for her. A married woman received a great deal of respect, and in light of all the trickery and mischief she'd instigated over the past few months, it was doubtful any other man would have her. Even though she was untouched, she had made some grave errors of judgment that could cost her dearly.

Laird Breccan's charge that she was not honorable echoed in her mind. Others might feel that way as well. But if she was married . . . then there could be a future for her.

"There will be no discussion," he informed her coolly. "I'll have my children in hand *before* you go to London."

"What if I return after three years?" she suggested. "We could have another child, then I'd return to London. That seems fair."

"Not if you expect me to pay your expenses."

He hadn't hesitated in his response. "That is a foul threat," she said. "And it is ungentlemanly of you to not agree with my wishes since it will be my body doing the birthing."

"You have already told me, my lady, that I am no gentleman, and I don't claim to be one." He ran a hand along his horse's neck before saying to her, "Besides, you've already cost me a pretty penny."

"*My father* cost you a pretty penny," she corrected. "Those are not my debts."

"I stand corrected, my lady."

"But will you agree to my terms?"

He shot her an assessing look from the corner of his eye. Beyond them, his two men craned their necks as if they had been trying to listen, but Tara doubted if they had overheard anything. Both she and Laird Breccan had been cautious.

"Two bairns born at Wolfstone," he said, "then you can have whatever I have. It will be yours to go wherever you wish.

He glanced back at the two men waiting for him. "This will be between us? Not even my uncles will know?"

Ah, so those men were relatives. "Of course I will be quiet. I don't want any word of this to be spread about." There were already too many who would gleefully slured what little she had left of her reputation.

But with marriage, even to the Black Campbell, there would be freedom. She would have a place in the world, and her father's capricious vices could no longer threaten to destroy her security—

Struck by this new thought, she asked, "Do you gamble excessively?"

He made an impatient sound. "I am not foolish with my money."

Spoken like a Scotsman. "Do you not fear you are being foolish now?"

He turned the full force of his gaze upon her. There was intelligence in his eyes and a touch of compassion as well. Perhaps he understood what it meant to be constantly judged?

"Not if I have my bairns," he answered. He held out his gloved hand. "Do we have a meeting of the minds, my lady?"

She realized he wanted to shake her hand, much like she'd seen men do between themselves at the few horse sales she had attended.

Tara searched his face. He seemed sincere. "Do you trust my honor now, Laird?"

"I'll take a risk."

She placed her ungloved hand in his. For the briefest moment, she felt a surge of a new confidence, of the sense she was making the right decision.

This was a momentous step. This man would be the father of her children.

They shook. His hand engulfed hers, and yet she did not feel threatened. He was the first to break their hold, taking up the reins of his horse.

"The reverend is waiting," he said. "Let us see this deed done."

Tara had almost forgotten that she was to have been married within the hour. He mounted, then offered a hand.

So here it was. The decision had been made. All she had to do was act.

Trust was not easy for Tara, but she had made

her decision. She reached for his wrist, and he lifted her up onto the saddle in front him. Her legs rested across his.

"We ride on," he told his uncles, who rode up to join them. "My lady, this is my uncle Jonas." He nodded to the smaller of the two men. "The other is my uncle Lachlan. Follow me," he ordered.

The uncles did as he bid, but Tara could almost hear the questions in their heads. It was to his credit that Laird Breccan did not see a need to explain. She wished she could be close-lipped around her relatives and not have them ask a hundred questions.

They easily covered the three miles to Annefield, a lovely home that her family had built less than a hundred years ago.

Torches lit the front door. A stable lad walked the Reverend Kinnion's horse in the gloom of a falling evening.

"Let me go in the servants' way," Tara said, before they came too close to the door, where someone would spy her in her disguise. She directed him on a path through the woods lining the yard. "Set me down here." Once her feet were on the ground, she looked up at him. "I will see you inside the house."

He nodded and turned away, the other riders following him. Tara watched him go. Had she made the right decision?

Did she have any other choice?

She escaped inside the house.

Upstairs, in her room, she found the housekeeper, Mrs. Watson, and her maid, Ellen, frantically whispering. They stopped when she entered the room. Mrs. Watson collapsed in relief, then her eyes widened in shock.

"Oh, my lady, don't tell me you have been running around the countryside dressed like a lad again?"

"Very well, I won't. Ellen, give us a moment of privacy."

The maid bobbed a curtsy and left, her eyes alive with curiosity.

Tara took Mrs. Watson's arm and led her away from the door, where they might be overheard. She'd known Mrs. Watson most of her life. Beyond her sister Aileen, the housekeeper was the closest Tara had to a mother figure. She was also someone Tara could trust.

"I am to marry," she told the housekeeper.

"I know. That's why we were worried when you weren't here. The bridegroom is expected at any moment."

"He will wait for me," Tara assured her. All men waited for her. "Besides, I have something more pressing I need to know."

"And what is that, my lady?"

"Please, Mrs. Watson, tell me, what happens in the marriage bed. And how quickly can one create a baby?"

Chapter Four

The hands on the earl of Tay's mantel clock ticked off the passing of time.

Breccan sat in a chair in the corner of the receiving room, waiting . . . waiting . . . waiting.

Almost two hours had passed since he had delivered Lady Tara to the house. He should have been married and halfway home by now.

After the first hour, the Reverend Kinnion had assured him the vows would not take long. "But also," he offered in a confiding tone to Breccan, "here is an observation from a man who has been married these past five years and more, women are a bit like cats. They have their own understanding of time. I find it easiest to not press my

wife to be anywhere at a certain hour. Well, save
for Sunday services." He'd laughed at that last as
if it was his own wee joke.

Breccan thought the reverend needed to take his
wife in hand. Time was a precious thing to waste.

However, since Breccan had purchased a special license for this marriage—*doing it the English
way so that it was very legal; after all, he was paying
a small fortune to wed the woman*—and because he
did not want to be accused of not respecting Lady
Tara, or of not following the procedures expected
of those of her class, or of doing *anything* that his
Campbell relatives would not, he waited.

And with every passing second, his temper built.

This room was not a comfortable room. The
portraits of proud Davidsons frowned down
upon him from the walls. The furniture lacked
the sturdiness of Wolfstone's, his ancestral home,
and he was not accustomed to needlepoint pil-
lows or fancy silver candlesticks.

Jonas had made fast friends with the earl of Tay
and his never-ending bottle of whisky, growing
louder and more boisterous as the time stretched.
They entertained each other with stories and lies
in front of the small coal fire in the hearth.

Lachlan was trying to herd Jonas in, but the

truth was, he savored a drop or two himself, so his shepherding was halfhearted at best. One would have thought the Campbells and the Davidsons were the fastest of friends to hear the three of them go on.

Of course, when Breccan had first arrived at Annefield, the earl had already been well into his cups. The man had actually stumbled and fallen to the floor.

His servant, a tall man with the hewn features of an aging Viking, named Ingold, had literally picked the earl up and physically moved him into the receiving room. Ingold had not behaved as if this was unusual behavior.

But it was to Breccan. He liked a drink as well as the next man, but he would never be slovenly about it.

The earl of Tay's hair was a mess. It blew every which way, as if he'd been pulling it straight up in the air. His waistcoat had stains of his last meal dribbled down it, or perhaps his last several meals. He smelled foul of stale whisky and body odor. He was a far cry from his beautiful daughter, and this was something else to give Breccan doubts. Sons were very much like fathers. Were daughters?

The Reverend Kinnion, after having Breccan grumble over his attempt to make excuses for the bride, had taken a seat by the front window. He appeared to be watching the misty evening give way to nightfall.

Breccan didn't know the minister well. The first time they'd laid eyes on each other had been the day Breccan had gone to the kirk in his pursuit of another glimpse of Lady Tara. He'd wanted to be certain that she was as he had remembered her.

She had been. That Sunday morning, seeing her dressed in her church finery, she had been every bit as lovely as he'd recalled. More so even. Seated in the back of the church, Breccan had not been able to take his eyes off her and had decided he had to have her.

After the service, the reverend had approached him. Breccan had been polite to the minister although he had not felt comfortable in the church. Many would have said it was because Breccan was the devil himself, but the truth was he did not like going any place where people could comment on his great size. The pews were too narrow and close for his long legs. He'd stood out. He couldn't hide amongst them, and it made him feel awkward. He knew they judged him.

But nothing made him feel more foolish than cooling his heels waiting for Tara Davidson to stoop to come down the stairs of her house and marry him. She insulted him. She thought she could treat him like one of her London swains.

Well, the blood of a thousand Highlanders flowed in his veins. He had pride.

Breccan rose. "I'm leaving. Come, uncles—"

"Wait, wait, you can't leave yet," the earl of Tay drunkenly informed him. "We haven't finished the bottle. We have a celebration here—" He paused. "Something's happening, but I can't remember what it is." He began giggling at his own ineptitude.

"I find nothing to celebrate," Breccan answered. "And you can tell your daughter, I've been here and gone."

"You can tell her yourself," Tay said, punctuating the word with a burp. "She is behind you."

Breccan turned sharply, uncertain whether to believe him. After all, how could Lady Tara arrive and he not be aware—?

She *was* there—and looked more beautiful than his fevered fantasies could have ever imagined.

He'd never seen a garment finer than the one she wore. The creamy gauze of her dress seemed to flow around her, emphasizing her trim waist and rounded breasts. He knew little of women's frills, but the lace over the skirt added the sort of femininity that highlighted the blessed differences between men and women. Her glorious hair was artfully styled high on her head. Pinned to it was a veil that trailed behind her with a grace saved for angels and muses.

She wore no jewelry. She needed none. The clear perfection of her skin and her vivid coloring were adornment enough.

He could not speak. He could not think. Every male part of his body had come alive, especially since she smelled sweeter than spring air to him.

This was how he'd pictured her, innocent and willing. What man would not want such a wife?

He ached to gather her in his arms and drink in the perfume that was uniquely hers. He didn't think he could ever tire of that scent.

And then, she pushed her advantage too far.

She'd accurately read his masculine need, and, with a canniness that would have made her wastrel of a father proud, she took a step in Breccan's direction and greeted him by lowering her head like a concubine flattering her lord. Long, dark lashes created small fans against her cheeks.

Any man who saw her this way would be affected. Certainly Jonas, Lachlan, and even the happily married Reverend Kinnion were stirred. Jonas actually whimpered, a sound echoed by the minister.

His uncle Lachlan breathed out the words, "You are a lucky, lucky man, Breccan."

And Breccan felt his temper explode.

Her behavior was too studied, too obvious. She'd kept them waiting on purpose, so that she could make this appearance. He'd wager she now expected him to offer slavish devotion, a sign she could behave however she pleased. Oh, yes, she would be pleased to make him dance to her tune.

And his reward? Why, she might gift him with a smile.

Well, he was not like one of his dogs who gratefully begged at the table for the slightest morsel. He knew when he was being teased, and it worked, damn it all. His manhood was as straight and hard as a yeoman's staff. Just the sight of her was enough to send him howling with desire.

But a man worth his salt could not allow his woman to have the upper hand. Not if he wanted her respect.

"Come, Jonas, Lachlan, we are leaving."

"*What?*" Jonas said, the word bursting out of him in his surprise.

But Breccan didn't repeat himself. He had said what he had to say once, and that was enough. He walked from the room, brushing right by Lady Tara.

$\mathcal{T}$ara took a step back, almost thrown off balance by Laird Breccan's *shoving* his way past her out the room.

Nor did he stop to apologize.

He continued walking right to the front door, snatching his hat up off the side table before a surprised Ingold could react. The laird opened the door himself and left the house.

She was stunned. He couldn't leave. They were to marry. The reverend was here. She'd made herself very attractive for the marriage, and this was after speaking to Mrs. Watson and having one of the *most disturbing conversations of her life*. He was lucky she'd forced herself to come down the stairs.

Furthermore, men did not walk out on her.

She walked out on *them*.

Laird Breccan's uncles began to follow. The shortest, Jonas, drained the drink in his cup before he left. He gave Tara a rueful, longing last gaze before slinking out the door.

Horrified thoughts of what Laird Breccan's desertion could do to her reputation filled her mind. She had already scandalized society by jilting one perfectly good man because she had loved another who, in turn, had rejected *her*. Oh, the tittle-tattlers had laughed with delight over what they considered her very deserved rebuke. But Tara did have pride. She would not, *could* not allow herself to be the victim of a third scandal-broth.

Especially when the man whose name would be attached to hers was the Black Campbell.

Didn't he understand she was doing him a favor to marry him? He was hairy and dark and three times the size of a normal man. He was also surly.

What other woman did he believe he could marry?

Her father yawned. "Oh, this is not good." He reached for the whisky decanter and appeared surprised to find it empty.

The Reverend Kinnion asked in a confused voice, "Should I leave?"

"Absolutely not," Tara snapped. "You stay right there." She charged out of the receiving room and through the front door Ingold had opened for the uncles.

By the doorstep's torchlight, she could see that the laird had not yet mounted. He had been in the act of offering vails for service, or tips, to the stable lads.

He noticed her come out of the house. His scowl deepened.

Well, she didn't give a care what he thought. She marched onto the drive and placed herself right in front of his horse.

He started to guide the animal around her, but she rashly grabbed the horse's reins and clutched them tight. She and the laird were practically toe to toe.

"Where do you believe you are going?" she challenged, her temper so white-hot the brogue she'd spent years struggling to contain reared its Scottish head. Nor did she feel fear as she stared up into his fearsome countenance.

"I'm returning home and to my bed," Laird Breccan said, attempting to pull the reins from her.

She wasn't going to let him have them. She would let him and his horse drag her to hell before she released her hold. "You are not," she replied. The horse danced a step but did not run over her. "You asked for my hand, and we are supposed to be marrying right this minute."

"We were supposed to marry *two hours* ago, my lady." Again he attempted to take the reins, his frown saying he could not believe she would defy him. But Tara was not about to let him have them, not without violence.

"I am *ready* to marry now," she said.

"I'm *not*." This time he used his superior height to his advantage, reaching around her with both arms—and their bodies bumped, her breasts against the flat planes of his chest and abdomen.

A jolt like a spark of fire shot through Tara.

He must have felt it as well. He yanked back as if burned, releasing his hold on the reins.

Tara didn't understand why there had been that charge of awareness between them, but she knew how to press her advantage. She held up the reins. "We have a bargain. Or are you going to run away from your money and your pride, Laird?"

An expression crossed his face that could be likened to the gathering of storm clouds. "I will not let you play me for a fool."

Tara looked up at this boulder of a man. He now represented her only course for living her life on her terms. Her life was crumbling around her, but Laird Breccan offered escape.

"You don't want me to play you for a fool?" she repeated. "Then the challenge for you is to tame me, sir."

It was a provocative statement. She'd meant it to be. Most men could not refuse such a gauntlet being thrown down before them.

He was no different.

Almost against his will, his gaze slid to her breasts. Oh yes, he'd felt the charge between them.

And inside her, at her very core, she felt a rippling of desire. It expanded through her being, filling those very breasts that had claimed his attention and bringing a warm flush to her skin.

He raised his gaze to her lips, and, for a second, she thought he would kiss her. She wet her lips, suddenly having a need to keep them moist, suddenly aware of a number of reactions she'd not experienced before . . .

"He puts himself in you, my lady," Mrs. Watson had told her upstairs.

"What do you mean 'puts himself in me'? How can he do that?" She knew that people who were lovers spent hours in each other's bed. She had

heard whispers. She could imagine it would be nice to sleep beside someone she liked. But she wasn't completely clear on the practical steps to breeding, and it was breeding that Laird Breccan wanted of her.

Mrs. Watson had hummed for a moment as if searching for the right words. *"He will use his male bits. Do you know men and women are different?"*

"Of course I do."

"Well, he will put his bits against your bits."

"That doesn't make sense," Tara had argued. *"Or are you saying we are like dogs or the horses and behave in that manner?"* She'd seen animals mating. She shouldn't have. The servants and Aileen had tried to protect her, but she'd grown up in the country, and, in truth, she had found their rutting too earthy for her tastes.

"Not quite," Mrs. Watson had said, to Tara's great relief.

"Then what is the difference? And for how long do we have to do such at thing?" Tara had asked with great distaste.

"My lady, your husband will know. Trust him. The bits go together nicely if it is done right. All you must do is lie quiet. It will be over before it has begun . . ."

Mrs. Watson's prediction echoed in Tara's

mind, even as she felt an unfamiliar tightening of muscles in her female "bits."

Laird Breccan took a step back, as if needing to put space between them, as if he, too, was suddenly very aware of her. His action seemed to give him room to breathe.

"Aye, we have a bargain," he agreed. "But I'll not be playing games. Do you hear? I'm a simple man, a straightforward one."

"There is no such thing as a simple woman," she was bold enough to say. "You may pull on your breeches and go out into the world, but it is more complicated for us."

A question came to his eye as if she was telling him information that he'd never considered before.

"I shall always want to be my best," she tried to explain. "And you will want me to be so. You would not like to hear people whisper that you had married an unfashionable woman."

The line of his mouth grew grim. "If she does my will, I shall not mind."

If he were any other man, by now, he would be praising her beauty and assuring her she could do anything she desired. He would not be challenging her with the obstinacy of a bull.

Or perhaps she was losing her looks and her ability to control men with them? If she was not attractive to men, then, what was left of her?

"Very well," she said, capitulating. "I shall be punctual before all else."

He sensed she mocked him, and she did . . . although she tried to sound sincere.

For a second, he hesitated. Then, he said to the stable lad, "Continue walking my horse. My lady, let us go inside."

"Aye, Laird," the boy said.

Tara released her hold on the reins to the lad.

Laird Breccan turned on his heel and walked with purpose toward the front door. All Tara had to do was follow. However, she discovered such docility was a bit alien to her nature. She was tempted to stand her ground and wait until he noticed she was not behind him, but then this man was her only hope for a life lived on her terms, whatever they might be. She would consider the details later. She started for the door.

His uncles had dismounted. Lachlan spoke up, "Breccan, are you daft? Escort the lady inside properly."

The laird turned as if just realizing he'd left her. Even in the torchlight, she could see a dull red creep up his neck.

To his credit, he retraced his steps to her. "Shall we go in?" He offered his arm.

Tara placed her hand upon it. The muscles under his coat were hard and solid. She didn't think she'd ever felt the like.

"I didn't mean to walk off," he muttered as an apology. "I can be a bit of an oaf."

Was that a warning?

If this was his poor behavior, Tara could assure him that she'd suffered through worse. She knew many men who were arrogant beyond boundaries, prided themselves on being difficult, were utterly selfish, and who would never have offered an apology even if their bare feet had been held to a fire.

Perhaps this *would* work between them.

Nor was she afraid. Not any longer.

She could manage him. He liked her breasts. She had just a wee concern about the marriage bed. She wished she understood better what was expected of her, but after she managed once, then the second time would not be distressful. The mystery would be gone.

And considering their bargain was for two children, Tara wouldn't have to worry about a third time. The deed would be done, and she'd be free to live her life as she chose.

Confident, she sailed to the house as he stepped

back to let her enter before him, proving he did have manners. She might be able to make something with him yet.

That thought of how she would change him occupied her mind as the Reverend Kinnion spoke the words over them that would make them man and wife.

But Laird Breccan seemed keen on listening to the reverend, as did his uncles.

For her side of the family, her father snored with little regret in the chair by the fire. However, Ingold was there in the doorway, as were Mrs. Watson and the other servants, and it seemed fitting. Even if Aileen had been here, the servants were more her family than anyone else.

The worst moment was when Reverend Kinnion asked, "Who giveth this woman to be married to this man?" He looked right at Tara's father. The earl's answer was a snort in his sleep.

"He is too gone in his cups," Tara informed the Reverend Kinnion coolly, but inside, she was humiliated. Her father couldn't think of anyone other than himself. "Must I have someone give me away? Can I not give myself away?"

"I don't know," the reverend said. "That would be unorthodox."

"She is an unorthodox woman," Laird Breccan said.

Tara looked up at him, uncertain if he was being complimentary. His expression was serious.

"Yes, well," the reverend started to say, as if wishing he did not have to make a decision.

"Excuse me, my lady," Ingold said, entering the room. He went over to her father, rapped him smartly on the cheek. "My lord, my lord?"

"Yes, yes," the earl said, coming to his senses with bleary eyes. "Yes?" he repeated addressing the butler.

"Say, 'I do,'" Ingold ordered.

"I do-o-o-o," the earl mocked the butler, before laying his head back on the arm of the chair and falling asleep.

Ingold looked to the reverend. "Will that do, sir?"

"It is the hoped-for answer," the Reverend Kinnion said. "But perhaps—"

"It is the right answer," Laird Breccan interjected in a voice that brooked no argument.

"Still," the reverend hedged, but then the earl raised his head to speak.

"Is it done? Is she married?" he asked in slurry

speech. "Will you give me the money to return to London?" He addressed this last to Laird Breccan. "Penevey won't like that, but damn it all, I'm allowed to go where I wish."

"I shall send you the money to go as far away from here as is humanly possible," Laird Breccan promised.

"Good," the earl replied, lowering his head again.

"Let us see this done," Laird Breccan ordered the minister, and he did. Within minutes, vows were repeated. She'd even learned that her new husband's full name was Breccan Alexander Campbell. It was a good name. A strong one.

The Reverend Kinnion had them kneel in front of him. The hardwood floor hurt Tara's knees.

"Do you have a ring, Laird?" the reverend asked.

"I do." He surprised her by pulling from his pocket a tiny velvet bag. He shook the ring out of it. It was a gold band that had been worn hard.

He noticed her studying it, and said, " 'Twas my mother's."

Tara nodded, still not completely connected to what was taking place. Her world was changing too rapidly. She heard herself murmur, "Then it cannot be replaced."

"No, it is the only one," he said, "and I treasure it."

She now learned something else about this man, about what he held dear. She could understand. She kept a locket that had belonged to her mother even though it was broken and in two pieces.

"Hold the ring over her first finger and repeat after me," the Reverend Kinnion instructed Laird Breccan. "With this ring, I thee wed."

"With this ring, I thee wed," he repeated.

"With my body, I worship thee."

"With my—" Laird Breccan hesitated ever so slightly as if realizing the import of the words. Then, in a firm voice, he repeated, "With my body, I thee worship."

"Trust him. The bits go together nicely if it is done right."

"With all my worldly goods I thee endow," the Reverend Kinnion read.

Laird Breccan had no problem repeating that vow. It was actually their promise to each other, Tara realized. Their bargain.

There are moments in life one never forgets.

As Laird Breccan slid the ring on her finger, Tara knew she would always remember every detail. Her senses were filled with him. Beyond the scent of food being cooked someplace in the house, of the coal in the fire and the smell of her father's whisky, underlying it all was her awareness of him. He smelled of fresh air and good soap.

The thin gold band fit. His mother must not have been a bigger woman than her. Funny to imagine such a giant could come from a petite woman.

The Reverend Kinnion began finalizing the vows by making the sign of the cross over their joined hands, but the laird signaled for him to stop. He turned to Tara, his hand still holding hers.

"I want you to know I shall be a good and faithful husband to you."

Tara nodded. In many ways, there was almost a dreamlike quality to this turn of events. She kept expecting to wake up and find her life back where it had once been, back in the days when she'd believed she'd been in control of her destiny.

Apparently he hadn't expected an answer from her. He'd made his declaration, a promise born out of his sense of honor. He looked to the Reverend Kinnion. "You can finish now."

The Reverend Kinnion waved a blessing over their joined hands. "In the Name of the Father and of the Son and of the Holy Ghost." He raised his hands over them. "And now, what God has joined, let no man put asunder."

And Tara was married.

In the space of a few hours, her life had been changed forever.

There followed an awkward moment of silence. Tara didn't know what to do now and apparently neither did Laird Breccan.

"Are you going to seal your pledge with a kiss, Breccan?" his uncle Jonas asked.

For a second, Tara panicked. She wasn't against a kiss, but not in front of this audience.

The laird seemed to understand, or perhaps he felt the same way because he said, "We are not here for your entertainment, Jonas."

"Aye, but you should kiss the bride." Jonas argued. "If you don't wish to do so, Breccan, I'll do it for you."

Jonas's offer brought heat to Tara's cheeks.

But it spurred the laird to lean over, and he barely brushed his lips across Tara's as if not wanting to touch her.

They were strangers. She told herself his kiss

was respectful, a formality . . . but it was also a far cry from the kisses she had once shared with Ruary Jamerson, the man who was, she reminded herself, the love of her life.

One life; one love.

Who she married no longer mattered . . .

Mrs. Watson took on the role of host since the earl was passed out. She announced, "Come now, Cook has prepared refreshments to celebrate. You will come this way, will you now, Laird Breccan and Reverend Kinnion?"

Laird Breccan frowned with distaste at Tara's sleeping father. His mouth was open, and he was beginning to drool. "I need to be returning home."

"But we can eat," Jonas protested.

"It's dark," the laird said. "I want to be on the road."

"Aye, Breccan is right," Lachlan agreed.

The laird looked to Tara. "Are you ready?"

Tara felt a discontent. He wanted to whisk her away too quickly. It was as if he was anxious to dismiss her family.

"I am not," she said stoutly. "I haven't even packed a valise." She hadn't really stopped to consider that Annefield was no longer her home.

"Then pack," he said. "Jonas, go fill your belly. You may go with him also, Lachlan."

"Are you not hungry, Breccan?" Lachlan asked.

The laird shot another glance of disgust toward the earl, and announced, "I'm hungry for my home. I shall be waiting for both of you outside." He walked out of the room.

It was a rude response. Mrs. Watson was surprised, as was Tara. "He means to leave now?"

Jonas nodded. "Breccan likes his bed. He never lingers. What does the cook have for us?" he asked, rubbing his hands. "Breccan may not want to enjoy good food, but I do. The cook at Annefield is famous."

"Then come this way, sir," Mrs. Watson invited. She didn't have to ask twice. Jonas was right at her heels as she left the room.

Lachlan followed although he paused in the doorway and looked back at Tara. "If I were you, my lady, I'd be packing. As you could tell earlier, Breccan doesn't like to be kept waiting."

"Does he always do exactly as he pleases?" Tara asked.

Laughter lit Lachlan's eye. "Usually. But then I have a feeling, you are as headstrong. This marriage will be interesting." He followed the others.

For a second, Tara wanted to rail against all that had happened. But then she realized protest was futile. Her decision had been made.

She looked to her maid, Ellen, who lingered in the hall, waiting for her command. "Come, Ellen," she said to the maid. "Help me pack."

"I've started doing a bit of it, my lady."

"Thank you," Tara said as she started up the stairs. It would not take long to prepare.

There was a footstep behind her and she turned to see Myra, another household maid, following. "Mrs. Watson instructed me to come help."

Tara nodded. Myra was a buxom lass who was a great favorite of the footmen. She took pride in her worldliness. She was not the best of servants, but right now, Tara needed help.

Upstairs, Tara's bedroom was a mess. Dresses, shoes, and scarves had been removed from the wardrobe. The valise was open on the bed. Tara realized she didn't know how they would travel. Nothing had been said about a coach. For a second, she debated having Ingold order one prepared, then decided to be quiet.

Laird Breccan's demands for her to pack with all haste, then his leaving the house to wait outside annoyed her. Especially after that pretend kiss, not that she had *wanted* to kiss him. Oh, no, kissing the air was fine with her.

Still, his imperial manner provoked her. All men were stubborn, but he behaved as if were a prince of the realm—which he was not. She knew the Prince Regent, and Breccan Campbell was no Prinny, especially with all that hair outlining the leanness of his cheeks and the hardness of his jaw. Didn't the man own a razor? Facial hair was *not* the style, although, she had to admit, the shadow of his beard was not unattractive on the Campbell . . .

Tara caught the direction of her thoughts and forced herself to think on the task at hand. No good would come from softening toward him. She'd be wise to keep her guard in place.

"Pack just the necessities in the valise," Tara decided. The bag was small enough it could be carried on a horse or stowed in a coach. "Tell Mrs. Watson to have Simon"—she referred to the footman who served many duties around the household—"deliver a trunk to Wolfstone on the morrow. In fact, who knows what the laird has in the way of luxuries at Wolfstone? For all I know, they sleep on animal skins." And considering Laird Breccan's boorish behavior, that could well be true.

Her comment elicited a giggle from the maids and gave Tara a bit of her spirit back. "Myra, fetch some linens for my new life. Bring them here so I can have a look at them. Ellen, help me dress." The details she had to consider were overwhelming. "I'll wear my riding habit; that way, I'm prepared for anything."

Soon, Tara was in her marine blue habit trimmed with gold buttons. She had Ellen braid her hair so it could be pinned neatly at the nape of her neck.

As Tara set the hat, a feminine version of a gentleman's curled-brim beaver, she said, "Remember to put my tooth powder in the valise. Where is Myra? She should have been back by now. Go see what she is doing. Also," Tara thought to add, "see if we have a fresh cake of that lavender soap I like. You know where Mrs. Watson keeps it."

"Yes, my lady." Ellen left the room.

Tara took a deep breath to steady her nerves and relieve the apprehension in her stomach. Her room overlooked the back of the house, so she couldn't see if Laird Breccan still waited for her or not. She assumed someone would come running for her if he decided to have another of his tantrums—and that is how she thought of his storming out on her earlier, a tantrum. She recognized it because she'd thrown a few of her own over the years. It was probably wise she was planning on living in London while he stayed in Scotland.

Still, one shouldn't pull on the wolf's tail, and it was past time for her to make her appearance downstairs.

Since Myra and Ellen hadn't returned, she tucked her tooth powder into her valise herself, closed it, and picked it up from the bed. She left the room, but wanted to tell Ellen she was leaving. She walked down the hall to the small room at the end of the hall by the servants' stairs that Mrs. Watson used as an office and where she kept the linen press.

The door was slightly ajar and she could hear Ellen's and Myra's hushed whispers.

"How do you know Laird Breccan is big down there?" Ellen was asking.

Tara had been about to let her presence be known. She now shut her mouth, listening and curious about what Ellen meant when she said, "down there."

"Annie Carr has seen enough to know he is. She says the man is a monster. She has to cut extra material." Annie Carr was the local seamstress.

"And," Myra continued, "there has been a lass or two that has had a go at him. They sing his praises." She dropped her voice a notch lower to confide, "They say he is a beast."

"But what of my lady?" Ellen worried.

"I'm thinking she'll have the time of her life."

"Or he could hurt her. If he is that big, why this night will be painful for her."

"Oh, yes," Myra readily agreed. "If he is as big as they say he is and her being such a petite thing, he could split her in half. Although *I* wouldn't mind having a go at him—"

Tara had stared backing away from the door, not wanting to be discovered eavesdropping, and shocked by what she'd heard.

Images of stallions mounting mares shot through her memory.

Mrs. Watson had been dissembling. Tara had asked her directly if the marriage act was such as that, and the housekeeper had assured her it was not.

No, that wasn't true. She hadn't answered the question at all. She had been deliberately vague.

As Tara went down the stairs, she knew she must behave as if all is well.

But it wasn't.

And she had a sinking feeling it never would be again.

"Just twice," she whispered, reminding herself of their bargain. "I have to lie with him twice."

Two bairns and she would be free.

Chapter Five

He'd been afraid to kiss her, especially with an audience.

Breccan stood in the night. The earlier gloom had dissipated, leaving a half-moon in a cloudless sky. The light would make traveling the way home easier.

The cold October air felt good on his heated skin. He didn't pace but rooted himself to the ground by his horse, waiting for her to come out.

Drapes covered the windows in the house against the chill and the damp, so he couldn't see the activity that was taking place. He could only guess.

Wolfstone didn't have drapes, or rugs on the

floor, or any of the frills he'd seen in the rooms at Annefield. His home was spartan compared to how Lady Tara lived here. He would tell anyone that his was a male establishment, and there was no need for softness.

But he did have a need for her.

He wanted her softness.

His parents had not been wealthy people. Breccan had been their only child, and he had seen how his father's laziness had made for a hard life for his mother.

She'd been a good and gentle woman, an educated one. She'd ensured that Breccan understood what his father did not. A chieftain cares for his people, she had told him. He puts their needs before his own.

His mother had also had a shrewd mind for turning a penny. She'd taught Breccan how to save and how to plan. She had urged him to imagine what Wolfstone could be.

"Don't let other people's expectations limit you, Breccan," she had said. *"Or their own conceits. Follow what interests you, and you'll be fine. You will be a good man."* To his mother's way of thinking, there was no higher goal.

He'd always been fascinated by how levers,

pulleys, and wheels worked. With his mother's encouragement, he'd actually created the design for the millhouse when he was as young as ten. A decade and a half later, he'd built that mill, almost according to his original design. It now served his clan and the surrounding countryside as well. He owned it, but he kept the prices fair and used the profit to build a school and pay two tutors.

He was also interested in new agricultural methods and using Wolfstone's land to the best of his ability. Aye, he'd brought in sheep like so many others around him, but he'd taught his clansmen how to grow crops efficiently so more could be harvested from the acres. He didn't need to toss people from their homes to graze animals. He believed he'd found a way for them to all live together, profitably.

The horse stables were a labor of love. He'd seen how the earl of Tay had benefited. Breccan liked good horseflesh and was interested to see what would happen if he bred Scottish resilience into a Thoroughbred's heart. Many laughed at him, but his two-year-old stallion, a bay named Taurus, was showing the signs of a champion. They were about to test Taurus's mettle in a few weeks at a race Breccan dearly wanted to win.

But he'd invested in his most challenging endeavors over the last year. First, he'd purchased two spinning mules and a power loom. Breccan didn't believe there was any sense in shipping his wool off when his own people could weave it into a cloth he imagined would be finer than any other in the world. The equipment worked off of water, something Scotland had in abundance.

He'd hired a weaver to teach his clansmen how to use wheel and loom. Then he had started building a row of cottages, again from his own drawings, so that those who worked together could live together. He had the idea from his studies of ancient guilds. Weavers were being trained, but so far the cloth produced had been of inferior quality. It was as if his people refused to master the equipment.

However, his latest venture was his most expensive one, and that was his marriage to Lady Tara. Buying the earl's notes had stretched his coffers thin. His mother would have warned him to not extend himself on the debts of another, and yet Breccan had wanted what he'd wanted.

Perhaps he did have some of his father in him because right now, at this moment, one tip of bad luck could see him in debtor's prison.

Worse, she might prove to be his greatest test.

He was a man who prided himself on being in control. She was a woman who just by breathing seemed to make his control disappear. He wasn't rational around her. Perhaps once he'd bedded her, *then* he might be able to think coherently—?

Aye, he had been angry with her for making him cool his heels while she'd readied herself for their vows. No Campbell took slights well. But he would have returned. He wanted her that much.

And then there was the moment when they'd argued over the reins, and their bodies had met— he'd never experienced such complete, unreserved desire. Just that swift touch had been enough for his manhood to almost embarrass him.

So, yes, he had hesitated kissing her . . . but he also couldn't wait to take her to his bed. God, he ached with need.

A groom brought a horse, a gelding, around from Tay's stable. "Lady Tara's mount," he said, taking a place by Breccan. The torchlight high-lighted the craggy features of his face. He had the height and solid body of an exercise rider, but he was too old. Breaking and exercising was a young man's game.

"She's a good rider, is she?" Breccan had to ask.

"Aye, Laird. We couldn't pull her off her pony when she was a wee thing. Yourself? You are a rider?"

"Of course . . . when I find a horse big enough for my carcass."

The groom laughed, then introduced himself. "I'm Angus Freeman, Laird, the earl's head groom. I've heard you have built quite a stable."

"Thank you." And then Breccan couldn't help himself from boasting just a wee bit, "I laid it all out myself."

"That is what I've heard. I've been told it is something I should see."

"You are always welcome."

There was a beat of silence and then Freeman asked, "Do you have a good stable master?"

Breccan knew the question was not asked in innocence. Freeman was obviously an ambitious man, one who may have learned a great deal in Tay's employ. The groom must know Breccan was searching for a new man. Perhaps these questions were his reason for personally bringing Lady Tara's horse from the stables.

"Actually, I could use one," Breccan said. "Now that Jamerson is gone, I am using William Ricks, but I need another good man."

"Aye, Jamerson was the best." There was a pause, then Freeman said, "I'd heard you were using Ricks. He's not half-bad."

"But he is not the best, either. Come see me if you are interested in my employ," Breccan said, just as the front door opened.

Lady Tara came out on the step. She held her own bag, and that was a relief to him. Here was a sign that she was not as much of a pampered miss as rumored, which was good. His clansmen, especially the women, didn't blindly offer allegiance. They made a soul work hard for their respect, but if she was willing to carry her own weight, she would do fine.

He stepped forward. "Are you ready to go, my lady?"

She nodded mutely. Her face was pale. For the first time, Breccan realized how much of a change to her life this marriage would be. She must have the same thought in her head.

"Your mount is over here." Breccan turned, and Freeman led the horse forward.

Lady Tara didn't move. She looked back to the door.

The butler came out. He had apparently been seeing to other matters and had not realized she was ready to leave the house. "My lady, may I help you?"

A frown formed between her eyes. She straightened her shoulders, and said, "No, Ingold, all is fine. Tell father I said good-bye."

"We shall see you again, will we not?" Ingold asked.

Her smile was forced. "Yes, of course." She walked down the step, but then stopped. She faced the door. "Thank you, Ingold. You and Mrs. Watson have been good friends to me."

"It was an easy task, my lady," he answered.

"And tell my sister," she continued, her voice taking on urgency, "that I care deeply for her, and I'm sorry that I had to marry before she could return."

"I will, my lady. But she will come see you when she and Mr. Stephens return."

"Yes, she might," Lady Tara agreed, but there was no hope in her voice. She walked toward Breccan, her face in shadows, her arms wrapped around her bag.

He stepped forward to help her mount. "Let me take your luggage," he offered.

She looked up at him, and he saw tears rimming dazed eyes. He reached for the bag, and, for second, she resisted. Then she sniffed as if struggling to compose herself and allowed him her bag although her hands followed him as if she wished to grasp it back.

Breccan didn't appreciate her behaving as if she was heading to the gallows. He was suddenly very anxious to be on his way before anyone noticed.

Fortunately, Jonas and Lachlan were leaving the house. "An excellent repast, Mrs. Watson," Jonas was saying. "Tell the cook everything they claim about her cooking is the Lord's truth. There could be no finer food in all the British Isles. Isn't that correct, Lachlan?"

Lachlan said something, but Breccan wasn't attending. Instead, after handing her bag to Freeman, he was trying to contrive a way to help Lady Tara mount. She offered no assistance but stood with her head bowed and her shoulders slumped.

This was not good. It embarrassed him, and so he did what he always did when uncomfortable, he took action. He picked her up and sat her on her horse as if she were a doll.

She looked up, startled.

He tensed, ready for a haranguing. Instead,

she lifted the reins and settled her leg over the pommel.

His uncles were mounting their horses. Jonas, full of whisky, kept saying his farewells to everyone. Breccan couldn't wait to leave this place. "Come," he said to his wife, and started off at a trot. She obeyed, riding beside him although she continued to be withdrawn.

Five minutes on the road home, she began weeping, the sound quiet, soft, and annoying.

Breccan didn't know what to do. Where was the woman who had shown such spirit? What had happened to her?

And he was afraid to acknowledge her crying because then he'd have to do something about it.

Jonas rode up beside him. "She's crying," he said in a whisper that if she had ears in her head she could hear.

Breccan tried to ignore him. This was his wife, his problem. His uncle needn't worry himself.

"You need to ask her why she is crying," Jonas prodded.

"I don't want to know," Breccan practically growled.

"Oh," said Jonas, and dropped back to ride

beside Lachlan, who had enough sense to keep his nose out of Breccan's business.

But his uncle's prompting made Breccan feel guilty. And, since he didn't have any other ideas, he did as Jonas had suggested. "Why are you crying?" he asked his wife.

"I'm not crying," she said with a sniff, her head bowed. Her horse was just following his. She was doing little to guide the animal.

"Then, why is there water running out of your eyes?"

No answer.

"You can visit Annefield anytime you wish," he offered, believing homesickness could be her problem.

"I know that," she said, her voice trembling.

"Then why are you crying?" Breccan had to ask again, knowing he had just gone in a circle.

"I'm *not* crying," she returned.

"Ah, then your face will *not* be blotchy from weeping," he responded.

She raised her head and shot him a look that would have skewered him if it had been a sword.

"I'll have to remember," Breccan said, "that when I want a response from you, I must appeal to your vanity."

He was mostly speaking his thoughts out loud, cataloging them for the future. He had that habit, but, for the first time, he realized there were some people, like his new wife, who might not appreciate the trait.

"I am not vain," she answered through clenched teeth.

Breccan decided he'd said enough, and so they reached Wolfstone in silence.

*H*e'd called her vain.

No one had ever said such to her, at least not outright. No one would have dared.

But she found she appreciated the laird's callous, unfair accusation. It *did* make her stop crying because she did *not* want her skin to be blotchy, and it helped harden her resolve against him.

He might be her husband, but he was the enemy. He was a Campbell, and she was a Davidson. She'd grown up on stories of the atrocities committed by the Campbells against their fellow clans—although at one time the Campbells and the Davidsons had been allies. And, yes, it had been centuries ago, but people still whispered that the Black Campbells were the worst, and here she'd been "sold" by her father to them.

Focusing on the drama of her circumstances helped her wrestle with her very real fear. Tara had never been one for pain. She did not wish to be "split in half." The horror of it unnerved her, and it didn't help that she was tired, hungry, and feeling very much alone.

Twice. She only had to let him have his way with her twice, the promise becoming her own little chant.

All too soon, they turned up a drive that led to Wolfstone Castle. It was located at the shadow of Schiehallion, the mountain that was also known as The Constant Storm.

The moonlight turned the castle's stone walls to silver. The building had to be hundreds of years old and a fitting lair for wolf.

The pace of Laird Breccan and his uncle's horses had picked up. The men seemed to lean forward, anxious to return home.

She toyed with spinning Dirk around and racing back to Annefield. But that would be cowardly.

A door opened, and a servant came out with a torch. Two more men followed him out. They moved forward to take the reins of the laird's horses.

Tara could feel that they watched her with great speculation. Ordinarily, this would not bother her. She was accustomed to people's staring at her, but this occasion was different than any other. She was their new mistress.

From hence forward, she would be known as the Lady of Wolfstone.

She didn't know if she liked the thought.

"My lady?"

The laird's deep voice surprised her. He'd already dismounted and reached up to help her off Dirk. She had no choice but to let him.

His hands seemed to encircle her waist. The contact was actually minimal. He lifted her out of the saddle and placed her on the ground, setting her on her feet as if she were a piece of porcelain he feared breaking.

She stepped away.

He did as well.

And for the first time, she considered that perhaps he found circumstances between them awkward as well.

He was not a bad sort. Indeed, he'd been gallant to her. It was just that he was so intimidating . . . and his reputation—

A herd of dogs came running out of the house. There were four of them in all shapes and sizes.

She remembered the dogs. When she had gone to his stables in search of Ruary Jamerson, his dogs had surrounded him.

She took a step back, but the beasts weren't interested in her. One was shaggy and gray and the size of a small pony. Two others were hounds; and then there was a black terrier who thought she was as big as the others. They playfully jumped on the laird, even the giant dog, anxious for his attention.

He laughed his enjoyment at such a happy greeting, rubbing the heads of his hounds and, finally, he picked up the smallest, a black terrier, and rubbed her head. She seemed the most territorial where he was concerned. She growled at the other dogs.

"Whoosh, Daphne, stop that," the laird ordered, and the dog obeyed.

Tara was not fond of dogs running loose. She was not accustomed to them and thought them quite wild.

Her father raised hunting dogs, but they were kept contained until there was a hunt. And she was even more unimpressed when she walked into the house and almost stumbled over a forgotten bone right inside the front door.

A serving girl in an apron with her blonde hair pulled back had been lighting a branch of candles. She heard Tara's soft gasp over stepping on the bone.

"*Och*, I'm so sorry, my lady. Those naughty dogs. They have no manners." She carried the candles over to Tara and handed it to her while she bent to pick up the bone, and the three others that were there.

It was cold in the house. The entry was all stone, without a rug or a small table to give it the feeling of a home. The room where the girl had been lighting her candles had a cold hearth and a table with several chairs around it. Again, Tara was struck by the hard bareness of the room, and there was definitely the smell of dog in the air.

The laird came up behind her. She realized she blocked the doorway and forced herself to move inside. His dogs followed him in, their tails still threatening to wag their rear ends off their bodies.

"This is Flora," the laird said, introducing the serving girl to her. He paused, then added, "You must be tired, my lady."

"I am a little," Tara admitted without thinking.

Jonas brought her back to her circumstances by saying as he entered the house, "Well, don't worry. Breccan will see you to bed." He grinned and winked his true meaning, and Tara felt her stomach turn inside out.

The irrepressible Jonas didn't stop in the hall but walked straight into the other room and threw his hat upon the table. Lachlan had entered, and he now joined his brother. He glanced at Tara and the laird, and said, "You two have sweet dreams. I'll keep this rowdy ape away from you in case he decides to try any wedding foolhardiness."

"Come now, Lachlan," Jonas said, as he threw himself down in one of the chairs and leaned back, setting his booted heels on the table. "He is our only nephew. Are you saying we shouldn't give him a blackening?" He referred to the country tradition of capturing the bridegroom and covering him with soot and whatever else could be found.

Flora giggled, Lachlan grinned and shook his head and Tara wanted to run.

She needed for this night to be done and over before her nerves caused her to embarrass herself. Tears had become her ever-present companions.

To his credit, the laird appeared equally ill at ease. "Do you need a private moment?" he asked.

Tara felt her heart lurch, uncertain what he was asking until she realized he wondered if she needed to use a water closet. "Aye," she answered gratefully.

"This way," he murmured. He carried her valise and led her through the sitting room, where Flora was lighting more candles for his uncles, and into another back room, and finally outside through a back entrance. "Here it is," he said, stopping in front of a stone building a few feet from the back door.

Tara was not eager to go inside. She'd been to places like this before, and she did not like them. Then again, she could use a private moment. Who knew when she'd have such an opportunity again?

She drew a deep breath and went in, closing the door behind her. To her surprise, the room was well kept and not a terrible experience at all. They had always said Wolfstone needed modernizing, and she now understood exactly what they meant. She almost feared what she would find in the rest of the house.

The laird waited respectfully for her outside. His dogs were not with him. Seeing she had noticed their absence, he said, "They heard a deer.

They took off running. Even Daphne, although with her wee legs, she can never keep up."

"Oh." She had nothing else to say.

He seemed equally awkward. "We will take these back stairs," he said, directing her back into the house. She lifted the heavy skirts of her habit and started climbing.

The stairs were not as narrow and winding as the front staircase. A draft of cold wind seemed to swirl around her. She realized that she had not thought to bring her cloak. Hopefully, Ellen would see that it was packed in the trunk. There were doors off the staircase. They were closed, probably to keep out the cold air.

"Here is my room," the laird said, and reached in front of her to open a door to Tara's right. The room was dark save for the moonlight flowing through two large windows. There were no draperies around them, and no welcoming fire had been lit in the hearth.

Holding her brace of candles, Tara walked in, her footsteps echoing on the hardwood floor.

Laird Breccan closed the door behind, and suddenly the room seemed very small. Tara worked to not panic.

He walked past her to the four-poster bed that

dominated the center of the room. It was not an ornate piece of furniture but sturdy and substantial, as one would expect for someone of his size. He set the valise on the bed.

"There is a trunk over by the corner for your things," he said. He crossed to the hearth and knelt. He began building a fire. He was using peat and wood and seemed to be deliberately busy, as if attempting to avoid meeting her eye.

Perhaps he was as nervous as she?

The idea seemed preposterous. What did he have to fear? He would be the one doing the splitting!

"I know the chest is not enough room for what you own," he continued, "especially with my gear in there. I'll move it out tomorrow, and I'll see if I can have another chest made or whatever you wish. You know more about your needs than I do."

I need to return to Annefield.

She stayed silent.

Smoke came from the hearth. He waved it away and checked the damper. It was open, but a peat fire was always smoky in the beginning. They didn't use peat in the house at Annefield.

He stood, and she could have sworn he was

taller than ever. She stared at the corner post of the bed. They stood not more than three feet from each other. She braced herself, waiting for him to pounce.

Instead, he said, "I'll give you a moment."

He left the room.

Tara found she could breathe again. She was so thankful, she almost sank to the floor. Instead, she set the candlestick on the chest.

The furnishings truly were sparse, and there wasn't any softness anywhere.

She walked over to the bed and tested it by sitting on the edge. The mattress was hard and rested on a bed of loosely woven ropes. They were a bit loose. She imagined the laird had to see these ropes tightened often. They would stretch with use and time.

She hadn't thought about beds before.

Whenever she had thought about marriage in the past, she'd had vague ideas of what married life would be like. Truthfully, she hadn't concerned herself with anything other than the wedding breakfast. She'd planned whom she would invite and what would be served, but she was realizing that she'd ignored many practical matters.

She rose from the bed, but as she did so, her foot bumped something on the floor. Bending down to see what it was, she discovered a stack of books piled haphazardly beneath the head of the bed where the room's shadows had hidden them. One was open and facedown. Aileen would have scolded him for treating a book in that manner.

Tara pulled the open book out to see what it was. She couldn't tell. It was written in Greek. Puzzled, she placed the book back. Laird Breccan didn't seem like the sort who would be bookish.

Then again, what else was there to do out here in the wilds of Scotland? She had even started sampling the books at Annefield although it was not a pastime she enjoyed.

A knock sounded at the door. "My lady?" her husband's voice asked.

Panic made her chest heavy. "*I'm not ready*. Not yet. Just a minute more."

"Very well."

She paced around in a circle and decided she must be brave. She opened her valise and removed her nightdress. Ellen had packed it.

Tara removed her hat and pulled the pins from her hair. Her hands trembled as she plaited it into one long, fat braid. She prayed she didn't embarrass herself when the time came for her to let him have his way.

Making quick work of undressing, she pulled the nightdress over her head and climbed on the bed. What did one do when sacrificing oneself? She pulled back the counterpane and climbed beneath the sheets. They were clean but not as fine and soft as the sheets from Annefield.

Tara studied the ceiling a moment, prayed for courage, and then said, "I'm ready." She closed her eyes and braced herself.

The door opened.

She could *feel* his presence. She pictured him standing in the doorway, hopefully clothed—

Or was he?

Could he be standing in the door naked? It was a *startling* thought—first, because she'd had the notion—she had never once in her life pictured anyone naked, even Ruary . . . and then secondly, if his clothes weren't on him, where were they? Would he have removed them on the landing—?

She had to look. She *must* open her eyes, even if she was afraid to because she didn't know if she would like what she saw. Still, Tara did have curiosity—

But before she could make up her mind, she heard Breccan shout an angry, "*No.*"

It was the only warning she received before a heavy, furry body landed on top of her, knocking the wind out of her.

Tara opened her eyes and found herself nose to nose with the laird's gray beast of a dog who happily slurped her face with his tongue.

In horrified seconds, other hairy, wiggling bodies with foul dog breath and rough paws bounded into the bedtime fray, climbing over Tara and trying to lick her everywhere they could.

She opened her mouth to scream, overwhelmed by the attack, but at that moment the ropes holding the bed on her left side broke, as if the extra weight and activity were too much. Dogs and woman went tumbling to the floor.

Chapter Six

From the moment Breccan had knocked on the door and heard her timid, "I'm ready," all conscious, deliberate thought had left his brain. Every drop of blood he had in his body, and certainly any intelligence he owned, had rushed straight to that part of him that was hard and stiff with wanting.

Indeed, from that day when he'd laid eyes on Lady Tara, this had become his normal state. He had only to think of her, and his body had yearned. The nights alone in his bed had been the worst.

And now here she was in it . . . and beckoning him to join her.

So could he be forgiven for not realizing that his pups had come up the stairs behind him?

He'd barely registered their presence. After all, they were a part of his life and, yes, it was true, he slept with them more often than not. He'd usually made them sleep on the floor, but there had been many times, such as during thunderstorms, when he'd let them join him. They had always relished the opportunity.

However, never had they charged the bed the way they did with Lady Tara in it.

They had barged past Breccan, Largo, his Danish hunting hound who was big enough and strong enough to almost knock him down, leading the pack. The others, the fox hounds and little Daphne, had been anxious to join.

It was as if they wanted to give Lady Tara an enthusiastic welcome.

However, cheerfully greeting her was not the activity Breccan had wanted to take part in this night.

He'd reached for the dogs, but they were too quick for him. They bounded on top of the bed, sending Lady Tara into a fit of screeching alarm.

And then the bed broke.

The mattress ropes had been frayed. Breccan

had known that. He'd meant to have them replaced, but what with juggling all of his plans for
the weaving and the horses and paying the earl of
Tay's debts, well, it was a detail that had slipped
his mind—unfortunately.

Lady Tara and dogs were dumped onto the
floor inside the bed frame. Tails, ears, red hair
and bare legs were jumbled up together as they
all scrambled to right themselves.

Even Daphne was in the mix. Her short legs
made it difficult for her to leap up onto the bed.
Breccan always had to help her. She'd been jumping on the floor the way she did, begging to join
the others. Now that everyone was on the ground,
Daphne bounded into the game, her round little
body quivering with excitement.

It was quite a welcoming, except Lady Tara
didn't seem to be enjoying it.

Breccan had started forward to help, but the
flailing of his young wife's legs, feet and toes riveted him to the ground. He remembered all too
well the sight of those legs clad in breeches and
tall boots. They were even more shapely without
them.

So he didn't move as quickly as he should have
to her rescue.

That was all right because she managed to free herself, showing an amazing resilience. She reached for one of Breccan's books and came to her feet, swishing it through the air like a sword, her braid over one shoulder.

"Stay back, you beasts."

They appeared to do as she said, tails wagging. Breccan knew they were just biding their time. "They think it is a game—" he started to advise, but at that moment the book came in contact with one of the foxhound's head.

She'd struck sweet Tidbit, a sensitive dog if ever there was one.

Tidbit yelped and fell back, as did the other dogs. Daphne spoke for all of them when she looked up at Lady Tara, her beady black eyes full of disapproval, and barked sharply.

Lady Tara's response was to threaten Daphne with a book beating.

And it wasn't just any book she would knock them with but it was a copy of *THE ELEMENTS* by Euclid that he had borrowed from a military engineer he had met in Glasgow.

Now, he moved forward, coming up behind her.

That was an expensive book, and he could ill afford, especially at this moment, to pay the man back. He grabbed the book just as Lady Tara pulled back to swing it again at his dogs.

She whirled to face him. *"Take them out of here,"* she ordered, wild-eyed.

"Don't be angry. They are just trying to say welcome."

"Very well, *I'll* leave," she replied, and started to step over the bed frame, her balance thrown off by the mattress beneath her feet. Breccan reached forward to help her, but she yanked her arm away—and that is when he realized her nightdress was made of very thin stuff.

He could see the shadow of her breast. He had seen her bare legs. She was naked beneath that gown.

Suddenly, Breccan had strong motivation to make her happy.

"Out," he barked at the dogs, lifting the book himself and threatening them.

His pets gave him quizzical looks. He rarely raised his voice with them.

"Go on now," he ordered, gesturing toward the door.

Tails stopped wagging. Largo and the foxhounds slinked off the mattress, moving toward the door. They looked back as if asking him if he was truly angry or just teasing them? Perhaps this was a new game?

"*Out,*" Breccan bellowed, the word ringing to the ceiling. He was indulgent with his dogs, his clansmen, everyone—but he did expect to be obeyed when he used that tone of voice.

They went running to the door, their tails between their legs.

Well, everyone went running save for Daphne. She still stood on the mattress, as proud of herself to be there. She gave a bark as if to punctuate his order to the others.

"I meant you as well, Daphne," he said.

She looked around as if there was more than one Daphne in the room, and she had no intention of going anywhere. Breccan knew his pet. She did not believe the order pertained to her.

With a sound of frustration, he dropped the book on top of Lady Tara's folded clothing on the chest and picked Daphne up with both hands. He marched the terrier to the doorway, placed her on the floor and scooted her out. He shut the door.

At last, he was alone with Lady Tara.

He turned to her.

She stood in front of the fire. She was so bloody

beautiful. He wanted her undressed with all haste—

Daphne scratched the door. He knew it was her. The scratching had an impertinent sound. "Go away, Daphne," he ordered, then apologized to Lady Tara, "Jonas was supposed to keep the dogs with him—"

"Those dogs are wild," she declared, wiping her mouth with the back of her hand. "Dog hair is all over me."

Breccan understood. Dog hair could fly everywhere, and he hated it in his mouth as well. Those short hairs could be pesky.

"They are good pets—" he started to assure her, daring to move closer to her. Her nipples were erect. He could see the outline of the points of them against her nightdress.

"Good?" She waved toward the bed with its mattress aslant. "Did you see what they did to me? They *attacked* me."

"No, they didn't—" he tried to soothe.

"They *did*," she shot back, the outrage in her eyes as sharp as lightning bolts.

Breccan didn't wish to argue. He yearned for her gentleness, for her affection . . . and to bury himself as deep as he could in her sweetness—

Daphne scratched again. One of the hounds howled a protest.

"Have you not been around dogs? Breccan asked. His gaze riveted on his lady's toes peeking out from the hem of her nightdress. She had cute toes. He'd not known toes could be special, but hers were. He took another step toward her. He wanted to worship every inch of her, but first he had to take her in his arms. "My pets were just greeting you—"

"*Fleas.* I'd wager they have fleas." She began itching madly. "I'm certain of it."

Visions of worshipping vanished. "My dogs don't have fleas," Breccan said, annoyed with the charge.

"You wish to know if I've been around dogs? Well, let me tell you, *I have.* I've been around *lots* of dogs." She tossed her head, as if in an act of defiance, as if she expected him to challenge her.

He wouldn't do that. He could barely focus on what she was saying. The vibrant color of her hair was a distraction. She had beautiful hair. He longed to run his hands through it and see if it was as silky to the touch as it looked—

"*Well-trained* ones," she continued, "that *know*

their place in life. They live *outside*. They are never allowed inside the house—"

Lust died. "*Outside?* My pets go wherever I go, especially on a cold night. I have outside dogs. But these? They need to be inside."

"You have *more* dogs? How many dogs do you have?" She made him sound unnatural.

"As many as I want," he said, put off by her attack.

Lady Tara held out her arms and looked around as if she did not know what to make of him. "Well, you can have your *dogs* or you can have *me*," she said. "I shall *not* live with dogs in the house."

If she had demanded anything else, Breccan would have given it to her. He would have thrown Jonas and Lachlan out the door without a backward glance.

But he liked his dogs. They were his confidants. Many a time when he'd felt backed into a corner, their loyal acceptance had helped him regain his sense of purpose. He could always count on them, something he could not do with people.

Something he had wanted to do with the woman who was his wife . . . and who really didn't have a care for him.

In one fell swoop of insight, Breccan realized

he didn't know this woman at all, and they had promised themselves to each other until death. Had he been mad?

No, randy.

There was something about her that attracted him in a way no other female had. He could study the curve of her cheek, the line of her neck, and the way she used her hands to express herself for all of time, but that didn't mean he could live with her, especially over his dogs.

"I don't take ultimatums, my lady."

"And I will not be mauled by animals," she informed him coolly, as if he were a mere lackey.

"Do you really believe I would allow that to happen to my wife?" The words exploded out of him.

Her eyes widened. Had no one ever raised a voice to her before? She drew three sharp breaths, then said, "I don't know if you would allow it or not. I know nothing of you," she added, echoing his own thoughts. "And after the evening I've had"—her voice was starting to shake—"I'm not certain I want to know you. Look at the *bed*. Look at this *room*. Look at *me*."

"I am looking at you, and I'm not certain I like you," he answered. "This is my house, woman. And my rules."

"Well, this is my bedroom, *man*. And here I have some say."

"And what makes you say that?"

"Because we are married," she said, giving a lift of her chin as if daring him to challenge her.

"We are *not* married yet," he growled. "Not until you are bedded—which right now, is *not* going to happen this night."

On those words, he yanked open the door and went charging out to the hall. He slammed the door behind him.

To his surprise, his dogs were not outside waiting for him, not even Daphne. He stomped down the stairs. All was dark save for the fire that was built for *her* arrival in the front room. He went in and there were his pups, curled up before the hearth. Tidbit and his foxhound brother Terrance were tucked in close to Largo's side. Daphne slept a distance away from them, as was her custom.

The hounds lifted their heads when he walked in, then laid them back down. Only Largo followed Breccan with his eyes as he moved to the table and pulled out two chairs.

Daphne was more to the point. She surveyed him with the disdain of a governess, then resettled herself so she was giving him her back.

"That's all right, lass," he said to her. "I have a feeling I'd best become accustomed to haughty, stubborn women."

Daphne sniffed her thoughts and feigned sleep.

But the others came back to him. As he settled his weight to stretch out between the two chairs, Terrance and Tidbit prodded his hand with cold, wet noses. He gave them a pat, and that was the invitation to Largo. The wolfhound came up to him.

He scratched the Largo's ear. The dog's expression was one of remorse. "Don't think you spoiled my wedding night. I know you were just giving her a greeting. She's not like us," he confided, "and I don't know what I am going to do. But I must be up before Jonas or anyone else. Do you hear me? Be certain I am awake."

The dogs stared as if they understood.

Breccan did not want anyone to know he'd spent the first night of his marriage sleeping in a chair. This would be his secret, a secret between him and his dogs, the only ones in his life he could trust.

$\mathcal{T}$ara could not believe that the laird had walked out on her.

She stared at the door, then muttered to herself, "It is just as well he left. I wasn't ready for him to bed me anyway."

And that was true.

However, she had sounded as shrill as a fish-wife. She could hear her voice now and was slightly embarrassed at her carrying on.

But the dogs had surprised her. It had taken all her courage to lie in wait for him and to find herself attacked—

Tara paused in her thought. "Attacked" was a strong word. So had been "mauled." She knew she had not been in any danger.

Still, dogs did not belong inside the house.

And the other revelation of all that had passed between them was that she was exhausted.

In less than five hours, her world had been upended.

She looked down at the dull gold band on her ring finger. "I don't know if I can do this," she whispered.

Of course, there was no answer. As was so often the case as she was growing up, when she needed advice or wise counsel, there was no one there for her.

Considering the age difference between Aileen

and herself, her older sister was always involved in her own pursuits. Nannies and governesses were fine, but they left. Sooner or later, they had to move to a new position, especially when the earl would fail to pay their wages.

Mrs. Watson was kind and good . . . but she was not how Tara imagined a mother would be.

A mother. Laird Breccan wanted children. That was their bargain. Tara would be a mother.

For the first time, she tried to picture what that would mean. Her own mother had died giving birth to her, and the laird wanted children.

A hint of a thought, a tiny inkling of an idea entered her mind. Some would claim that over the past few months she had been behaving erratically. She'd accepted the proposal of one man and run off for another. Truthfully, if Tara could have put off marriage, she would have. She had only accepted the marriage offer because, amongst the debutantes and other young women in society, she had been growing long of tooth. It was past time for her to marry.

But in missing a mother's presence in this moment, Tara found herself considering that she might had avoided marriage because it has been marriage to her father the earl that had taken her mother's life—a woman she'd never known.

No one talked about her, not even her father. She'd asked him a question once, but he hadn't answered. Instead, he had chastised her for having morbid thoughts. Life was for the living.

She studied her wedding ring a moment longer and wished she could have known the woman who had worn it. Like it or not, this ring was a connection between the two of them.

"Would you allow dogs in the house?" she asked, speaking to the memory of the laird's mother; and then she laughed at herself. She was exhausted.

Tomorrow, she would deal with this marriage. Tonight, she needed to rest.

She tugged the mattress so that it landed on the floor, the frayed ropes hanging from the bed frame. Climbing on it, she brought covers over her head.

Snuggling in, she toyed with the thought that maybe, when she woke, this whole day would disappear. It would prove to have been a dream, and with that pleasantry on her mind, she fell asleep— only to wake and discover on the next day, things were worse than she could have imagined.

Chapter Seven

*E*ven on the floor, the mattress was lumpy, as if it had never been turned. Tara knew exactly where the laird slept because the wool-stuffed mattress was contoured to his form. She'd spent the night curled in what would have been the center of his body. It had been the only comfortable place.

However, with daylight came optimism.

She'd learned a long time ago that her wisest course was to the make the best of things.

The hour of the day when she woke was not as late as she usually slept in London, but not as early as she usually woke at Annefield. She'd started the habit of an early-morning ride. That would not happen today, and she found she missed it.

Pushing her sleep-mussed hair out of her eyes, she clambered to her feet and stepped off the mattress. There were no drapes on the windows, so the sun of what promised to be a fine autumn day streamed through panes of glass that could use a cleaning. The floor appeared clean enough until she spied some dog hair. Its presence did not surprise her.

There was work to be done here, but it wasn't as dire as she had anticipated from her misadventures last night.

The fire had died out. However, it had been built in a clean hearth. That was a good sign. This might have been a bachelor's household, but a sense of Scottish cleanliness and good order prevailed . . . beneath the dog hair.

Then again, it was now *her* house. She was the mistress, an interesting concept since she had no relationship to the furniture in the house. This bedroom wasn't like hers at Annefield, where James Stuart had slept on the bed, and, therefore, it would remain forever in that room. She could make changes here.

Of course, as was often the situation in drafty old castles, the bedroom was not spacious. However, a washstand with a privacy screen could be fitted in the far corner by the bed. There was also room on the wall by the door for a dresser and perhaps a wardrobe.

In London, she'd been attracted to furniture designed in the style of the ancient pharaohs. She'd liked the gilded sphinxes and the graceful carvings on the chairs. She was certain the furniture was expensive, especially since it must come from London, but Laird Breccan was a wealthy man. After all, he'd paid her father's debts. Would he not pay for a bit of elegance in his home?

Furthermore, this style would suit him. The laird was a big man. He needed strong, masculine furniture. She could picture him in a cross-framed chair. He would look a bit like a warrior general, a fanciful thought that caught her by surprise.

She remembered he was in church one Sunday. Her father had enjoyed making a jest over Laird Breccan's presence. In some way, a tiny corner of her brain had noted him. Her mind's eye recalled his sitting in the back of the congregation. He was not a man who could hide, even in a crowd. He always stood out.

Of course, that Sunday, she'd been distraught over hearing Ruary had eloped . . .

Tara pushed the memory from her mind.

Ruary's rejection still hurt, and with that hurt came an almost overwhelming sadness for what she'd lost.

Instead, she forced herself to think of furniture.

She didn't look in the direction of the broken bed with the mattress on the floor and the lattice-worked ropes broken and frayed. The sight of it reminded her of the fight they'd had, the one in which he had warned her, *We are not married yet. Not until you are bedded.*

Tara released her breath with the heaviness of acceptance. She was going to have to let him have her. She had no choice. Two children; her freedom.

But for right now, her first move was to dress.

There was no maid, and she hadn't expected one this morning. She dressed herself in the long-sleeved day dress of a soft, peach-striped cambric with a gauze fichu at the neckline. Some people claimed women with her coloring should not wear the rose and peach hues, but Tara enjoyed defying convention. She also liked the way these colors gave her skin a soft glow.

Swiftly braiding her hair, Tara fashioned it in a knot at the base of her neck and walked to the door. She stood a minute, trying to listen through the heavy wood. She didn't hear any movement. She dared to open the door, cracking slightly and bracing herself for another wild-dog attack.

No one was in the hall.

She went out onto the stair landing. There was barely room for two people to stand on it. The stairs wound up to another room not far above her, and there was a door that opened into another room on her level.

The stairs were as drafty as she remembered them to be because of open arrow slits in the wall. Someone should have closed them up or put glass in to block the air. She doubted anyone would be firing arrows at their enemies from the towers in this day and age.

Curiosity propelled her to open the door, to discover a long room that was larger than the receiving room at Annefield and almost empty of furniture. There were desk and chair and a huge, leather-upholstered chair in front of the carved-stone fireplace that dominated the center of the interior wall. Once again, there were no rugs on the floor.

Opposite it was a bank of three arched, mullioned windows. Tara quite liked them and walked over to investigate. They overlooked a charming garden that she had caught a glimpse of from the bedroom window.

Late-season roses bloomed over a trellised gate. There were well-tended beds of flowers that were sadly losing their vigor with the coolness of the season, and herbs were being allowed to go to seed in preparation for winter. Beyond the garden was a road that must lead to the stables. A bank of trees at a curve in the road blocked her view.

People had told her that Wolfstone needed modernizing, and she could agree. There was plenty of room here to build a water closet, especially one that could be accessed by the laird's bedroom although it would mean moving a wall—

A footstep sounded on the stairs.

She turned just as Laird Breccan started to pass the doorway. He must have been on his way to check on her because, catching a glimpse of her in the main room, he came to an abrupt halt. He stepped inside the door, having to duck as he did so. The doorframe had not been designed for a man over six feet in stature.

For a moment, they seemed to take each other's measure.

He was a well-built man. Because he was so tall, he intimidated. However, now, she discovered he was not all that scary. Yes, his shoulders were broad, and he had an air of true power, but his manner was unassuming. He wore work clothes—buff breeches, worn boots and a hunter green waistcoat over a homespun shirt. He hadn't bothered with a neckcloth.

She wondered if he had been out exercising the horses. The smell of fresh air was about him. He had also still not shaved. She wondered when he would, although the few days' growth of beard on his face was not unattractive. Besides, if a man wouldn't shave for his wedding, when would he?

As for him, he seemed to be taking a truly good look at her for the first time . . . and she sensed he wasn't entirely happy with what he was seeing.

It was not vanity for Tara to believe she was an uncommonly beautiful woman. Almost everyone of her acquaintance, including the Prince Regent, said it was so. Why should she doubt them?

But she did.

In moments of blinding self-honesty, Tara knew they were wrong. She clearly saw her defects . . . and lately, not just the physical ones.

Now, someone else seemed to see them as well. He spoke. "The dogs are outside."

That was a concession. She recognized that she might have overreacted the night before. Having not been around dogs as pets, she didn't understand those who doted on them. Thinking back, she had sounded a bit churlish last night. "Thank you. I know they mean a great deal to you."

He nodded but didn't speak. Was he waiting for a compromise from her? The only person she'd ever met halfway was her sister Aileen.

Then again, wasn't a husband at least of the same importance as a sister?

We are not married yet. Not until you are bedded.

Those words seemed to hang in the air between them. Especially, "not until you are bedded."

But if he was thinking in the same direction, she couldn't tell. Instead, he said, "I thought you might need some private time and your breakfast. That is why I came for you."

"Thank you." She hesitated a beat, then heard herself say, "I was thinking, you could put a room for a water closet here. I mean you have the room, then it would be there for the bedroom."

A part of her must have wanted him to exclaim over her cleverness, a desire that caught her off guard—but then, maybe it shouldn't. He was her husband, and shouldn't she want to make the best of a bad situation?

His response was a frown. "These are stone walls. They are a foot thick."

"They have done renovations to royal palaces. I'm certain something can be done here," she replied.

"Palaces," he repeated, as if with that one word he could dismiss her suggestion as gibberish.

"Yes, *palaces*," she answered. "Is this not a castle?"

He shook his head, not even entertaining her idea. "This way." He started out of the room, expecting her to follow.

And she did. She didn't have a choice. It was either follow him or wander aimlessly around Wolfstone.

But when she had a chance, she was going to repeat her water-closet suggestion. Just because he was mired in his ways didn't mean her idea lacked merit.

He took her down the staircase and outside to where the garderobe was located. It was only a step or two from the back doorway, but still, certainly he could see how more convenient it would be if the room was upstairs.

Also waiting outside were his dogs. They sat in a line by the door, the tallest to the smallest, like children waiting to greet a new governess. Their tails began wagging as he came out of the house, but their heads dropped when they caught sight of Tara following him.

Well, not all heads dropped.

Daphne, the black terrier, lifted her nose to glare with shiny black button eyes. She even gave a growl—

"Daph-ne," the laird warned in a low voice.

The terrier stopped the growling but not the glaring.

The dogs' reactions startled Tara. They acted like individual people. They seemed to understand everything that was happening and had formed opinions. But that couldn't be. They were dogs.

She disappeared into the garderobe to see to her business. It was barely a more pleasant place in the light of day. There were narrow windows close to the roofline that allowed for air.

When she came out, she saw that the laird waited a respectful distance from the building. The dogs were gone, save for Daphne. The terrier appeared to have taken it upon herself to protect all from Tara.

She barked and went running to the laird as if warning him.

"She doesn't like me," Tara said to the laird as she approached. They stood on a stone-paved walkway that connected the castle to several outbuildings.

He didn't argue. "You've placed yourself on her bad side. Daphne can hold a grudge. She'll forgive you by and by."

"She's a *dog*," Tara felt she must point out.

"And what does that have to do with anything?" he said, indicating with a nod for her to follow him.

"A dog can't have human emotions," Tara explained.

"Obviously they can. You just said you felt she doesn't like you. Dislike is a human emotion."

Tara frowned, certain he was deliberately trying to vex her. He had to be upset about last night. She'd always heard men cared about the marriage act more than women. She'd overheard more than one matron complain as an explanation for a husband's pouty mood.

She skipped a step to catch up with him, putting her hand on his arm to beg him to stop for a moment.

He turned.

"I'm sorry last night didn't go the way it should

have." There, she had apologized, and it was prettily done in her mind.

"Do you think this is about me?"

"Yes," Tara answered, as if it was obvious.

"Well, perhaps it is," he said, facing her. "This is my home, my lady. I understand I am not your choice of a husband, but we have a bargain, one I regret making."

He would have walked away again, his haughty terrier leading the way, but Tara was not done. She tightened her hold on his arm.

"You are being unfair," she accused. "This is all new to me. You—" she started, ready to hurl a few choice comments about him and his dogs, but then thought better of it. What purpose would it serve?

And she realized, her sister would have been proud to hear her bite her tongue. Aileen had set the example of a woman gracefully accepting responsibility for her own actions. Tara must act in that manner as well.

"You must be patient," she finished, covering up what she could have said. "Please."

She didn't meet his eye as she added that last. He'd see what a struggle being contrite was for her.

He reached down for her hand on his arm and gently held it in his own. He ran the pad of his thumb along the line of her nails. "This is all new to you. I imagine it is a bit of a comeuppance. It's not London."

"Not yet." She found the courage to meet his eye and was surprised that instead of being cold and gray as she'd originally thought, they were blue. A light blue.

Their children would have blue eyes.

The unbidden thought astonished her. Her mind had never traveled in that direction before, but it did now . . . with him.

"So all is not lost?" she asked. A hint of her old self, the woman who could prettily command any man's attention, was in her tone.

And he responded to that woman. The iciness left his manner. "No, it is not lost at all. We shall do better with each other." He raised her fingers to his lips and kissed the tips.

A warmth spread through her, a response to being this close to him. He would not have been her first choice of a husband or her second or third—but he was the man she had married. They could do well together, at least until she left for her life in London.

At their feet, Daphne sniffed her disdain, but Tara didn't worry about her anymore. The laird was choosing her over his dogs. He might not realize it at this moment, but he had.

"Come, you need something to eat." He directed her toward the open door of the kitchen, which was attached to the main building. Perhaps at one time it had been separate, but one of the laird's ancestors had seen fit to build a walkway, and from that walkway had come a hall, then a room.

The kitchen was one long space with a good-sized table in the center for kneading dough and arranging dishes. There was a good deal of bustle. The cook here was a male. He had two scullery girls to help him turn the meat he must have been preparing for dinner. Meat pies were cooling on the table. The laird's uncle Lachlan sat at the table eating one of the pies. He rose as Tara entered the room and greeted her by asking if she'd slept well.

"I did," Tara lied, but that was fine because by the twinkle in his eye as he shot a glance at his nephew, he had apparently not expected an honest answer.

The laird cleared his voice as if he, too, was a bit embarrassed.

That was a change. She'd not thought of a man of his stature as being anything but confident. But then, the laird wasn't like most men she knew. There was a humility about him. He was probably strong enough that he could break any man's neck, and yet, there was a touch of gentleness about him as well, and some of the tension she always held deep inside her eased . . . to be replaced by the spark of interest.

With the right clothes and a good barber, why, he might even be handsome beneath his scruffiness.

"We take most of our meals in here," the laird explained, nodding to the table. "There is only the three of us, so we don't stand on ceremony. Of course, now there are four of us."

She liked the way his deep voice had warmed over "four of us." He included her.

Of course, that didn't stop her from thinking it might be nicer to eat in the dining room inside the house, but she had to remember she was not planning on staying.

The laird was introducing her to the cook, a man with a barrel-shaped chest by the name of Dougal. The girl Tara had met the night before, Flora, was also one of the scullery maids, as was another young woman close to Tara's age named Agnes.

Dougal was most anxious to see to Tara's breakfast. She noticed that Daphne and the other dogs were not in the kitchen. Daphne lingered outside the door, eyeing Tara as if she was evaluating all the attention the human mistress was receiving and was not pleased.

So perhaps dogs had more human attitudes than Tara had supposed?

She focused on her breakfast and not the unhappy terrier outside the door. "I would be pleased with just some tea and toasted bread," she said.

"Aye, we can do that," Dougal answered, and started giving out instructions for Flora to make the toast and Agnes to see to the tea. "Use one of the good cups. And the saucer, too."

Dougal turned his attention back to entertaining his laird's new wife. He was attempting to be very gallant. This was the reaction Tara expected from men.

Lachlan watched the interaction in the kitchen with a bemused air.

Benches served as seating for the table. Tara asked Lachlan, "May I sit across from you?"

"I would hope that you would," he answered.

She was about to slide onto the bench when the

laird's other uncle Jonas came charging into the kitchen. He addressed himself to Lachlan, who could be seen easily by anyone passing the doorway.

"God's balls, Lachlan, you should see Breccan's bed. He and the Davidson lass *destroyed* it. He must have pounded heerrrr—" He drew out the last word as he caught sight of Tara at the table with the laird off to one side. Apparently, they could not be seen from the walkway.

His eyebrows hitting his hairline, Jonas closed his mouth. There was a moment of awkward silence.

Tara's face flamed with embarrassment. She could feel the interest of the cook and the maids. A legend had been born. She knew the story of the broken bed would now take on a life of its own. And there was nothing she could do to stop it other than to tell the truth, and that meant admitting the marriage had not been consummated. She knew to keep her mouth shut.

Jonas tried to overcome his lapse of manners. It was never good to be caught gossiping. "Why, good morning, my lady," he said with false heartiness. "And you, Breccan. I thought you were down at the barn."

"I have a bed to fix," the laird said dryly.

Such a statement would have dampened the spirits of a lesser man, but Jonas recovered. He smiled. "Well, that is not a bad thing, is it?"

"Perhaps you should go to the barn, Jonas," the laird suggested.

"I should," Jonas readily agreed, obviously eager to escape. He picked up a meat pie off the table, toasted Tara with it, his grin having returned, and popped out the door.

"Why couldn't he have been born mute?" the laird grumbled.

"Because God is wiser than we are," Lachlan answered.

The laird looked to Dougal. "Isn't my lady's tea ready?" he asked pointedly, a reminder that the cook should mind his business.

"Aye, Breccan. It is almost." Dougal snapped his fingers for his girls to stop gaping and finish their tasks.

Tara had been studying the wood grain in the table, but now that her initial shock over Jonas's boast about the bed had passed, she realized the incident was humorous. Jonas's expression at seeing her in the kitchen was one to be remembered, and she couldn't help but smile.

The laird sat on the bench beside her. He was

disgruntled. It swirled in the air around him. He leaned close to her to confide, "Jonas should mind his own business."

"That is *not* the way of families," she answered. Flora set a cup of tea in front of her. She picked up the spoon resting on the saucer.

"They know too much about my life," he answered.

"That *is* the way of families," she said.

He looked at her with new eyes. "You are taking this well."

"So are you . . . considering."

He studied her as if uncertain how to accept her comment, then must have decided she was teasing, as she had been. He smiled.

His smile transformed him. She hadn't realized how tense he was, how serious, until that moment. He had a dimple, just one. She had not noticed it before, but she now found it charming.

"You surprise me," he confided.

"I confound myself," she admitted. And then she dared to lean close to him and say, "But we do have a bargain. I will honor it."

Men were easy to read. His glance said he hoped she was being serious. Yes, he wanted her, and she was beginning to sense the attraction between them might be mutual. She just needed to take hold of her nerves.

She could feel the approval of the others in the kitchen. They liked their laird. The Scots were egalitarian amongst their clansman. There was often a proprietorial air toward their leaders. They wanted him happy.

Breccan. She said his name in her mind. They all called him by his given name. Even the cook called him Breccan.

Could not his wife? Especially since she liked the sound of his name. His was a strong name.

And she would have used it. A sentence was forming in her head so that she could hear herself speak his name aloud—but at that moment, a young lad charged into the kitchen. He was breathing hard as if he'd come a good distance. He looked around wildly, his gaze settling on Breccan.

"Laird, Mr. Ricks needs you at the stables. It's Taurus. He's standing on three feet. Mr. Ricks says it is bad."

The lad did not have to repeat himself. Breccan shot up from the table and moved for the door. "What has happened?" he demanded.

"He has pulled up lame," the lad answered.

"Damn." With that one word, Breccan was gone without a backward glance toward Tara.

Lachlan started to rise as well. "Excuse me, my lady, I need go to the stables."

"What is it?" Tara asked. "What is happening?"

"Taurus is an important stallion," Lachlan said. "I'd best go and see if I can offer assistance." He left, and Tara felt like a great wind had come through and sucked everyone out of the kitchen—save for Dougal and the maids.

The cook made his feelings known by throwing the pronged fork he'd been using to lift a pot from the fire into the corner of the kitchen. Flora and Agnes froze as if expecting another outburst.

Tara slid off the bench to rise. "What is it?" she demanded of the cook.

"A catastrophe, my lady. Without that horse, we're ruined." He didn't explain more but joined the other men by running out of the kitchen as well.

"This doesn't make sense," Tara said. She looked to the maids. Agnes appeared ready to burst into tears. "What is happening?" Tara demanded.

"We need Taurus, my lady," Flora said. "There is to be a race in three weeks' time. If the laird doesn't win that race, why, he could lose every-thing."

"What do you mean 'everything'?" Tara asked.

"It is Owen Campbell's fault," Agnes said, jumping into the conversation. "If he hadn't said the things he did about the laird, there wouldn't be a wager."

"A wager," Tara repeated, focusing on this key bit of information. "The laird gambles?"

"Not often," Flora hurried to say in his defense. "But this was forced upon him."

"In what way?" Many a time, Tara's father had claimed he'd been forced to gamble—and nothing could be further from the truth.

"Owen Campbell said terrible things about our horses in front of everyone in Aberfeldy one day," Agnes said somberly. "Then he challenged the laird to a race, one our pride says we must win."

"Well, if this Taurus is lame, he can't run," Tara answered. She took a sip of tea. *Breccan was a gambler.* She'd lived all her life with one in the person of her father. She knew and abhorred the hand-to-mouth existence. A gambler was one sort of person she had *not* wanted to marry.

"It is not that simple, my lady," Flora said. "The laird had to put up the money to enter the race. If

Taurus doesn't run, he loses his stake. We may all lose. Dougal and all the others have made wagers with the other side of the family. We want Taurus to win."

"If he doesn't, the laird will be poor again," Agnes added.

"Poor?" Tara frowned. She had no desire to be poor. She didn't even like the sound of the word. The laird could not afford to let her live her life in London if he was poor. "The Campbells are not poor. They are many things they are, but lacking in money is not one of them."

"You might be wrong there, my lady," Flora answered, a wisdom in her eye that belied her youth. "There is many a poor Campbell. We were once, but then the laird had made things good for us. But lately, Dougal says he has been spending his money . . ." Her voice trailed off, and her eyes widened as if she realized she was saying too much, and Tara had a suspicion of what Dougal had *actually* been saying.

Flora turned around suddenly and furiously started to pretend as if she were busy with knives and pots. "I forgot to cut your bread and make your toast, my lady."

Agnes's eyes had gone round as if she was

alarmed by Flora's furious activity—but Tara was not fooled. She walked over to the maid and placed a restraining hand on Flora's as she was about to cut the bread.

"Yes, my lady?" Flora asked, the picture of innocence.

"What Dougal told you is that the laird paid my father's debts?"

Flora's mouth rounded as if she didn't know what to say, but then she finally conceded. "Yes, my lady. Most of us know that."

"But you are all worried now because you know the laird has overextended his purse?"

"Overextended, my lady?"

"He doesn't have the blunt to meet his debts if that horse doesn't win," Tara said, speaking plainly.

Tara could see the thought go through the girl's head that she should just deny all knowledge. With a lift of her eyebrow, Tara dissuaded her.

"I have heard that could be the case," Flora admitted.

Tara began moving toward the door.

"Don't you wish your toast, my lady?" an anxious Flora asked.

"I'm not hungry."

"Please, my lady, have I upset you?" Flora pleaded.

Tara stopped in the doorway. "No, Flora, you haven't. But I'm about to upset Laird Breccan." She left then, following to the stables, where she would discover for herself the exact state of the laird's finances . . . and woe to him if he'd promised her London and could not deliver.

Chapter Eight

$\mathcal{B}$reccan was a fair enough horseman, but there was much he didn't know. Lameness was one of those issues. When he'd left the barn an hour ago, Taurus had been fine. Now, the horse moved under the lad riding him in the paddock as if he was a three-legged stool.

"What is causing this?" Breccan asked.

"There could be a number of reasons," William Ricks answered. He was of middling years with a horseman's flair. His wide-brimmed hat and red waistcoat had become a common sight around Wolfstone.

"Pick one," Breccan answered, ready to grind the man to a nub. He wanted answers.

"He could have a stone bruise. Or have pulled a muscle. Since the lameness is in his left front, he could have rolled wrong and injured his neck."

Injured his neck? Breccan did not like the sound of that.

"Can he run in the race?" Breccan had to know.

"I can't say, Laird," Ricks answered. "There is no knowing."

Breccan wanted to roar his rage, and it didn't help that he was the one who had put his pride on the line with a senseless wager.

"Then what are you going to do for the horse?" Breccan asked in a voice that could strike fear in any man.

Ricks was no exception. "We'll rub him down and keep him on stall rest. We might be lucky and it is only an abscess although I can feel no heat. However, I have a trick of drawing the poison out. I'll have the lads press a wedge of potato to the bottom of his hoof and tie it in place. That could do the trick."

"A potato?" Breccan repeated with a hint of disgust. The man was guessing, and considering how much Breccan was paying him, that guess was costing him dearly.

Not for the first time did he wish Ruary Jamerson was still in the area. The horse master had a gift. It was as if the horses communicated with him. He would have understood what Taurus's injury was.

He would have also told Breccan he'd been a fool to take Owen Campbell's challenge. Jamerson had wanted Breccan to race Taurus in the Derby in the coming spring. That was where Breccan's plans for the horse should have been. Instead, he'd allowed his pride to make an unwise choice.

His pride had been doing a bit too much of that lately.

Well, it was too late to change the game.

"Do as you say," Breccan said to Ricks. He turned to where Lachlan and Jonas stood by the fence. They were not alone. A dozen or so of his clansman had gathered around the paddock to watch Taurus move. Their grave expressions showed their concern.

Aye, the Derby at Epsom would be a fine race to win, but for the Black Campbells, the only race that mattered was the one against Owen Campbell and his ilk. Breccan did not want to think on how many wagers his clansman had made on Taurus. He wouldn't be the only one with empty pockets.

"So?" Jonas demanded, wanting a report.

"He doesn't know," Breccan answered.

"Doesn't know?" Jonas snorted his opinion. "The lads are telling me the horse was fine this morning."

Breccan shrugged. "A horse can change in a blink. He might have been hurting and not showing it."

"But will he be able to race?" Lachlan asked, and the men around them leaned close for the answer.

"So you've placed a wager as well?" Breccan asked his uncle.

Lachlan acted as if the question was a foolish one. "Of course I'd put money on you, lad. And I can't wait to see Owen Campbell's comeuppance."

Several heads nodded.

However, Breccan was saved from a reply by a stirring amongst the men around him. Breccan turned and looked to see what had caught their attention and saw Lady Tara walking with purpose toward him with the air of an avenging Diana, goddess of the hunt.

Men gaped in open admiration. Breccan could understand how they felt. He still had difficulty looking at her without his mind leaping to a hundred fantasies. Perhaps even two hundred.

If she was aware of her impact on his men, she gave no indication, and perhaps that was good. Someone muttered something about the bed having been broken, and now he understood why. Ah, yes; Jonas's tongue had been busy.

And there was more than one whispered comment and a snicker or two as Breccan moved forward to meet her.

In truth, he did not need her distraction right now. He had a busy day ahead of him, one already disrupted by Taurus's injury. Who knew what would happen next—?

"I wish to talk to you," Lady Tara said without preamble.

"Can it wait?"

"Would I have come out here if it could?" she replied tartly. She started walking between the paddocks, moving away from the stables, where they could be overheard. She didn't look back but expected him to follow as if he were a pet monkey.

For a second, he debated letting her stew in her own vinegar, but then curiosity propelled him forward. His dogs started to trail after Breccan, but he sent them back with a word. There was no sense in antagonizing her more than she was.

From behind him, someone called, "Make her purr, Laird."

The randy bastards. If they knew what had really happened last night, they wouldn't be so proud of him. Thank God for Wolfstone's thick walls.

Lady Tara had stopped at the far paddock post. She waited impatiently. He could swear she tapped her toe.

He slowed his step. He had to. He was male.

Her jaw tightened, but he gave her credit that she waited until he reached her before she lashed out, "What is this about you not having any money?"

"I have money."

She shot him a look that said she believed he was lying. It made him bloody angry.

"*Are* you done up?" she asked, rephrasing the question.

"*No.*"

"If you don't win that horse race, will you be?"

Breccan wondered where she'd heard the story. He decided not to prevaricate. "Money will be tight."

"What of our bargain?"

"The damn bargain," he said with disgust. He had more pressing concerns than her bargain.

"That is not how you spoke yesterday."

"Right now, yesterday seems like a lifetime ago. Wait, I remember. Yesterday at this hour, I was still a single man. I didn't realize life was so good."

Her brows came together like two angry lightning bolts. "You can still be single. I'll go speak to the Reverend Kinnion now. I'm certain he'd be happy to annul the marriage." She started off as if she would walk all the way to Kenmore Kirk to plead her case, but Breccan caught her arm and swung her around.

He placed both hands on her shoulders. "You do not want to do that, my lady."

Her chin lifted. "What I don't want is to be poor. I thought you were different from my father. Now, I find out, I left one gambler to live with another."

"I'm not a gambler—"

"Did you wager on your horse?"

"Of course—"

"And if you have to forfeit the race, will you lose your money—?"

"Are you always a *nag*?" The words just shot out of Breccan. In the short time they'd been together, she'd demonstrated an amazing ability to slice right through reason and common sense.

Her back stiffened. She took a step away from him. "I am *done* with this marriage," she announced in a voice that would have made the queen proud.

"And I am saying, that you and I have no choice but to go on. That is, not unless you want to be the laughingstock of the valley."

"I'll tell people the truth. They will laugh at *you*."

"It doesn't work that way, my lady. Aye, they will think I'm a fool. But there is already a good number in this valley who believe that of me. And, considering how much I spent to marry you and what I've received so far for it, well, I agree with them. Of course, on the other hand, if you return to your father, I should receive my money back. And then I could lose a thousand races and come out ahead. Come to think of it, toddle on. Go see the Reverend Kinnion.

She shook her head like a young filly evading the bit. He could tell she wanted to do exactly that. Righteous indignation had her up in arms.

But then common sense took over.

"I can't go, and you know it," she said. "Between my jilting my last suitor and marrying you, well, who else would have me?"

"Aye, you are running out of men to walk over," he agreed.

"Walk over?" She crossed her arms against her chest. "I've tried—" She started to protest, but then stopped. For a long second, she was quiet, and then, as if willing herself to patience, she said, "You don't like me, do you?"

Her directness startled him. "Why would you accuse me of such?"

"Because you've challenged everything I've said."

"Perhaps your thinking deserves challenging."

"My thinking? You don't know what I think at all."

"I know you are unhappy."

"And you would say without good reason?"

Now it was Breccan's turn to make an impatient sound. "*No*. There is no good reason. You didn't want me to touch you last night and this morning, you are now carrying on as if you have a say in how I spend my money."

"We have a bargain—"

"One that you have yet to uphold," he pointed out.

"I *will* uphold it. But I—"

"*When?*" he asked, cutting her off.

"What do you mean 'when'?"

"When will I bed you? I have time right now. Let us see to the matter." He took a step toward the house, but she skittered backward.

"It is the morning."

"As good a time as any," he replied, and reached for her arm, feeling a bit triumphant because he was giving her something to think about.

She moved to place the corner post between them, bracing herself as if ready to run. "This is not why I came out here."

"I thought you wished to discuss our agreement," Breccan answered.

"I wanted to discuss why you can't honor it."

"I will honor it, my lady," he said, putting steel in his voice. "My horse *will* win that race. What *you* should worry about is honoring your vows to me."

She glared at him as if ready to carry on, but then the fight left her. "You sound like every gambler I've ever known. You all are always certain that fortune will favor you."

"I am not like other men," Breccan assured her.

She tossed him a look that made her doubts clear. It was as if she could see how much he'd placed on the line lately. He was stretched thin, and well she knew it.

"Why did you offer to marry me anyway?" she asked.

Now it was Breccan's turn to take a step away.

She came around the paddock post to say, "I

bring no dowry. We barely know each other, and, from your own admission, paying my father's debts might have ruined you."

That was true.

"So, I'm asking," she continued. "Why do you want *me*? There are half a dozen women in the valley more suited to you than I am. And they would have added to your coffers."

"Are you asking for honesty?" he questioned. "Or are you looking for a weapon to use against me later?"

A spark of anger lit her eye. "I'm trying, Breccan. I *am* trying."

The sound of his given name on her lips surprised him. He liked it, and it was an indication of sorts that she was willing to be open to him.

"Perhaps I am as besotted with your beauty as any other man?" He made the truth sound like a suggestion. He assumed she would be flattered.

He was wrong.

She crossed her arms tightly against her waist. "I am not beautiful."

Breccan started to laugh off her disclaimer, but she said, "I don't see myself that way. But in truth, I don't believe anyone else sees *me* at all."

"Of course we see you. Tara"—her name was like

a caress on his tongue—"you are a hard woman to miss. You know that."

A frown line formed between her eyes, a frown that wrinkled the perfection of her skin. "Everyone assumes my life is easy because I have good looks. They believe that because men like staring at me, I could not want for anything else. But while men are writing poems to my earlobe or offering to drink wine from my shoe—which is the most disgusting idea—they don't do the one thing I wish they'd do."

"Such as?"

"Letting me have an opinion. Or giving me an honest hearing when I do say what I think. Even my sister Aileen will patronize me. *Silly* Tara. *Headstrong* Tara. *Lov-lee* Tara. Those aren't compliments, are they? And I'm expected to be perfect at all times. I'm judged for it. Someone will meet me and comment about my imperfections as if finding fault with me is a sport. Of course, if I strive for their good opinions, I am considered difficult or conceited." She shook her head, and said with bitter mockery, "Oh, no, I must *not* be conceited, even though all everyone else focuses on is the arrangement of eyes, nose, and mouth on my face."

Breccan could understand. The first thing

anyone thought of him was about his size. The conversation was always about his height, his strength, and there were many who described him as a great beast of a man, which was not a charming epithet.

But this was not about him. And she spoke of wanting something more than platitudes.

So, he admitted the truth. "I'm guilty."

"Of what?"

Breccan knew he could be treading into dangerous territory. "I wanted to marry you because I *like* looking at you. That is not a sin."

"But what if I were ugly? What if I become ugly?" Her magnificent blue eyes lit up with the idea. "What if there was a fire, or I was set upon by brigands—?"

"Brigands?" The word amused him.

"*Brigands,*" she reiterated. "And they carved my face up or cut out my eyes."

"That's bloodthirsty."

She shrugged his protest away. "Brigands are bloodthirsty, but that is not the point. What if I become unattractive? Then what happens?"

"Then nothing. I took a vow. You are my wife."

"You can't say that. You don't *know* me . . . and shouldn't vows mean something more?"

"Like what?"

She searched the ground as if looking for an answer, then said, "Like love."

Breccan almost wanted to laugh. "Love? Love is an excuse for bad behavior."

"And why do say that?" she asked, acting disconcerted by his response.

"My father fell in 'love' with a woman from Glasgow. He didn't hesitate to leave Wolfstone for her. Walked right away from his responsibilities here, and it ruined him. It almost ruined all of us."

"What happened?"

A hard lump of resentment formed in Breccan's chest. He did not like thinking about it, but Tara should hear it from him. "It turns out the woman was married. Her husband was a soldier who came home and discovered the affair. He shot my father in a rage of passion, and the law found the murder justified. It is not one of the best stories in the family, but when you want to mock people or make them feel belittled, it is a good one to trot out."

"I'd not heard this tale," Tara said, and her commiseration sounded genuine. "How terrible for your mother. The humiliation must have been painful."

"It destroyed her. Few ever considered her feelings. She was not an attractive woman, but she was the best of mothers. My father's taking up with another and abandoning his family broke something inside her. They blamed her. She blamed herself. I believe she thought if she were more good-looking, her husband might have strayed, but he wouldn't have left. She became a recluse."

Tara raised her hand and touched her chest over her heart. "I can understand."

The note of empathy in her voice humbled him, an emotion Breccan did not trust. "It doesn't matter now," he said briskly. "She's been dead ten years and more." And he missed her wise counsel every day.

He sidled away. He kept those memories at bay for a reason.

But Tara was not done with him. "My mother died giving birth to me," she said.

No one with any conscience could walk away from that statement. "I'm sorry."

She nodded as if agreeing with him. The line of worry had returned between her brows. "I fear there are important things I should know that only a mother can tell you." She glanced at him as if wanting confirmation.

"My mother was important to me."

"I wonder what kind of mother I will be?"

Breccan took a step toward her. "Some things are instinct."

"That's what they say." She hesitated, as if turning something over in her mind. "You said during the sacrament of marriage that you promised to be a good husband to me."

"I did."

"Thank you." She let the words hang between them a moment before adding softly, "I pray your horse can run."

"I do as well."

And he had a sense that an agreement had been struck between them.

From the moment she'd ridden into his stables looking for Ruary Jamerson, she'd rarely been far from his thoughts.

However, in his dreams, she hadn't talked, she hadn't had opinions, or likes and dislikes. The Tara Davidson of his imagination had never challenged him or spoken of loss or expressed an understanding of what it meant.

No, the woman of his fantasies had just let him love her—wait, that wasn't true either. The woman of his imaginings had let him roger her, and he'd rogered her well . . . something he now realized had been the musings and hopes of every suitor who had crossed her path.

He also caught another bit of insight—yes, he lusted for her, but the reason he'd really wanted to marry her was to prove *his* worth.

She'd been right. He didn't know her. He'd promised himself to her . . . but had he truly wanted a wife? Or another way to prove to his Campbell brethren that the Black Campbells were every bit as good as they were?

And then she asked a question that wiped every conscious, sensible thought from his brain—

"Will the bed be repaired by tonight?"

The flood of excitement that rushed through Breccan dumbed him of speech.

She waited for his answer, and it was as if the sun shone down upon her head with a special ray of light. She was so lovely, so perfect, so everything she did not want to be.

And was it his imagination, or did this talk between them make her more intriguing?

Because now she wasn't just the musings of his lustful mind. She'd taken on dimension—

"Laird, *Laird!*"

The demand for Breccan's attention seemed to

come from far away. He registered the voice, but it wasn't until Tara stepped forward, and said, "There is a lad coming for you," that he realized he was needed.

He turned and saw Davy Erroll running toward him. That is when he remembered he had been due at the mill close to an hour ago. There was a dispute between a tenant and Erroll, Davy's father, that Breccan had promised to resolve.

He held up a hand. "I'll be right there, Davy." Without waiting for a reply, he turned to face Tara. He began walking backward, saying, "And I'll have the bed repaired by tonight." He'd see it done if he had to do it himself and use his own shirts.

And then, because he couldn't help himself, because she was all he'd ever let himself want and because *now*, finally he would have her, Breccan changed direction and instead of walking backward, he moved forward. He marched right up to her, placed his hands on her arms, and kissed her.

Yes, he kissed her.

It wasn't a big kiss. He knew every man jack around the stables had been watching them from the moment they had walked away. Well, now they had something to chew on.

Nor was this a self-conscious kiss like the one he'd given her at the wedding. It was one born out of joy and anticipation. It was a hard buss but an enthusiastic one—and it sent a shot of desire straight through him. From the stables, he heard shouts of encouragement.

One of the hardest things he'd ever done in his life was to set her down. "Tonight," he promised. *Yes, tonight.*

He turned and walked to Davy before he lost all control of himself.

He'd picked her up and moved her.

Tara wasn't a big woman, but she was bigger than a chair. He'd lifted her up as if she weighed nothing. He was that strong, that huge, that powerful.

All over.

He could split her in two.

No, she didn't believe that, but she knew that consummating their marriage would be painful. She had been warned that it would be, and Tara already knew that Breccan was said to be larger than other men. If she hadn't believed before, she was certainly convinced after how easily he had picked her up.

But she had to go through with it. Their bargain aside, she'd married the man. It was what was expected.

She raised her fingers to her lip. Even his kiss was hard. When he'd kissed her after the marriage ceremony, he'd barely brushed her lips; this time, he'd bruised them.

It had not been an unpleasant kiss, but it had promised an enthusiasm that churned her anxiety—

"Are you all right, my lady?" Lachlan's voice asked her.

Tara turned to see that Breccan's uncle had approached from the stables and eyed her with concern. "Yes, yes, I'm fine."

"The lad likes you," he observed, referring to his nephew.

His comment confused her. "He seems to."

Lachlan stepped closer. "No, I mean, he likes *you*. He's a busy man. He has many projects going at all times, but don't think he doesn't consider you a priority."

The problem was, she wouldn't mind Breccan's turning his attention elsewhere, at least until she could regain her equilibrium. "My life has changed so quickly," she murmured, feeling the need to explain.

"Well," Lachlan said, "sometimes fate plays tricks on us that way. We think we are going in one direction, then another presents itself."

"And when it does, what do you do?" The question just burst out of her.

"You face it," he said as if it was obvious. "You can't live in fear."

"Who says I'm afraid?"

His expression softened. "Lass, it's etched all over your being. You remind me of a young doe, always ready to bolt. Look at you now. Your weight is on one foot, and you half turned from me as if you would run if you could."

When he said this, Tara became aware of her stance. She *had* balanced herself so that if she wished to dash off, she could. Indeed, she realized, she was usually ready to be the first to leave. She'd learned that she could control situations better that way.

"I must protect myself," she said, reasoning it out. "I don't like it when people leave me."

And yet, that was what had happened in her life. Her mother had left from the moment Tara had entered the world, and her father had stayed just long enough to bury his wife before leaving for London.

There had been a succession of nannies and governesses. They had moved to new positions when they tired of her father's forgetting to pay their wages.

Aileen had been constant in the beginning, but then she'd had to leave because she had wanted her own life—and at some point, Tara had grown to understand that it was important to leave, and if one left first, there was no pain.

She shifted her weight, rooting herself to the ground with both feet. It felt odd . . . and slightly scary.

Lachlan gave her a gentle smile as if he understood. "I don't know you well, yet, my lady. What I see, I like. You have spirit. You are not afraid to stand up for yourself, and that is unusual in women of your class. But I'm going to offer you a wee bit of advice— You can never build anything meaningful in your life if you are always ready to run from the challenges." He took a step away. "Let me know if there is anything you need. We want you to be happy at Wolfstone."

"And why is that?" she asked as he started to walk away."

He didn't break his stride but glanced back over his shoulder to say, "Because Breccan is happy."

"And is that enough?" she asked.

Lachlan paused, gave her a grin, and said, "There is nothing more important." He walked on.

Tara watched him leave, uncertain whether he was encouraging her or warning her? And she wasn't certain she agreed with him about happiness being of any importance. She'd seen the wider world. There were many in London who would argue with him.

Besides, what was happiness? Who could define it?

If she thought about it, she'd never known a moment when she had truly been happy—well, save for when she had believed Ruary had returned her love.

And she knew there *must* be more purpose to life than simple happiness. Lachlan sounded as if he didn't think life was hard, and it seemed terribly hard, especially right now.

Nor did her attitude change as returned to the house and discovered that a workman was busy repairing the broken bed.

Chapter Nine

There was more to keep Breccan at the mill than a simple dispute. The pulley system he'd rigged for moving equipment had not been repaired properly. Breccan had been forced to reorder the whole thing himself.

Then there was concern over a drainage ditch that had collapsed. He'd worked with a few of his clansmen to rebuild the retaining wall. He sensed there was a better solution to the problem of redirecting springwater, but he couldn't think of what it was.

Over the course of those events, he'd also checked on Taurus. He kept working over in his mind what could be the matter with the horse.

And, never far from his thoughts, was Tara.

God, he adored the sound of her name. It was like an embrace to the tongue and inspired his usually practical mind to couplets of poetry.

Of course, he received a good amount of ribbing from his clansman about his marriage. Ribald suggestions came from every quarter. Most had heard about the broken bed and reached their own conclusions, none of them based in fact. Thank God.

But tonight . . . *tonight*, Breccan would see the deed done.

It took all his willpower to stay at the task at hand. He was tempted to return to Wolfstone, throw her over his shoulder, and make mad love to her with a good release of seed. He'd have her with a bairn before Boxing Day and enjoy the process.

Yes, that is what he wanted. He wanted to stake his claim to her, to seal this holy sacrament between them with the joining of bodies and souls.

Breccan was not sorry for the conversation they'd had. It had given him the chance to know her a little better. He'd not realized her mother had died in childbirth. He'd known that the earl of Tay was widowed, but he hadn't understood what that would mean to his wife. She'd sounded lost when she'd mentioned her mother, as if she longed for family.

Well, he was her family now. His clansmen would be loyal to her.

And when the time came for her to think about leaving Wolfstone to move to London, he was determined she would choose to stay with him. A woman who understood how important a mother was in a child's life would not leave her bairn. Breccan would have staked everything he owned on that one fact.

It was well past dark by the time he was able to return to the castle, his dogs trailing behind him. The late hour was not unusual for him. His responsibilities were vast, and most of his own making. He'd designed pulleys and levers and cogs and wheels, and only he understood how they worked. They would break, or the equipment would stick, and he'd have to fix it. He enjoyed this role but not tonight.

Flora sat by the kitchen fire waiting for him. Breccan was a bit disappointed. In his fevered longings, he'd pictured that Tara would be the one waiting for him.

He wanted her to be the one.

As Flora placed a plate piled high with venison, bacon, peas and bread in front of him, Breccan asked, "Has everyone eaten and gone up to bed?"

"Aye, Laird," the girl answered.

"They must have straggled in here and there," Breccan suggested, tucking into his food. He felt bad that he wasn't able to be there for Tara. He imagined her sitting at this table, lonely and eagerly waiting for him. He should have escaped from his duties sooner.

"No, they all ate together," Flora informed.

"Who 'all' ate together?"

"My lady, Jonas and Lachlan."

Breccan grunted a response. Of course, his uncles would share their meal with Tara. Jonas was such a scoundrel, he'd probably orchestrated eating his meal with her. Lachlan was a quiet, thoughtful one. He would follow Jonas's lead—

"Lachlan and Jonas were here first," Flora offered. "But then Lachlan went in search of my lady and asked her to join them."

"Lachlan did that?" Breccan asked, uncertain if he'd understood her correctly.

"They had a fine time," Flora assured him. "Jonas and Lachlan had her laughing."

"And what did she laugh at?" He hadn't made Tara laugh.

"They were telling her stories about when Jonas taught you to ride. Did you really loosen the saddle while you were on the horse, then end upside down? Is that true?"

Breccan failed to see the humor in that story. "I was a wee lad," he informed her. "I wasn't always brawny."

"That is what my lady said," Flora answered.

It mollified him that Tara would come to his defense. However, Flora spoiled that by informing him that his uncles also shared the story of how his mighty steed Jupiter had tossed him into Loch Tay.

Now that was a humorous story, but Breccan wanted to be the one to tell her.

He put down his fork.

"Is something wrong with your supper, Laird?"

"No, it's fine." He stood and walked over to the door. He began tossing the goodly amount left of his meal to his dogs, making certain the portions were equal according to their size. Daphne never agreed to this arrangement, but Largo thought it fine. "Have they all gone to bed?"

"Jonas and Lachlan went over to Alec Allen's,"

she said. Alec was an old friend of theirs, and the men spent many a night together telling stories and drinking.

That meant that he and Tara were alone.

Breccan handed his now-empty plate to Flora. "Good night, lass. I'm done for the evening." This meant she could go home. He left the kitchen, moving with an intent purpose for his bedroom.

His dogs fell into step beside him. They followed him into the castle, climbing the turret steps with him, but at his bedroom door, he stopped. "I'm sorry, pups, you can't come in here again tonight."

Largo understood exactly what he meant. He circled as if looking for a place on the narrow landing to lay his huge carcass. The foxhounds had an inkling of the new circumstances of their lives. They sat on their haunches, tilting their heads as if asking if he was serious.

Daphne was oblivious. She trotted up to the door and stood there wagging her tail, ready to go in. When he didn't open the door immediately, she scratched the door with her paw, her command for him to hurry and do her bidding.

"Not tonight, Daphne," he apologized, and

opened the door to the sitting room on this floor. Largo went in. The hounds followed him, their heads low as if they had done something wrong.

But Daphne stayed although her tail no longer wagged. She knew what was coming, and she was not pleased. He picked her up. She growled a protest.

"You can complain all you want," Breccan told her, "but this is the way it must be for now." He gently dropped Daphne inside the door and closed it.

Her reaction was immediate. She scratched on the door, an insistent command that she wanted it open—but Breccan had already turned his attention to his bedroom door.

And then he rubbed his jaw.

He needed to shave. Tara had told him so. He didn't want to delay this evening with her, but he also wanted all to be good.

In truth, he'd meant to shave the day before, but he'd forgotten. He claimed he wasn't a fussy man, but he'd been defiant in his habits. He liked to be clean, but shaving was a chore. It took time he felt he couldn't spare.

Or could he?

In the corner of the kitchen was the washstand

he and his uncles used for shaving. It was easier to do it there because it saved having to carry hot water up the steps.

Breccan returned to the kitchen.

Flora had already left, but there was water in the iron kettle. He poured it into the bowl and lathered up with shaving soap. His whiskers were as tough as thistles, so he sharpened the razor on the strop while he waited for the soap to do its work.

He applied the blade to his face. As he worked, he wished he hadn't spent the day on his duties and responsibilities. It would have been good to have had dinner with Tara . . . and perhaps the time had come for him to change his ways.

Breccan liked to work, but he had a wife now, and he found he longed for the comfort of her company.

Finished shaving, he wiped his face with a linen towel hanging off the stand. He glanced in the mirror. He'd never be a handsome man, but, hopefully, he would find favor in his wife's eyes.

He went back upstairs. Daphne still pawed at the door. She would not give up, but she had to understand that things had changed.

Breccan started to open his bedroom door,

but then paused. His wife was gently raised. He needed to be considerate. He knocked on the door.

There was a moment's pause, then a hesitant voice said, "Come in."

Good, she was there.

He drew a deep breath. "Don't ruin this," he ordered himself and, ignoring Daphne's still-persistent scratching at the door—that dog never gave up—he entered the bedroom.

There was a small fire in the hearth. His clothing chest had been pushed up to the bed to be used as a bedside table, and his books were stacked neatly there. He'd never thought of doing that. He used this room for sleep and little else, but he had a feeling he'd be spending a good deal more time in here now.

Slowly, savoring the anticipation, Breccan brought his gaze to the bed—

And frowned.

He had expected a compliant, alluring Tara, wearing his sheets and little else. He'd imagined her smile.

Instead, she lay on top of the bed's counterpane in her long nightdress, which covered her from neck to toe. She'd crossed her hands and rested them on her chest, and her eyes were closed as if she had been prepared for burial.

Her vibrant hair spread out across his pillow as the only color to this scene because her face was as ashen white as his sheets.

He was beside the bed in a blink. "Are you ill?"

"Do it," she urged him, not bothering to open her eyes. "Please just do it, do it quick, and be done with it."

"Do what?"

"Consummate the marriage."

He frowned. She expected him to plow into her as she acted like a corpse? Was she refusing him any willingness?

Breccan's temper rose.

This was an insult. She was making him feel like a pig because he *had* purchased her and he did want her.

He couldn't move. He could barely breathe.

And then he began removing his clothes.

So, this was the marriage he had? Why should he have expected anything different?

He was an ugly ox who was receiving his just deserts. And it was his weakness as a male that he was going to take her. Aye, he would have her and hate himself for his weakness afterward.

She lay rigid, her face turned away. He considered blowing out the candle, then decided, damn her to hell, he would not hide behind darkness.

This was who he was.

A tear slid from the corner of her eye, but her lips were pressed together as if she'd promised herself she would not scream.

Breccan stood naked, his irrepressible manhood ready for his bride.

And he hated himself . . . because with her like this, it would be rape—and that was not what he wanted. He'd dreamed of something else between them. At the very least, he had hoped for a companionship that would be meaningful.

Instead, he faced rejection . . . by his own wife.

He could leave. He could walk away now, his pride intact.

Or he could give in to base desire.

She obviously didn't reciprocate any feelings for him. She acted as if she feared him, and that, too, made him angry.

Breccan placed his knee on the bed. She didn't flinch, but every muscle in her body seemed to be pulling away from him.

Grimly, he made himself stretch out beside her. His manhood had a mind of its own. It seemed guided toward her.

Her breathing had grown rapid and shallow.

He steeled himself against pity. This was his wife. He had a right to her. She'd taken the vows. And if he didn't do this deed, if he did not make her his wife in more than name, then the marriage could be annulled.

When she'd threatened him earlier, he'd been angry. He'd been even angrier the night before when she'd denied him. Disappoint was a bitter pill.

Let it not be said that he could not make her his wife in more than name. They would laugh at him, and Breccan had worked too hard to the butt of jests any longer.

He thought about pulling on the drawstring of her gown around her neck and then asked himself why? He'd be torturing himself to reveal her flesh, knowing she abhorred his touch—because that was how she was acting. She behaved as if she'd shrivel if he placed a hand upon her.

The kiss he'd taken from her earlier had lifted his spirits all day. But now, in reflection, he'd been the one to kiss. She had as of yet to offer one morsel of feminine kindness.

And she'd made him keep his dogs out of his bedroom.

Damn, damn, *damn*.

A new thought hit him. "Is there someone else, my lady? Is your heart attached?" He'd ground the words out, had loathed asking the question, because if she responded yes . . . he didn't know what he would do. Jealousy could make him mean.

She gave a quick shake of her head, no, and he was relieved.

Then she whispered, "Please just do what you must. But do it quickly."

Quickly? His body was so ready, so needy, he'd explode in a second. And she would do nothing to help?

Bitterness filled him. He had come here searching for warmth, and instead faced the worst sort of rejection, one laced with his humiliation.

He reached down to pull her nightdress up. Her legs were pressed together tightly as if she would deny him admittance.

His response was to rip her gown. He dug his fingers into the material and pulled. The fine cloth tore easily, revealing the sweet curve of her hip and the secrets of her sex. Secrets, she would deny him if he let her.

Well, it was not going to come to that. She might despise him, but she was going to be his wife in more than name only.

Sourly, he rose up over her, positioning himself, ready to use force if necessary. A bead of his seed wept from him. He was so primed, the deed would be quickly done—but it was not how he wanted it.

He had dreamed of so much more, and yet this was all she offered.

And then the scales of outrage and insult fell away when he realized she was shaking. She was afraid.

Of him?

Or of what he could do to her?

Breccan lowered himself to her side, studying her and seeing her anew.

"It isn't me, is it?" he asked. "You are afraid."

She didn't answer, she didn't have to.

He rolled out of the bed, a fluid, swift movement as if he couldn't wait to put distance between them. He frowned at his obvious sign of desire even as it lost its drive. His manhood was a belligerent character, but even it had not wanted rape.

She'd heard him move away. For a second, she appeared confused; and then she'd opened her eyes. She sat up, gathering her nightdress around her. She was blushing. Tara Davidson, the woman who set all male hearts racing, was actually very modest. Here was something else he knew about her that others didn't.

He reached for his breeches. The torn gown embarrassed him. He'd lost control. He prided himself on never losing control. He was not like his father. He pulled his breeches on and fastened the top button.

For a long moment, they took each other's measure. She broke the silence first.

"What is the matter? Are we going to do this?"

"You tell me. Why are you so afraid?" And then, because he couldn't help himself, he asked, "Or are you just averse to me?"

Her eyes widened. She shook her head, then stopped. Her brows gathered. "You are a big man," she whispered, then added, "They say it is painful, especially, the first time."

Breccan experienced a mixture of emotions. On one hand, he could understand the fear of the unknown. He had heard that the first time could be very painful for a woman.

Furthermore, Jonas's obnoxious claims aside, Breccan knew he was well favored, a characteristic that usually worked to his benefit. But it did not now.

He was not one to sow his seed everywhere. However, he'd had lovers. There had been a young widow in Aberfeldy who had gone off to marry another man. They had parted on good terms, and there had been a few others.

But he'd not bedded a virgin. He'd only been with women who were willing and knowing.

And he could understand her concern. Tara was petite when compared to him.

"Aye, I've heard that it can be," he answered her, not that he'd been thinking that way when he'd entered the room. He was as selfish as the next man.

"Then let us do it now and be done with it," she answered, lifting her chin like a brave soldier preparing to go to war. "I want it done now. Then I won't have to worry about it again until I need to give you a second child."

"You won't?" Breccan echoed, wondering where she'd taken ahold of the idea that they would share a bed only for the act of creating children, not that he didn't consider that a good goal. Still, he liked pleasure. He opened his mouth, ready to correct her impression, then he closed it again.

This afternoon, she had told him a great deal

about herself when she'd shared that she was a motherless child. He understood what it meant to lose a parent and, if it had not been for his mother, or his uncles, he would be half the man he was.

She couldn't claim to have a father. Everyone knew the earl of Tay felt little obligation to his daughters. He didn't know about her sister, but he'd heard rumors about the Lady Aileen. She was a divorced woman, and she'd married the man that Tara had been betrothed to. This was not a doting sister.

Breccan was a big man, but he had a bigger heart, and he now saw Tara in the same light that he would a motherless kitten. She may have been feted and lauded in London, but she didn't understand what truly mattered between a man and a woman.

He wasn't certain he did as well.

But because of his father, he'd done some thinking. He'd watched other men, those who truly valued their wives. He wanted their relationship for Tara and him, but he sensed that, in the same way care had to be taken to properly train a colt, care must be exercised to bridge the divide between being just a lovely plaything or becoming a woman full born.

And it was on his shoulders. She was his wife.

He was feeling his way now, uncertain and yet determined. He pulled the covers back, then took off his breeches.

Apparently, she had not noticed his manhood before, but she did now. The color left her face, and she looked away. He didn't blame her. It was not a pretty thing right now.

As it was, his little guy began to stir.

Breccan climbed into bed, pulling the covers up to his waist before he embarrassed himself and sent her flying to the corner of the room to escape him.

But he couldn't let her be afraid. He wouldn't.

He patted the bed right beside him and said to his wife, "Come here."

Chapter Ten

$\mathcal{T}$ara stood, her arms across her body as she held her nightdress together. "I should change."

"No." The word shot straight out of Breccan.

He'd had a glimpse of thigh. *Oh, God.* She was delicious.

It would be a kindness to let her remove her torn clothing. It might also be the only way to cool his hot blood.

But if he let her move away from him, if he let her keep barriers between them, if she thought she could maintain her distance, then they would never have a child.

He also surprised himself by wanting something more from her than what he'd anticipated—he wanted her respect. He yearned for her companionship. There was a pull between the two of them that he could not yet name although she didn't seem to be aware of it.

However, if he let her keep scooting away, there might never be anything meaningful between them.

And he certainly didn't want fear in her eyes.

"Stay on the top of the covers, if you wish. I won't—" He paused, uncomfortable, but then forced himself to say it, "I won't attack you. That is not how I want things between us."

"Then let me change."

"*No*, lass. We are part of the most intimate union there can be between a man and a woman. I can't let you have room to run. At some point, we must learn to deal with each other."

She flipped her hair over her shoulder as if denying what he said.

"Then change," he told her, "but I'm not leaving the room. This is my bed, Tara. We are to share it."

"That is a strong invasion of my privacy." The small line of worry appeared on her brow. He was growing accustomed to seeing it. It marred the perfection of her features, but enhanced them as well. Here was the true woman—

What if I become ugly? she had asked.

He could have told her, she would never be

ugly in his eyes. He'd vowed to care for her, and so he would.

"I don't mean to cause discomfort, Tara, but at some point you need to let me earn your trust."

"Like you attempted a few moments ago?"

"You test a man." He could feel his temper, and it took all his patience to not lash out at her. "I deserve some scorn, but you must also see your own part."

"I was willing," she argued.

"It is not willing to be frightened out of your wits. I didn't understand at first. I thought . . ." He let his voice trail off. Breccan was not in the habit of expressing himself. He'd learned that sometimes the less said, the better—and that might be the case with her.

But then she challenged him. "You thought what?"

Did he dare share the truth? He'd look like a fool.

But if he expected her to risk feeling safe in order for him to earn her trust, should he not put some of himself into the game?

"I thought you were mocking me," he said.

"Why would I do that?"

"*Och*, lass, don't be thickheaded—" The word was out before he'd thought of the insult he was paying her, and he immediately raised his hand to beg for quarter. "I don't mean that. You are not thickheaded. I'm not good with my thoughts and my mouth." He ran a frustrated hand over his face.

"You shaved." Her statement sounded as if she had just discovered the fact.

"Aye. You wanted it." He was surprised she had noticed, and here was proof of how panicked she had been.

She studied him with a slight frown, then said, "It changes you."

"For the better, I hope."

There was another moment's pause, then said answered, "Yes, it does. You have a strong face."

She said it as if it was a compliment. Another beat of silence, and she admitted, "I *am* frightened."

"Of me?"

Tara shrugged; he understood what she held back. "You shocked me."

"I'm a bit shocked at myself." Now it was his turn to ask the difficult question. "But you were afraid before I came in the room and said a word. Am I that distasteful to you?" Because if he was, they were done.

To his relief, she appeared genuinely stunned by his question. "It's not you."

"Then what frightens you?" he asked softly.

She shifted her weight, and answered, "The housekeeper, Mrs. Watson, told me what to expect. I mean, I understand about animals, but I didn't realize that people were the same way.

Breccan considered that. "And when did Mrs. Watson explain this to you?"

"Yesterday evening."

He looked at the room, silently cursing all people protecting their daughters. He'd heard of this before. The idea was the less known about the marriage bed for young women, the better.

But at sometime, someone had to explain—and Breccan wished the earl and his staff had chosen a better time than right before the marriage ceremony.

"I was warned that it could painful," she said. "I'd heard about the pain before, but I never understood why."

"Ah," Breccan answered because she seemed to expect a response from him. But he was also wondering if this had more to do with her than reasonable fears. His lovers in the past had been eager. But he'd met men who complained that their wives were not warm and willing. These women did not enjoy the intimacies.

Here was a new fear for Breccan to consider. If Tara was not willing, he'd pack her off to London posthaste.

At the same time, he was fair enough to realize that what happened between them now would set the tone of their marriage.

"I'd also heard your male bits were very, very large," she said, whispering the last words.

For a second, the label "male bits" startled him. Who had ever heard of such a silly name for proud and noble manhood. At the same time, he could see how a suggestion of size would concern her on top of her other fears. "Who told you that? Jonas? I'll tan his hide."

"I overheard two women discuss it."

"They were discussing my d—?" Breccan caught himself. "Male bits," he finished.

"You are blushing," she noted.

And so he was.

Breccan threw his legs over the side of the bed, turning his back to her. He kept the sheet discreetly across his lap—thank God—because his male bits were acting up. Again.

He looked over his shoulder at his wife. "I want

you to know I don't show myself to everyone," he said.

"All right," was her uncertain answer. Then she said, "They predicted you would split me in half."

"*What?*" Breccan jumped to his feet in outrage, carefully keeping the sheet around him, which meant he could not stray from the side of the bed. "I wouldn't hurt you. I've never hurt anyone. At least, not that way. And I couldn't hurt you. It is the way God made us."

To his surprise, she'd placed the back of her hand over her mouth to hide her smile, her torn night-dress momentarily forgotten—by both of them.

"What is funny?" he demanded.

"You are still blushing." And she started laughing.

Breccan could have roared his outrage, except no sound was more musical than Tara's laugh. It was like the chiming of the finest bells, or the music of angels.

He stood transfixed.

Her laughter slowed as she realized he stared. She tried to silence herself, and he wanted to tell her no. He wanted to urge her to laugh forever.

Now, she was the one to blush, as if she knew what he was thinking.

"We'll do fine together, Tara," he said. "But I'll not rush you. When we make love, I don't want there to be fear, only desire."

She didn't believe that day would come. He could see it in the play of emotions in her eyes . . . and yet, he had roused her curiosity as well. She'd let her gaze linger over the hard planes of his chest.

Breccan climbed back into bed. He stretched. "Come, Tara, let's sleep."

Her gaze swept to the pillow beside him.

"I'm not going away," he said. "We must learn to be at ease with each other."

Again her brow furrowed with indecision.

Breccan closed his eyes, seemingly uncaring what decision she made—which was not the truth. He wanted to jump this hurdle between them. And if she had a doubt, all she had to do was look at his wily rod, which, with a mind of its own, was begging for release. If he wasn't careful, not even the covers would hide it.

A minute went by. Then another.

He struggled to hide his annoyance. He was trying everything he could to regain her trust, but it was hard. Or, at least, *he* was hard—

The mattress gave as she sat upon it. She hadn't moved the covers but lay down on top of the counterpane.

He looked to her. She was on her side, her back to him and as close to the other edge as she could be without falling out of bed.

Breccan willed himself to patience. If he was wise, he would go to sleep. Certainly, he'd done enough throughout the day to overtax every bone in his body.

She didn't move, but he sensed she was awake.

And, finally, he could not take it any longer. "Are you asleep, Tara?"

There was no answer, but he could see her clinging tighter to her portion of the mattress.

"I know, I can't sleep either," he said as if she'd answered him. He knew too well how silence could become a wall between two people. He'd seen it in his parents.

He drew breath and released it. He rolled over toward her, punched his pillow, sighed again.

She remained inert.

Breccan stared at her back, willing her to face him.

There was the silence of the room but not the gentle breathing of sleep.

"I think I liked you better when you laughed," he said. "Or when you were teasing about blushing. That is the way I want things between us, Tara."

Her shoulders tightened as if she had crossed her arms, shutting him out.

But Breccan would not be deterred. "I've never been called friendly. It's a way to protect myself. When you come from a clan where everyone sneers when they say your name, you learn to keep your guard in place. Then there were the stories about my father. That was a difficult period of time for my mother. She was hurt."

He paused, watching her, wondering what it would take to bridge the gulf between them.

It wasn't a distance he wished, but trust took time to build.

Rolling onto his back, he studied the ceiling for a moment. He'd meant what he'd said about wanting her to become accustomed to him—and he wasn't about to fall asleep as long as she was awake.

"When I had trouble sleeping, my mother would tell me stories." The memory was a good one for Breccan, and it helped to take some of his attention off his silent bedmate.

"She was from the north," he said. "They have these animals that live in the water. They call them selkies, and she said they often could be seen swimming in the sea or on a sunny day basking on rocks. But, Mother, warned me that things weren't what they seemed. She said that the selkies might look like seal creatures, but at special times they can take off their skins and become as human as you and I, except the men are very handsome and the women more beautiful than can be imagined."

He could hear his mother's voice as she'd spin the story.

"It is said that if a man can steal a selkie woman's skin, then she is his to do as he wishes. They love the sea, but, from time to time, they dance upon the water in their human form, and that is when a young fisherman caught himself a selkie wife. Oh, she was very lovely, fair of hair and skin, with blue, blue eyes."

Eyes as blue as Tara's. He could picture them in his head, expressive eyes that reflected every emotion going through her being. It was very easy to see his new wife as the selkie in his mother's story.

"He captured her," he repeated, which was what he'd done to Tara. He'd claimed her in the only way one such as himself could have captured a mystical creature. "And he hid her selkie skin from her by locking it in a trunk. He wanted to keep her forever."

There was movement on the other side of the

bed. Tara shifted her body weight and repositioned her head on the feather-down pillow. The mattress had an indentation in the center for where he usually slept. Even her small movement drew her closer to him.

Besides, the bed was not that big. He could feel her body heat, knew that she listened.

And then, as if to prove him correct, she turned her head on the pillow and looked at him with somber eyes. "What happened after the fisherman captured the selkie?"

A shot of elation brought a smile to his face. He tried to hide it by leaning over and blowing out the candle. The only light in the room now came from the glow from the hearth and the moon in the window.

"They were happy," he told her. "They had a bairn. A little boy. The fisherman was proud of his wife and his healthy son. Of course, there were some problems?"

"Like what?"

"Let us not forget, his wife was a seal at heart. Aye, a selkie, but she truly belonged to the wild. She liked being in the water, and, late at night, she would steal from the bed to go swim. Of course, the fisherman always knew when she was gone. He'd follow her and find her on the beach, dancing in the moonlight. Her selkie brethren would be there, but they would run and hide when they saw her fisherman husband."

"Was she a good mother?"

The question was not one he'd thought of before. But he knew the answer. "She was the best. A good and loving soul. There was one thing else she did differently, and it is important. The fisherman would keep them well fed with his catch. He worked hard, and he'd come home and cook up the fresh fish for their supper but his wife always ate her fish raw. It was how she preferred it, and even though she seemed happy and took care of her bairn, the fisherman should have noted those small differences and been warned."

He dared to roll onto his side so that he faced her.

She did not pull away.

"It was the middle of the summer," Breccan said. "There was a storm brewing, and the sea has its own music. The fisherman did not go out that day, but he noticed that his wife kept opening the door and listening, and tears would come to her eyes. He asked her what was wrong. She said that she could hear her family calling her. Well, he did not like that. He told her that he and their son were her family. She didn't need the sea. But when he looked into her eyes, he saw that they had changed. They were no longer the blue that delighted him so but an icy gray, as if the life was leaving her."

"So what did he do?" she asked.

"He did what a man in love would do. He went to the place where he'd hidden the sealskin and brought it out to her."

"Did it make her happy?"

"It made her very happy. She gave him a kiss and whispered good-bye. Then she ran out the door to join her people."

"She left the fisherman and her son for her people?"

"I'd asked that same question when my mother told me that story."

"Did she have an answer?"

"She always had answers. She said we all must be who we are. The words carry a heavier importance than they did when I was a lad. In those days, I didn't understand. Now, I know I can't keep a person from feeling what she feels or wanting what she wants."

"What happened to the fisherman?" Tara wanted to know.

"He was sad, dismal—especially when she

didn't come home that night or the next, or the next after that. He waited, but she was gone. Then several months later there was terrible storm, and the fisherman was out in his boat. His rudder broke and he was left at the mercy of the heavens. He feared he would not see his son again. He knew he would be lost. And in the middle of the storm, with the wind blowing and the rain slashing at him, he thought of his wife. He longed to see his wife and know that she was happy. In his unhappiness, he cried seven tears."

"Seven tears?"

"Yes, which is magic to selkies. The moment his tears touched the sea, a great calm settled over the water. The wind stopped blowing, and the rain gave way to gentle mist. Up from the water came a seal, as fine and dainty as can be. She looked at the fisherman, and as he stared into her eyes, they turned the deepest blue—and he knew she was his wife. She had come for him."

"Did she want to return home?"

"No, lass, but she loved him in the best way she could, and she knew their son needed him. She pushed his boat to safety; and then she returned to where she wanted to be."

As he finished the story, he thought of Tara's

desire to go to London. Aye, there was a part of him that was not going to let her go. He assumed that a woman would stay with her children. That was one of the reasons why he had made the bargain he had. He'd thought he'd not have to pay the price.

Perhaps Tara was right. He was a gambler . . . and gamblers always lose. He knew that.

Breccan rolled onto his back, feeling a chill go through him. He had not thought of this story for a long time.

It was as if his mother had reached from beyond the grave to remind Breccan that few things in life were ever as we wanted them to be.

And there were some things that could break a person. His father's defection and death had done that to her.

And now, here he was with memories of a story about a blue-eyed selkie. The *deepest* blue. That is what his mother had always said.

He turned his head toward Tara. Her eyes were closed in sleep. The tension was gone from her body. She no longer leaned away from him.

That was good.

Reaching over her, he picked up the far edge of the counterpane and pulled it over her body. She didn't move but slept. For a second, he was tempted to touch her cheek. Her skin was so soft . . . and he was man who longed for her softness.

Breccan lay back on his side of the bed. He listened to her breathing, wondering how he would ever fall asleep with her this close to him, but he did.

A sense of peace fell over him. Tonight had been difficult, but they understood each other better. It would take time for them to be completely comfortable, but it would be time well spent.

He fell into a deep, dreamless sleep.

Tara opened her eyes from feigning sleep.

Breccan filled the bed. There didn't seem to be much room for her. At first, that had alarmed her, but his story and the calm deepness of his voice had settled her.

He could have forced her. The violence in him had frightened her, but then he'd pulled back. She'd been aware of the struggle inside him. His discipline had won.

Having lived with her father, she could admire that quality in a man. And she couldn't remember one time when her father had been aware enough of her needs to have done something so simple and considerate as to see the covers were tucked in around her. She couldn't even remember being carried in her father's arms.

But where Breccan had surprised her is when he had told her a story. A beautiful story about a man who could love his wife enough to let her be who she was.

Had he calculated his use of the story? Or had it just been something out of his nature . . . his *kind* nature?

She had never thought of kindness as a particularly admirable quality in a man. Her standards had been set by others. A gentleman was accomplished if he came from a good family, had a fortune and was fair of face. The rest was ignored.

She'd known what to expect from her life in that society. She was important until she married. She was important in her marriage until she bred an heir. After that? She was nobody. She could host salons and preside over society, but that sort of life suddenly seemed aimless.

The selkie knew what she wanted. She'd returned to her people.

Tara had grown up in this valley and yet, her people—or at least the ones who saw her having any worth—were in London, weren't they?

She watched him breathe a moment, his face relaxed in sleep, the glow from the fire in the hearth casting shadows.

His was a strong face. His beard was already beginning to form on his jaw. There was nothing soft about him. He was Highlander through and through, and she was not surprised his mother was from the north.

Tara snuggled deeper under her covers.

She had a secret of her own. When she'd had her eyes closed while he'd been over her, she'd peeked. She'd seen him—her first completely nude man who wasn't carved from stone and wearing a discreet fig leaf.

Breccan had appeared powerful. And that which made him a man had alarmed her. His male bits. They *weren't* bits.

But at the same time, she wasn't repulsed. Indeed, she found herself curious. His male bits; her female bits. If it was such a painful, disgusting thing, then why did so many women willingly venture to a man's bed. Was Breccan just different? Or could the maids Ellen and Myra have been silly?

Tara reached forward and tentatively placed her hand on his shoulder.

Breccan slept on, seemingly unaware of her presence.

His skin was warm and even relaxed, there was the hardness of muscle about him. Her husband was a strong man. In ancient times, he would have been considered a great and able warrior.

The thought made her smile because in this age, he was the harried chieftain of a small segment of a powerful clan—

He turned toward her and captured her hand. He tucked it in against his chest. With a sigh, he seemed to fall deeper into sleep.

Tara didn't know what to do. She feared pulling her hand away. He might wake and misunderstand her curiosity, and then she would be babbling about selkies and other things that this all-too-perceptive man might draw out of her.

So, she let him hold her hand and soon found herself in a restful, relaxed sleep.

The next morning when she woke, she discovered that although Breccan was nowhere to be seen, his side of the bed was now occupied by a disgruntled Scottish terrier whose black, beady eyes were full of malice.

Chapter Eleven

Tara blinked sleep-filled eyes, thinking the dog was a dream. The terrier lay on the bed, her paws in front of her but her hind legs positioned as if she could spring at any moment and snap at Tara's nose.

Her hands on the mattress, Tara started to push herself up.

Daphne growled, her eyes brightening.

Tara paused, uncertain. Her hair fell over one shoulder. Keeping her eyes on the animal, she reached to set her foot on the floor on the opposite side of the bed.

The dog growled again, twitching her whiskers around her nose as if daring Tara to go one inch farther.

Breccan's clothes from the day before hung on a peg, but his boots were gone. The door was open a crack. That must have been how the dog entered. She wondered how long Daphne had been watching her.

A part of Tara wanted to dismiss Daphne as just being a silly dog. But another part sensed that the terrier felt slighted. There was an air about her of a scorned female. Tara knew the type. She'd had more than her share of exchanges over the years from young women whose suitors had lost interest. The women assumed that Tara was the reason, and sometimes she was. But could Tara help when a gentleman decided to transfer his affections from one woman to her?

Apparently, Daphne thought she could.

"Where is Breccan?" Tara asked. "Shouldn't you be with him?" She wondered what time it was and where he could be found?

Of course, Daphne didn't answer, but her little body was tense with intent, and Tara knew it was up to her to escape this dog's anger.

Carefully, she reached for the feather pillow.

Daphne glanced at her hand, then whipped her attention back to Tara as if worried about a frontal attack. She growled.

Tara halted her movement, forcing herself to wait. This dog was not a dumb animal. Daphne appeared to have more intelligence than most people Tara knew.

Attempting to smile, Tara said, "Nice dog."

Daphne did not appear placated.

Tara took a deep breath, then moved as fast as she could. She flung the pillow at Daphne's head, even as she jumped off the bed. There was a second where Tara's foot caught in the counterpane, but, with a hop, she shook it loose. She dashed around the bed, heading toward the door.

Daphne snarled at the pillow and jumped toward the foot of the bed. Barking madly, she put her paws up on the footboard and appeared ready to leap viciously at Tara.

Tara gave a small cry of alarm. She couldn't help herself. The terrier was after a piece of her. Tara stepped back. Her only escape was the door, and to reach it, she had to run by the dog.

However, at that moment, the partially open door opened wider. Flora came into the room. She didn't see Tara at first but crossed to the bed to pick up the barking dog. "Daphne, what are you going on about? And what are you doing here anyway? The laird is at the stables—"

Her voice broke off as she turned and saw Tara standing in front of the hearth.

"My lady, I'm so sorry. I didn't mean to come barging in."

"It's fine," Tara assured her. "I don't know what is the matter with the dog. She's growling and acts as if she would like to chew me to pieces."

"She's jealous, my lady. Agnes and I were talking about that yesterday. Daphne is used to doing whatever she wants, but now she knows the laird has favored you."

"Daphne is a dog," Tara felt she had to say. "She can't feel emotions, or least not human ones."

"So you say," Flora answered with some humor. "Then what do you believe she is doing now? Because it appears to me she has singled you out."

She held Daphne up to prove her point. The terrier leaned forward, her front legs pawing the air as if she could fly through the air toward Tara. She showed her teeth and rolled her beady eyes.

"I think she doesn't like me," Tara could agree, sidling away from the dog.

"Daphne is always the last one to be warm to a new person. Largo and the foxhounds are always adoring, but Daphne is like a great-aunt who has seen too much and has an opinion on everything."

Flora's words brought Tara's aunt Lucille to

mind. The woman wasn't even a true relative. She was the aunt of her half sister Aileen's mother and the dowager duchess of Benningham. During her first season, there had been many times when Tara could have used her assistance. However, the dowager did not like Tara. She seemed to take her suspicions about the earl of Tay and cast them on his youngest daughter. Tara understood the woman was free to dislike her, but when the dowager had actively been moved to use her influence in society to exclude Tara, then they had a disagreement.

Fortunately, by that time, Tara had made enough friends she survived. Also, the dowager's power was not what it had once been, especially amongst the smart set.

That Tara connected Daphne to Great-Aunt Lucille did not bode well for the dog.

"She won't bite," Flora stated. "She always carries on, but she knows there is a line she'd better not cross. The laird would not tolerate her bad behavior."

"Perhaps she believes I'll keep my mouth closed about the matter," Tara wondered.

Flora laughed. "She might—" Her laughter came to an abrupt stop. Her eyes opened in shock as she looked at Tara.

Crossing her arms protectively against her chest, Tara said, "What?" and then realized, to her horror that Flora was looking at her torn nightdress. Tara had been so caught up in the dog, she'd forgotten the seam was ripped from thigh to ankle.

She now lowered a hand to hold the edges together. She couldn't imagine what the maid was thinking. At the same, the truth was not a wise thing to share. The truth would lead to even more questions.

"I tore it when the dog startled me, and I jumped out of bed. Silly of me," Tara said. "I caught my toe in it." She attempted to laugh at her own foolishness.

"Do you wish me to take the garment to Dougal's wife? She is handy with a needle," Flora offered.

"That might be good," Tara said, feeling ridiculously guilty. After all, it was a small little tale and one that saved embarrassment.

But it did earn her some approval from Daphne.

The dog's ears picked up. She stopped urgently pawing the air and gave Tara a knowing look, as if she knew the truth. And perhaps she did. Dogs had keen hearing. There was no doubt in Tara's mind that Daphne had spent the night straining to hear whatever had been going on between her and Breccan.

"Very well, my lady. If you leave it on the bed, I'll take care of it. And I'll take Daphne downstairs with me."

"Thank you," Tara said, as Flora left the room with Daphne on her shoulder. The dog's eyes never left Tara until the door was closed.

With a thankful sigh, Tara came around the bed and sat on the edge. She surveyed the damage to her gown. Needle and thread could not repair the thin lawn. Her other nightdress was made of heavier stuff, and perhaps, after last night, it would be wise to wear it.

She quickly dressed, folding the nightgown and placing it in the bottom of her trunk.

Now the question was, what should she do with her day? She thought of the selkie who had made a home for her husband. Tara knew there were a number of tasks she could perform to make Wolfstone more comfortable. She would be living here, and she needed to make the best of it.

With a sense of purpose, she left the room in search of the kitchen for her morning meal. As she circled down the staircase, Daphne's head poked out the door of one of the side rooms. Flora had not taken the dog very far.

Tara moved over to the wall. Daphne watched her and let her pass without incident. Relieved, Tara was several steps down before she realized Daphne was following her.

Attempting to be calm, Tara pretended she didn't notice the dog as she walked through the rooms to the back entrance. Daphne fell into step beside her. Together, the reached the kitchen. Daphne sat by the door and let Tara enter.

The door to the kitchen was usually open to release the heat form the cook fires.

"Ah, see, my lady," Flora said in greeting. "Daphne has made a friend of you. She has decided you are fine after all."

Dougal and Agnes both nodded, as if agreeing with her. Tara looked back at the dog. Sitting on her haunches, Daphne didn't move her feet as she watched a fly circle around her. She snapped at it a few times, then grinned at Tara.

The dog *grinned*.

That was astounding to Tara. Daphne had approved of her, and the only reason could be because Tara had not tattled on Breccan.

"I'm flattered to earn her approval," Tara said

as she nodded to Dougal's silent offer of porridge for her breakfast. Agnes brought her fresh cream to go with it. "I just hope she isn't fickle."

The others in the kitchen laughed at her wee joke, and something tight and fearful inside of Tara began to unwind. She was finding a place for herself here.

Taurus was more lame than ever.

Ricks had no explanation except to advise placing more slices of potato on the bottom of the horse's hoof. "We haven't drawn out whatever it is."

"Is there not an ointment we can use?" Breccan asked. He wore his usual attire of breeches, shirt, and waistcoat. He did not have on a neckcloth. He'd thought about putting on one, but he'd woken late and had needed to hurry to see the morning rides.

"Aye, we can try, but we don't know what it is," the horse master said.

Breccan had to turn away from the horse, swearing under his breath, words that died quickly when he saw his wife standing in the stall doorway.

She was a vision. Of course, he could never tire

of looking at her. She wore her hair down. He had not realized it was as long as it was or had the curls. Her dress was a sensible loden green cambric and with her coloring, she reminded him of a wood sprite. His mother would have been amused.

Nor was he the only one impressed.

Ricks had removed his hat. The stable lads gazed at her in wonder, as if an angel had appeared amongst them. Jonas was there, and he was grinning from ear to ear like a monkey. He was probably spinning his own story.

"Breccan, do you have a moment?" she asked.

He gave Taurus's neck a pat, then asked Ricks, "Are we done?"

"For today, Laird," Ricks said. "The lads can wrap the hoof. I'm needed over at Annefield unless you have something else?"

Ricks had informed him only that morning that he would now be overseeing the training of the earl of Tay's horses. Breccan wasn't pleased. After all, he was the one who had found the man in Glasgow and invited him to come—and a pretty penny Ricks's services were costing him, a goodly amount more than what Ruary Jamerson had charged.

Then again, Breccan didn't feel he could complain. Ruary Jamerson had offered his services to many in the valley. It seemed only fair to let Ricks earn a living.

"Aye, we are done," Breccan said, anxious to see why Tara had come to the stables this day. When last he'd seen her, she'd been snuggled in his bed. She snored. It was a soft, gentle sound, like a kitten sleeping hard, but it was a snore nonetheless, and something personal and unique to her. He cherished the information.

Ricks nodded to him and to his wife, put on his hat and left. Tara barely acknowledged the horseman. Instead, her attention seemed to center on Breccan.

Furthermore, the strain around her eyes appeared to have eased. There was an awareness of him, but it was without her earlier tension. She stepped into the stall and, to his surprise, Daphne was with her.

He'd wondered where the terrier had been. Sometimes, Daphne didn't come to the stables with him. She didn't like the walk; however, here she was.

"You made a friend," he observed.

Tara smiled and, for a second, Breccan went

light-headed. Out of all her lovely attributes, her smile was her best.

The stable lads acted as if this meeting between man and wife was also for their enjoyment. They openly watched.

Breccan reminded them of their duties by growling, "Don't you all have something to do?"

They moved quickly, well, save for Jonas. His uncle took his time loitering around the tack room across from Taurus's stall, picking out a bridle and carrying it down the aisle.

Tara didn't seem anxious to discuss her purpose with others around. She reached up and scratched Taurus's ear. The stallion groaned his pleasure. Breccan could understand why. He wanted his wife to do the equivalent to him, only he'd prefer if she would use her tongue.

He tried not to let any of that show when she faced him. They were alone now.

"You slept well?" Breccan asked.

"I did. And you?"

"I slept fine." Damn it all. He was anxious for the day when he could claim he hadn't received a wink of sleep.

"Dougal told me there was some furniture in the attic. Is it all right if I go though it?" she asked.

"There might be some things we could use in the rooms downstairs.

"Most of it is old. My mother brought better furniture into the marriage and moved the other to the attic."

"Where is your mother's furniture?"

Breccan hesitated a moment before admitting, "I sold it for my stake to start the mill."

"Oh."

"You are welcome to use whatever you wish. I'll send one of the lads to help you move it. I haven't really worried about furnishings."

She nodded, thoughtful a moment, and asked, "What's wrong with the horse?" She had her hand upon Taurus's mane, and the horse nuzzled her hand as if wanting more pats. Breccan knew how he felt.

"He's come up lame. Ricks doesn't know what it is. He has me padding the horse's hooves with potatoes, but it could be in Taurus's neck. It could be anywhere." He shifted his weight, then confessed, "This is the horse I need to run against Owen Campbell."

"Can he run?"

"It's doubtful."

She frowned. "What of your money?"

"The stake I've already put up?" Breccan took his time answering, stretching the tightness in his back. "If he doesn't run, I lose it."

"And no one in the stable has an idea of what the problem is?"

Breccan crossed his arms. These were all questions he'd chased in his head. "He was fine for the ride yesterday morning, then he pulled up lame. The lad doesn't think he did anything. He noted Taurus had seemed a bit slow but still sound. I'm glad you came out to see me," he said, wanting to change the subject. He was about to almost ruin himself. Money was hard-won at Wolfstone. He should not have been so foolish. If he could have hidden it all from her, he would have. "Daphne has warmed up to you."

Tara sent a distracted glance toward the terrier. "Apparently," she murmured. "She seems to have forgiven me."

"For what?"

With a shake of her head, Tara changed the subject. "Which leg is bothering the horse?"

Breccan wanted to tell her that this was not her problem. He sighed. "The left."

Tara bent over and lifted the hoof. "What's his name?"

"Taurus." He didn't want her involved in this, but Tara was headstrong.

She let go of the hoof and straightened. "The problem isn't in the leg," she informed. "It is the hoof. I think you have a hot nail."

"A what?" Breccan knew a little about shoeing, but he left that up to Ricks and the stable lads. It wasn't that he didn't pay attention to how his horses were trimmed, but this was a new endeavor for him, and there was much to learn.

"A hot nail," Tara explained, "is when the shoe is nailed wrong. The nail goes into the soft part of the hoof instead of the hoof wall."

"What do you do for it?"

"You take the shoe off."

That was an easy solution, and one Breccan was surprised they hadn't tried yet. What the devil was Ricks thinking?

Breccan moved to the box of tools for the shoe puller as she asked, "Who did his shoes?"

"Ricks. He says he likes to do his own." Breccan picked up Taurus's hoof, put it between his legs to hold it in place and pulled the shoe off. "Look at this. It is obvious where the nail had gone in wrong."

"It happens," Tara said. "Sometimes they shoe wrong. You will have to let the horse rest," she advised, as Breccan pulled the other shoes off. "And keep your eye out for infection. It could get worse."

"How long will it take to heal?"

"It could be a week. It could be months."

"I can't afford this," Breccan said more to himself than to her. If it was months, even more than a week, he was in trouble. He threw the shoe puller into the box of tools, disgusted with himself for having made such a wager. "Are you certain it could take so long to heal?" he asked. "How do you know this information?"

"Mr. Jamerson."

She said it curtly, as if it wasn't a name she wanted to think about.

For his part, Jamerson's name from her lips inspired a jagged jolt of jealousy. He focused on the horse.

"Do you have any idea how I can hurry the healing?"

Tara frowned, then said, "I wouldn't use potatoes. Are those the ones you took off him?" She nodded to the corner, where the bandages taken off Taurus still were. "They smell." As if agreeing with her, Daphne sneezed.

"Mr. Jamerson often used a salve made out of

comfrey leaves," Tara continued. "He put it on sores and cuts, almost anything."

"Comfrey leaves," Breccan repeated.

"Angus, the head groom at Annefield, may have some of the salve."

"I hope so. And if not, there is the apothecary in Glasgow."

"You would go that far? Perhaps you can find someone who knows herbs closer?" she asked.

"If there is, I will search him out," Breccan vowed.

"Angus will advise you to soak the hoof in salted water. He recommends that as a remedy for everything."

Salt water. It was a common cure. Breccan should have thought of that himself. "Thank you," he said to her. "You may have saved my race."

She smiled modestly and demurred, "It is in my own best interest."

Aye, it was, and yet he liked the idea that she was willing to help him.

She took a step toward the stall door but then stopped. "Thank you for last night," she whispered. She hurried away. Daphne went gamely after her.

Breccan wanted to chase after her as well. He

wanted to walk her to the castle and spend the afternoon with her, but he had to see to finding comfrey leaves and to soaking Taurus's foot. He prayed her advice bore fruit.

He started to call one of the stable lads to help when Jonas popped his head around the corner of the door. " 'Thank you for last night?' " he teased.

"Don't you have anything else to do?" Breccan countered.

"Aye, but I've done it." Jonas grinned. "*Och*, Breccan, you are a lusty lad. You ripped the gown form her body. I'm proud of you—"

"*What?*" Breccan almost backed into Taurus in horror.

Jonas laughed happily. "I knew you had it in you. I *knew* it. And I noticed today that the lass is more at peace. A happy wife is a well-plowed one."

Breccan wanted to pick his uncle up and give him a shake. Instead, he used his formidable height to lord it over his diminutive uncle. "Say one word more about my wife and her pleasures, and I will pull the teeth from your head." He enunciated each word so there would be no doubt in the irrepressible Jonas's mind of his intent.

His uncle eyed him as if waiting for the laughter or a hint of a smile.

There was none. Breccan could not imagine what would happen if Tara overheard such a conversation. "Do we understand each other?"

Jonas's brows rose to his eyebrows. "Aye, Breccan."

"*Good.*" There was a wealth of threat in that one word.

Feeling as if he had settled the matter, Breccan closed the stall door and started for the yard. He wanted to send some lads to help Tara in the house and one to soak Taurus's hoof. He'd ride over to Annefield himself and confer with Angus. Angus Freeman. Indeed, he remembered the conversation he'd had with the groom the other night and Angus's suggestion that he was not tied to Annefield. Perhaps the time had come for a new stable master at Wolfstone.

However, as Breccan was about to step outside, Jonas must have decided he had to have the last word. "Of course," he threw out, "if gown ripping can bring one of those rowdy Davidsons to heel, we should have done it a long time ago—Whoa, wait, Breccan. *Breccan.*"

Jonas had not had a chance to finish whatever cleverness he had in mind. Breccan had spun on his heel and been upon his uncle in a thrice. He picked Jonas up by the scruff of his shirt and the seat of his pants and carried him out of the stables to the small pond. Ducks scattered as Largo, Tidbit, and Terrance returned from their rounds and excitedly followed him.

"Breccan? What are you doing?" Jonas protested. The stable lads now saw what was going on. Work came to a halt.

Breccan answered Jonas by stopping at the pond's soft bank and tossing him into the murky water. Jonas's shout was cut off by a loud splash.

The stable lads cheered. Jonas's teasing could annoy everyone. Breccan had once heard his uncle described as the black fly of Wolfstone, and, today, he had bitten the wrong man.

Jonas shot up out of the water. "You've made your point, lad," he said.

"About what?" Breccan challenged.

"Your wi—" Jonas started but then caught himself. "About my mouth."

"Good," Breccan answered, and climbed the bank. A short while later, he had donned neckcloth and jacket and was on his way to Annefield.

*A*ngus had agreed to come to Wolfstone, but it had not been a simple discussion. He'd assured

Breccan that he would need to consider the matter over a pint or two or five. The brew at the Kenmore Inn was potent. For all his advantage of size, Angus could have put him under the table.

In the end, Breccan had a small pot of the comfrey salve and a stable manager . . . a good one.

He noted that just as Tara had checked the shoe after hearing the vaguest description of Taurus's lameness, Angus, too, had assumed the issue could have been a hot nail. So why hadn't Ricks? The man who had shoed the horse?

After the third tankard, Breccan had said as much to Angus. "Here now, it happens," the horseman had said. "Even the best of us have put a nail in wrong."

Breccan wasn't certain.

What he did know is, that once again, he was returning home later than he had planned. Not even his dogs were waiting up.

Once again, he ate alone in the kitchen from a plate Flora prepared. "Has all been good here?" he asked the maid.

"It has been busy. My lady found some furniture in the attic. She's worked us hard today."

"Did she?"

"Well, no harder than she has worked herself."

That was good news. Breccan didn't know

what he would do if he'd had a lazy wife . . . and the thought reminded him of Tara's warning that looks faded.

But what was left had to be valued.

Flora said, almost shyly, "She's a worthy woman, sir. A fine mistress."

"Thank you." Thoughtfully, Breccan said his good night to Flora and made his way into the castle. Fortunately, he'd carried a candle because otherwise he would not have found his way in the dark. Tara had been busy.

The first room he entered no longer had the simple table and chairs. In their place was a table big enough for a banquet and seating for ten and more. There was even a carpet on the floor. He wondered what else she had changed.

Upstairs, he found his dogs sleeping outside his closed bedroom door. They all rose to greet him, tails wagging sheepishly as if they were guilty of defecting from him. Well, save for Daphne. Daphne expected her pat, unrepentant that she had spent her day following Tara and left him to fend for himself.

Women.

Breccan opened the door carefully. He didn't want to disturb her if she was asleep—and yet, he hoped she was awake. He had a picture of her in his bed that was rarely far from his mind.

Of course, in his imaginings, she was naked, and he'd had yet to see that about her yet.

He was not going to see it tonight either. She was already asleep. She slept on the counterpane with the spread flipped up over her as it had been the night before. She was on her side, facing the door.

A candle had been left burning for him in the room. He blew his out and set the candlestick on the new table beside the bed.

There were other changes in the room as well. There was another table, with a washbasin and pitcher on it. His shaving kit was laid out beside it.

Tara was a persistent woman.

He ran a hand over his rough whiskers but he was tired and still had the ale in his veins. Shaving could wait until the morrow. He did use the water in the pitcher to wash. A bar of scented soap was by the basin. The scent reminded him of his wife.

Breccan began undressing. A new chair in the corner afforded him a place to remove his boots. He liked the furniture. It was heavy oak and appealed to his masculine tastes. He set his boots aside, unbuttoned his waistcoat and hung it on a peg before tugging his shirt hem from his breeches—and that is when he noticed movement from the bed.

He studied her a moment. Her eyes appeared shut, but he had a sense she was not asleep.

And then he noticed the barest movement of her lashes.

Could she be watching him?

He decided on a test. He untied his neckcloth and pulled his shirt over his head.

There was no response from the bed. She seemed to be sleeping soundly—and yet he could not shake the suspicion that she was awake.

Breccan moved to the side of the bed. By now, his manhood was alive with a mind of its own. He could not have hidden if he tried, so he didn't.

Instead, he freed the little beastie by unfastening the first button, and the second . . . knowing his instincts had not been wrong when a rush of the most becoming pink stained her cheeks—and the game was on.

Chapter Twelve

*O*f course Tara had heard Breccan come in. She'd been waiting for him. He'd not been far from her thoughts all day.

She'd organized the carrying of chairs and tables from the attic with an eye of concern for what he would think. Would he be pleased? Was she overstepping boundaries?

Tara found she liked the task. Many of the rooms were bare, so she'd felt free to imagine what they could be.

Of course, such an endeavor had involved a good number of servants, but many had offered to help. The stable lads Breccan had sent to the castle had attracted the maids and other lasses working on different parts of the estate.

They had been a merry group. Once they'd felt comfortable with Tara, they had worked hard, but they had also teased each other. In short order, she has discerned which couples were sweethearts and which would like to be. There were even the disgruntled. The game was the same whether it was played on London's ballroom floors or in Scotland's Highlands, and she found herself, curiously, relieved to not be involved in it. She was someone's wife. The struggle, the need to prove herself acceptable was over.

Freedom was a sweet dish.

Lachlan had approved her changes. Jonas had been uncharacteristically quiet over dinner, which they ate in the actual dining room and not in the kitchen. Tara had asked Jonas if he felt well, and he'd answered, "I'm guilty, feeling guilty."

It was a cryptic response, but Lachlan had advised her not to ask too many questions, and so, for once in her life, she hadn't.

Indeed, she found herself relaxed and looking forward to the morrow.

She no longer feared Breccan. Yes, he was a brawny man, but she was beginning to respect him . . . something she discovered she'd never felt for a man before.

Today, when she'd given her opinion on Taurus's injuries, he'd surprised her when he'd acted upon her advice. Another first in her life. It was gratifying to have her opinion valued.

So, even though she was tired when she went to bed, she listened for the sounds of his return.

Had she meant to pretend to be asleep?

Not at first. However, when she heard his voice in the hall, she'd become nervous, and she wasn't certain why, so she'd shut her eyes—until she had heard him starting to undress.

Curiosity had always been one of her besetting sins.

There had been times today when she had recalled the sight of him naked. Her husband was a well-formed man. There was a part of her that wanted to purr her interest like a cat.

However, although her fears of him had abated, she was still cautious. She needed to hold on to her wits. She did have reservations. She was more than a bit shy.

But was it wrong, since he seemed so nonchalant about undressing, if she didn't watch?

He actually seemed to be performing for her.

The candlelight highlighted the hard lines of his chest. She did like the way his waist tapered.

She could recall his weight upon her last night. His actions had alarmed her, but the physicalness between them had stirred her senses.

Breccan unbuttoned his breeches.

She stopped breathing as the rounded tip of his manhood protruded. She wanted to open her eyes and stare. She'd couldn't. She wouldn't.

Last night, she'd had a glimpse. In her mind, everything the maids had said was true . . . expect this part of him wasn't always prominent. He'd be unable to wear his breeches if it was. She wondered if he was like a horse and pulled it in and out?

That was a strange thought, and it almost made her giggle.

And then he lay down upon the bed beside her.

Tara had assumed he would climb under the covers as he had the night before. But no, he was right next to her on the counterpane. Naked.

Now her whole body blushed. She didn't know what to do. They were so close together that if she rolled over, she'd bump into him, especially *that* part of him.

So she continued to do what she was beginning to do best—she feigned sleep—hoping it would come even though her senses were full of him, of his scent, his warmth, his presence. The man didn't just lie on a bed, he overtook it—

"I know you are awake, Tara."

No, he couldn't have caught her. He didn't have a clue last night.

"I know you watched me undress." He turned on his side toward her. "Now, look," he cooed, "your whole body has turned as red as an apple."

He placed a hand on her shoulder. She tried not to tense, but she failed. She opened her eyes and gave him a frown.

Breccan laughed. "My purpose is not to embarrass you. But you don't have to hide that you'd like a look at me. I'm yours, lass." He rolled on his back, presenting himself. "We are married, and what is mine is yours."

And as if agreeing, his male bits seemed to nod.

Tara fought panic. This was so open. It was almost too much. She concentrated on his face. He hadn't shaved, but the attractive dimple had shown itself again, giving him a roguish air.

She had never been attracted to the rakes. She had too much common sense. However, that dimple made something inside of her all fluttery.

She had to guard herself against it . . . and she didn't understand why.

And if his goal was to make her feel more comfortable with him, then it was working. Yes, she had some apprehension about the marriage act, but that was fading. Her inquisitiveness was too lively to keep her in fear.

So why did she resist?

It was a lack of trust. This man was not her choice. She'd saddled herself with him, lured by the promise of his returning her to where she had once been successful. Her return to the valley had not been as she wished.

She must keep in mind that her future did not lie with this man. She must protect herself and keep a respectable distance between them.

"Would you please put yourself between the sheets?" she asked primly.

His smiled widened until it appeared positively wolfish. "No."

"Then I shall sleep between the sheets," she announced. She climbed off the bed, lifted the covers and put herself between the sheets.

"Then I shall use the counterpane," he said, and wrapped it around himself, pulling a portion off Tara. "There is a chill in the air tonight, but I feel snug and warm here," he said, wiggling his body as if he would burrow into the mattress. "Of course, we could be warmer . . ."

She knew what he suggested. She tried to ignore the way her pulse picked up at the hint of proposition in his voice.

Only a matter of weeks ago, she'd vowed her undying love for Ruary Jamerson. Now, her traitorous body reacted to Breccan with a yearning so strong, it took all her willpower to not lean forward into his body heat.

His appeal was the fact he was naked, she decided. Humans were animals after all. That last statement had been the claim of one of her London suitors, an obnoxious, pretentious man with aspirations for science. He adored repeating the "animal" declaration as if he believed it made him sound clever. But now, she considered there might be something to the statement.

If Breccan were wearing clothes, well, perhaps she would not give him a second glance—but she knew that was no longer the case. The men she had favored in the past might have been elegant of form, but she was finding Breccan's solid muscle enticing as well.

She was also becoming at ease with the part

of him that was so distinctly male. So obviously animal.

"Does it hurt?" she asked abruptly.

He came onto his side, propping his head up with one hand. "Does what hurt?"

"You. Being the way you were."

The light of a thousand devils danced in his eyes. "Aroused?"

"Stop it," she ordered.

"Stop what?"

"Words like that."

"Like 'aroused'?" he repeated.

"It is unsettling." *Aroused*. It described how she felt. "I need to sleep," she answered him.

"Then sleep," he replied.

"I will." She closed her eyes, then opened them again. "I can feel you watching me."

"It keeps me aroused," he answered.

Tara reached for her temper. It was a safe way to keep distance between them. "I'm happy you find all of this so humorous." She flipped over to her other side, giving him her back. Unfortunately, she lay wrong on her braid and had to lift herself up to free it from being pulled by her own body weight. The gesture defused the drama she had planned.

For a moment, silence reigned between them.

She wondered if he'd fallen asleep. She couldn't,

and she believed it was his fault. She'd been perfectly at rest before he'd brought his naked self and plopped it into the bed.

But her thoughts could not quiet.

Tara found herself wondering if he'd had lovers. Most men had, or so she'd been told. It was all part of being male. But a married woman could have lovers. Perhaps she would have lovers when she returned to London. Slim, manageable lovers. Not big and brawny ones with a swollen sense of themselves . . . and their arousal.

Of course, she and Breccan were not lovers, not yet—

Her braid came over her shoulder. It just fell across her face.

She rose up, mystified, until he explained, "It was across my pillow. I didn't like it there. You need to keep your hair to yourself."

Tara sat up. "Are you mad?"

He seemed to consider the matter. "Sometimes, yes."

His candor caught her off guard. She didn't know how to respond other than to lie back down, muttering about "Obnoxious, ill-behaved boors—"

"That I must share my bed with," he finished, mocking her with his agreement.

Tara pulled the covers up as high over her head as she could. She huddled down, arms crossed, legs tucked, and willed herself to go to sleep . . . except what she was really doing was waiting.

And he did not disappoint.

"Would you like a story?"

"I'm sleeping," she said.

He leaned close to her, his body almost cradling hers. She could feel his knees in the indent of her own. His chest was against her back.

She could not feel his arousal, but she knew he was aroused.

"Do you have another story?" she suggested. It might take her mind off him. It had worked last night.

"I have a good one." He moved onto his back, once again claiming more of the bed than he should. But she was learning not to quibble. For all his great size, Breccan had a quick wit. He easily used her complaints against her.

"Do you like bannocks?" he asked, referring to the small round oatcakes. "They are my favorite when they are hot from the griddle with some good butter."

Tara frowned. She liked them as well. It was dangerous to have something in common with him. It bought them closer.

Breccan launched into his story. It was one she'd heard before, but she didn't mind listening to it again.

"The crofter's wife had made a big bowl of dough," he said, "and she shaped it into two round loaves. But then, she noticed she'd left some dough in the bowl and so she made a wee bonnie bannock. Now, when the bannocks finished baking, she saw that wee one, and she thought to herself, I'm going to have a taste of that. But her husband had come in from working hard. He saw the wee bannock as well, and he wanted it. They both reached for the bannock at the same time—much like you and I seem to be pushing and pulling over who will sleep where in the bed."

Tara had been picturing the couple and the bannock. His poke about the bed annoyed her. "Is our arguing over the covers part of the story?" she demanded, coming over on her back.

He chuckled, the sound masculinely wicked. "I was trying to make the story more personal."

She had to struggle not to smile. "Shall we keep the commentary out of it?"

"'We can try." He looked to the ceiling as if placing his thoughts before saying, "Well, when two people argue, they upset things." He shot a side glance in her direction, questioning if she accepted this.

Tara did not respond. She knew when she was being baited.

"They upset the pan where the wee bannock was," Breccan continued. "The bannock did not want to be eaten, especially by greedy folk. It started rolling away. He rolled out the door and was on his way down the road, feeling very clever as he traveled. Now he passed a young girl who was doing her knitting. She saw him, and she, too, said to herself, I would like to eat that wee bannock, so she tried to grab our friend. But the bannock was clever. He made circles around her and caught her in her own knitting and off he went again."

Breccan's voice was lively. He was enjoying the telling of the story.

Tara was enjoying the hearing. "Is the bannock ever going to stop?"

He held up a finger, begging her to be patient. "He traveled on until he passed a smithy. The blacksmith was a hungry man. He had just been thinking that he'd like a wee bannock, and here one was. He dove for the bannock. But the bannock was wise to him. The bannock went around in circles, passing between his legs until the smith was dizzy and forgot about his hunger. On the bannock rolled. On and on, until he spied two hungry children. They were thin as posts and very sad. They had not had a meal in three days."

"Three days?" She turned on her side to face him.

"Aye," he assured her. "They were very hungry children. The bannock said, I'm sure they would like a wee bannock, and so he hopped into their basket. And then do you know what happened?"

Tara shook her head.

"They *ATE* him," Breccan said, leaping on her and giving her sides a tickle.

Tara shrieked her surprise, and Breccan fell back laughing. She laughed as well.

"I was not expecting that," she said.

"I waited for it, but every time when my mother did it, I was always surprised as well. I liked the giggle."

She could picture him as a young boy with curly black hair and laughing eyes. Their children would look like him. Well, they might have her smile, and she hoped that if they had a daughter, she would have her nose. His nose was fine for a man but would be unfortunate for a woman.

He noticed her staring. "What is it?" he asked, his gray eyes still alight with humor.

Tara could have told him . . . but then where would that lead? She wasn't ready. Not yet.

"I'm tired," she offered weakly. Was it her imagination, or did he appear to understand what she hadn't said?

"Then good night," he said. The counterpane had fallen to cover his hips. He now pulled it up and slid back down into the covers.

She did the same, except he appeared to fall asleep immediately. She didn't.

The candle on the bedside table still burned. Tara started to rise from the bed to go around and blow it out, when something irrepressible inside her took hold. She lifted the counterpane for just a peek at his male bits. She'd been afraid to look earlier, although they had been hard to avoid.

They were odd-looking, but not threatening. Not any longer. And when he was relaxed, they appeared soft as squishy fruit. The thought almost made her laugh, and she carefully lowered the counterpane before a draft of air stirred him.

She rose and walked around the bed to blow out the candle. There was no fire in the grate this night. The servants had been busy helping her. She had a list of tasks as long as her arm. She was also enjoying the changes she was making to the house. She felt productive.

The scent of melted wax in the air, Tara used her hand on the footboard to guide her way in the dark to her side of the bed. She tucked herself back in, but because of the darkness, she ended up closer to Breccan than she liked.

His arm came around her. Its weight rested on her hip.

Her breath caught in her throat. Her first thought was that he was awake. She expected him to move on her as he had done the other night. Her heart gave a double beat against her chest.

But he did not move. He appeared and sounded as if he was in deep slumber. He was far more relaxed around her than she was with him, but that was changing.

Tara found herself falling into a deep sleep.

However, her night was not without interruption.

At one point, she woke to discover that her body was cradled next to his, their legs intertwined. Her drowsy mind registered this, but all she did was smile, strangely content. She fell back into sleep and dreamed of bannocks rolling around blacksmiths chasing girls who knit and a powerful stallion who no longer frightened her.

Instead, in her dream, she thought him a magnificent creature.

That morning, she woke to the sound of rain on the windowpanes and, once again, discovered herself alone in the bed.

"*I* want to make bannock cakes," Tara argued.

Dougal frowned. "I am happy to make them for you, my lady, especially if you want little round ones.

Tara made an impatient sound. "I don't want you to do it. I wish to bake them myself."

"Do you know how to cook?"

"No."

"Then perhaps you shouldn't."

Tara had a swift retort for the cook, but Jonas's voice behind her said with a yawn, "Help her cook them, Dougal. What's the matter with you, man?"

"My lady has taken all my help," Dougal complained. "She has them cleaning every room in the castle."

"Which need cleaning," Tara pointed out.

"Then how am I to do my tasks for supper?" Dougal said, addressing the question to Jonas.

But Tara was not going to accept this silliness.

She placed her palms on the sides of his jaw and turned him around to face her. "You talk to me."

There was a stubbornness in Dougal. He didn't like the order. Then again, he had little choice but to obey. "Yes, my lady." He looked to Jonas and ground out, "You can see to your own breakfast."

Jonas held up his hands, begging for quarter, but he was laughing as well.

In short order, Tara found herself learning how to make bannocks. "These are the laird's favorite, right?" she asked Dougal. He had been about to stir the dough with a porridge stick himself, but she had commandeered it.

The idea to make bannocks had come to Tara while she was dressing. She wanted to do something for Breccan, to please him.

"Is this good?" she asked Dougal, showing him the mixture in her bowl.

He was very surly over having his mistress in his kitchen. She knew the changes were disrupting him, but he was going to have to cope.

"Good enough . . . my lady." He added her title as an afterthought.

Tara gifted him with her sweetest smile. She was not going to let him destroy her good mood, and she was very aware of the power of her smile.

"I'll heat up the griddle," Dougal said.

It had been raining steadily outside. The kitchen door was usually open because of the heat, and today was no exception. Daphne had made her way to sleep curled up inside the door.

"So what has Breccan done to earn such a favor?" Jonas asked. He sat at the table, the hair on his balding pate going every which way, holding a mug of cider.

"He likes bannocks," Tara said. "With butter. That's why I am making them."

"Aye, so you are. That lad is a lucky man," Jonas said, and Tara frowned, sensing that there was more to Jonas's words than what she heard.

She also could feel Dougal's reaction behind her. She turned to catch him winking and make an odd gesture to Jonas, who just grinned.

"I don't have time for nonsense," Tara said. "Is the griddle ready?"

"It is, my lady," Dougal said.

"Then what do I do next?"

He taught her how to knead. Tara found she liked working the dough. After what seemed a good half hour, Dougal declared it ready to be cut it into pieces. Tara performed the chore while Dougal smeared bacon fat on the hot pan. They dropped the dough into the grease.

"Will it take long to cook?" Tara asked, fascinated by the process.

"Not since they are so wee. I usually leave the pieces larger."

She grinned. "But I want *wee* bannocks." She hoped Breccan would be pleased.

The rain had stopped. The sky was still overcast, but this was Scotland. Overcast days were to be expected.

Jonas was watching her, an amused expression on his face. She sat in the chair next to him. "You look as if I've surprised you."

"I was just thinking how nice it would be to have a lass as fine as yourself cook for me."

The compliment brought heat to her cheeks. "I've never cooked before."

"Breccan's a lucky man," Jonas said, as if just now reaching that opinion.

"Did his mother cook?" Last night, she had pictured her making bannocks.

"I suppose she could. Certainly, she could have cooked better than Dougal. A goat could cook better than him."

"*Hey,*" was the cook's warning. He then tempered his tone and said, "I'll turn these over."

"No, no, I wish to do it." Tara hurried to the fire. Her first attempts were clumsy. She lost one into the fire and a few bannocks were a bit black. "I've never seen them like this."

"Don't worry, my lady," Dougal said. "They are the way Breccan likes them. That's why they call him the Black Campbell."

Tara knew he jested. She would not take these to Breccan, and she was determined to do better. She wanted them round and not as misshapen as the ones she was cooking. The next batch turned out not as burnt and a bit better. She could imagine them rolling down the road, although their travels would not be as smooth as she had imagined when listening to the story.

Lachlan looked in the door. He saw her cooking and smiled, then nodded and went on his way.

"Were you or Lachlan ever married?" Tara asked Jonas.

"I couldn't find one lass who could tame me," Jonas declared.

"And with good reason," Dougal chimed in. "There isn't a woman alive who doesn't have something better to do than stand for his nonsense."

"I'm certain you are right," Tara said with a distracted air as she turned the oatcakes, then looked up with a smile to show she jested.

The men laughed . . . but it was a different kind of laughter than what she had usually experienced. In London, they laughed to woo her, to placate her, to feel accepted by her.

Here, they laughed because they found what she said amusing. They laughed because they were including her as one of them.

Tara was so taken with the moment, she burned her bannocks again.

"You have to watch the fire at all times, my lady," Dougal cautioned. He helped her with the last batch.

"So what of Lachlan?" Tara asked, wiping dough off her hands with a linen towel. "Has he been married?"

Jonas became sober. "Aye, he was. He had a wife and three children. They all died of the fever. He was in the navy in the Indies. He was out to sea when the fever hit. When he returned home, they were all gone."

"That is a terrible story," Tara said.

"It is not a story, my lady, but the truth of it," Jonas answered. "He returned to Wolfstone shortly after that. Said he'd lost his desire to go to sea."

"What does he do all day?" Jonas she saw often, but Lachlan would disappear until dinner.

"He's a tutor at Breccan's school. You've not seen the school yet, have you?"

"I haven't," Tara answered.

"Well, ask him to show it you," Jonas answered. "And while you are at it, ask to see the weavers' cottages he is building."

"Breccan is doing that?" she said.

Jonas laughed. "All I have to do is look at you to see why the lad doesn't spend his night talking when he is with you. But, aye, he has many irons in the fire. You might urge him to slow down."

Tara digested this advice. Apparently, there was more to her husband than she had imagined. He didn't come home until late, but she hadn't minded that he was so busy.

"Your bannocks are done, my lady," Dougal said. He brought over the last pan. These were brown. They would do.

"Do we have a basket for me to carry them in?" she asked.

"One moment." Dougal fetched a basket with a handle and started to line it with a towel.

In the meantime, Tara tried to break one of the bannocks. It had been a long time since she'd had one. Years, in fact.

The oatcake was hard to break. Perhaps it would soften as it cooled. She took what she'd broken off and offered a piece to Daphne. Terrance and Tidbit, the foxhounds, had taken to following her around as well. They had been lounging outside the kitchen. Dougal said they preferred the outdoors. They now came rushing over to taste the treat.

Tara divided the other piece of bannock between the dogs. They accepted it but after a taste, let it drop from their mouths.

"They don't like it," Tara said.

"Dogs know nothing," Dougal answered. "They eat squirrel innards."

Tara made a face at the thought. She straightened and took her cape off a hook on the wall. Dougal had the basket ready. "Now I just need to find Breccan," she said.

"I would start at the stables," Jonas advised.

"That's what I shall do. Oh, did you place butter in here, Dougal?" she asked, moving to take the basket.

Dougal jumped as if just remembering the butter and hurried to prepare a small crock of it for the basket.

Tara took one last look at her bannocks. They definitely looked as if they could roll down the road. And she was proud of them.

She took off out the door to find Breccan.

Chapter Thirteen

*B*reccan raked an angry hand through rain-soaked hair. He wore an oilskin coat and stood in the center of one of the cottages being built for the weavers. He'd been there for a good two hours studying the structure.

Beyond the partially finished structures, several of the crofters, male, female and some children, most of whom had been eyeing these buildings as new living quarters, waited for his verdict.

Amongst them was the weaver Ian Ewing, who Breccan had hired to organize the work. The man lived in a crofter's hut less than a mile from here. Part of the agreement for him to come to Wolfstone had been the promise of one of these cottages.

But they were all going to have to wait.

His uncle Lachlan stood close at hand. "What are you going to do, lad?"

Breccan surveyed the careless work that had been performed by the builder, a man he'd just chased off with the threat of stringing him up by his bollocks if he ever saw him again. The walls had been set on dirt. There was no foundation beneath them, and that was only one of the problems.

"I'm going to finish them," Breccan vowed.

Lachlan leaned close. He had invested in the project with Breccan. "I've given you all I have, lad. Do you have the money?"

"I have some of what we have left. I'm too canny to pay the man all."

"That is a relief."

"I was told he was good." Breccan had a mind to ride to Glasgow and ring William Govan's neck. The man had assured him that Thom Roberts could build the cottages to Breccan's design.

"I know."

"But," Breccan said, surveying all that still needed to be done, "I'm also glad that the man didn't finish. If he had left that ceiling beam with the crack in it in place, then the roof could have fallen in. I'll finish this. I now know I have as much sense as that ass had."

"Breccan, do you have the time?"

He looked to his uncle. "Do I have a choice? Do you see them out there? They are waiting. I promised them this."

"No one is going to hold you responsible—"

"I hold myself responsible. We've invested in this, Lachlan. If it is successful, then we'll all do well. All of us, the crofters, too. But that weaver is going to leave before we know enough about how to operate the machinery if I don't deliver on a promise."

"But what of money, Breccan?"

"I can't let the money we've spent go to waste," Breccan said. "And it is my fault it is tight. If I'd kept my mouth shut when Owen was going on, then I wouldn't have put the stake up for the race."

"He put you up to it. The man is always pushing."

"Aye, but the knowledge doesn't help us now. My pride is what is really at stake, Lachlan, for both the race and these cottages." He considered the matter. "The lads will need to take down these walls, and we'll put a proper foundation in. That won't cost much. I hate to think of how much of our money the man put in his own pocket." But there was enough left.

"With all willing hands at work, we can finish these before Hogmanay," Breccan said, referring to the end of the year. One advantage he had was that, since the building had started, he'd been approached by a number of men with the skills he needed who had been looking for work. He'd referred them to Roberts, who had insisted he use his own relatives. Well, that was done.

"You can do this?" Lachlan queried.

"I'm anxious to try my hand at it."

"It will call for a good amount of time," his uncle warned. "You have a new bride, and you've not joined her for dinner yet."

If anything, supervising the building of the cottages would give Breccan one more task to keep his mind off his bride. He'd not tell Lachlan he hadn't bedded her yet. Any man would think he was daft. They wouldn't understand that Breccan wanted more than just Tara's body, he wanted her love.

Of course, a beauty such as hers could claim every man's heart. However, she understood that her physical appearance wasn't permanent. She had wished for a man who could love her fully for the person she was.

Breccan was just biding his time until she realized *he* was that man. Until then, hard labor would relieve some of his frustration. It was damn difficult to spend the night beside such an enticing creature as his wife and keep his hands off her.

He'd almost broken his vow to let her come to him in her own time when she'd lifted the covers on him last night. He'd known what she was looking at, and it had taken considerable concentration to not react. He was fortunate he'd been on his side. If he'd been on his back, he would have created a tent out of the counterpane.

"What has you smiling?" Lachlan asked, reminding Breccan to stay in the moment.

"A random thought," Breccan murmured, then said, to reassure his uncle, "I'll see the work done. And in truth, I will appreciate the challenge." He turned to the men awaiting his verdict—some of his clansmen who had been helping Roberts. "We need to take it down. All of it. This time, we'll do it right. Now that the rain has stopped, let's see how much we can get done." The weather had been dismal earlier, but for the undertaking of moving rock and timbers, one didn't need dry ground.

They came willingly to help. Apparently, the

big fear had been that Breccan would abandon the scheme.

Breccan was about to set to work with them, Lachlan at his side, when he noticed a figure walking on the road toward them—his wife.

Her hair was like a beacon. She'd styled it up on her head and had not bothered with a hat, perhaps because she would have covered it with her cape if it rained. She carried a basket, and his pups, Terrance, Tidbit and Daphne pranced at her heels.

Largo roused himself from where he'd been resting, waiting for Breccan. With a bark, he trotted up to her.

Tara stopped and gave the big beast a pat, before looking up and smiling at Breccan.

He could swear his heart was in danger of stopping every time she looked at him as if he were the only man in the world.

Was there any woman more beautiful than his wife? He thought not. He never tired of looking at her, not with those large blue eyes.

He left the work and went walking to greet her.

Lachlan and the lads said a few teasing things in his wake. Breccan didn't care. He'd barely heard them.

He approached his wife. Her smile, just for him,

had widened in greeting. Her skin was so perfect, her teeth so white.

She held up her basket. "I made you some wee bannocks."

"You what?" He wasn't certain he'd heard her correctly. He took the basket and, with his hand at her elbow guided her to where they could have some privacy away from the prying ears of the others. From here, he could still see the work being done on the cottages but have a quiet moment with his wife.

"I baked bannocks," she repeated, "like in the story last night."

"I didn't know you could cook," he said, lifting the cloth over the oatcakes.

"I've never cooked anything before," she confessed. "This is my first effort. But I rather liked doing it. There is satisfaction in making food. Of course, Dougal and I argued. He wanted to make two big bannocks, but I insisted on wee ones."

"Oh, so these are Dougal's bannocks," Breccan said with a sense of dread. Dougal was not a good cook. He was fine with meat, but his bread was tough and his bannocks in the past had been harder than rocks.

"No, they are mine," she countered. "And they are still hot. I brought butter as well."

She had made bannocks for him, and she'd taken to heart his description of how he liked them. No gift could be finer.

Breccan set the basket on the ground and pulled out a bannock and the small crock of butter. For a second, he feared the dogs would stick their nose into it, but the hounds and Daphne took a sniff, then turned away.

If the dogs didn't want it, then Breccan knew it would be bad. He dipped his bannock in the softened butter. He smiled at Tara.

She smiled back, her eyes brimming with pride.

He crunched into the bannock. His teeth did not make much progress. True to Dougal's talent, the oatcake was dry and hard, but Breccan was determined. He managed to bite a bit off and gnawed away with his side teeth. The champing of his teeth sounded loud in his ears, but Tara didn't seem to notice.

Breccan swallowed as soon as he could.

Such chivalry certainly deserved a kiss, and that is what he had in mind. A proper kiss. He hungered for it.

"They are tasty," Breccan said, wishing he had some ale to wash it down—or to soften them.

Tara looked up at him with the trusting eyes of a child who was delighted to have accomplished something. "I wanted to please you," she said.

No words could be sweeter, even if the heavens had opened and angels appeared to sing a chorus of hosannas. *I wanted to please you.*

His strategy had paid off. His wooing had worked.

And now for the kiss.

Breccan leaned down to meet his wife—

A crack was the only warning before the crashing sound of stone walls caving in.

He pushed Tara behind him, even knowing she wasn't in danger, and, a beat later, he was racing for the cottages. The front wall of the corner cottage had caved in. A woman started screaming even as more of the walls crumbled.

Breccan shouted, "Stay back." He ran forward. To his relief, he saw Lachlan and Jonas. They were coughing and looked around, then Lachlan shouted. He pointed, and Breccan could see that the ceiling beam had fallen. It rested at an angle, half of it on the floor, the other half still being held by the wall, but not for long.

"*Breccan,*" Lachlan said. "The beam fell on Ian."

In horror, Breccan saw Ian beneath the heavy beam. Ian was trapped. He gasped as if breathing was difficult through his panic. "I'm pinned," he warned them. "I can't move."

His wife had been the one screaming. She now tried to climb across the rubble to her husband.

Breccan said, "Move her out of the way."

His uncles and the others were attempting to lift the end of the beam on Ian. Other men were on their knees trying to dig beneath him.

Breccan saw that way would not work. They needed leverage and they must hurry because the wall holding the other end of the beam threatened to cave as well. If that happened, Ian would be crushed. As it was, who knew what injuries he had already suffered.

There was little time to waste, so Breccan used himself for that leverage. He went directly beneath the beam even as Lachlan warned him to stop.

"If that wall caves, you are both gone," his uncle warned.

Breccan's answer was to brace his shoulder against the beam, raising his arms to grasp it with his hands. In this way, he hoped to direct the fall once the beam was lifted. It would not serve to throw it off and have the heavy wood land on Ian's head.

"When I give a shout, pick up your end," he said to his uncles. "Ian, be ready to move."

"I don't know if I can."

"Help him," Breccan ordered those who had been trying to dig.

They nodded understanding.

Breccan drew in air and released it. There had been a time when Jonas had him picking up heavy objects for sport. He'd once lifted two anvils, one stacked on the other. This would be different, but the weight would be about right. It was a matter of believing he could do it.

He released his breath, and said, "*Now.*" He put everything he had into his back and his shoulders.

It helped to groan, to rage against this accident that could take a man's life. Breccan gave all he had. Everything. He would not cry quarter.

After a few agonizing seconds of doubt, the beam moved. "*More,*" he roared. He could no longer tell what the others were doing. His whole being was invested in his battle with the beam.

And then, miracle of miracles, he raised the beam.

There were shouts. Someone said, "We have him, Breccan. He's safe."

Only then did Breccan release his hold and

move out of the way. He practically fell forward and not a moment too soon because the weak wall holding the other end collapsed, and the beam fell like deadweight to the ground.

Breccan looked around. "Is everyone safe?" he asked, panting, as he tried to catch his breath. His every muscle had been strained to its limit. He started to fall to his knees, then caught himself— and that is when he saw her.

Tara stood by the side of the cottage. Tears streamed down her face, and her eyes were dark with concern.

He tried to smile, to reassure her, but he knew it looked like a grimace.

Her response was to come forward. She took his great face in her hands and gave him the kiss of which he'd dreamed.

$\mathcal{T}$ara had been shocked to see the building caving in. She'd heard the screams. The wife had begged for anyone to save her husband, and there were those who believed that Ian would die. There were those who ran from the collapsing house.

Breccan had moved forward.

And then she'd witnessed the most amazing

sight. This man who could entertain her with the gentlest of stories, who struggled to control himself, who showed patience to her, now placed his own life in danger.

Anyone could see that the beam was in peril of falling to the ground. It was huge, massive, and strong enough to hold up the floor of a house. It would have killed the man on the ground.

But Breccan had saved him.

If she had not seen him lift the beam with her own eyes, she would not have believed the story.

And now she came forward, struck by how fortunate she was to have this man in her life. The realization was just that clear.

He was no ordinary being, and she knew that even before he had displayed the strength of a Hercules.

She went to him. She went in gratitude, in amazement . . . and, most, surprisingly, in love.

Yes, love. She was falling in love.

And love surprised her. She'd returned to Annefield and the valley because she believed she loved Ruary.

But now, she wondered if she'd ever loved before.

Breccan was *the one*. One life; one love.

With the clarity she'd never experienced before, Tara saw that while she might have once cared deeply for Ruary, their connection had been actually a safe haven at a time when her world had been turned upside down.

And she'd never felt any deep emotion for any of her suitors, including the man she had almost married . . . because they had never engaged her in the manner Breccan had. They'd not captured her imagination or proven they could think of anyone's needs over their own.

Breccan had worked to earn her trust at a cost a more selfish man would have refused to pay.

Certainly, she had never been in *wonder* of a man. Or admired one because of his kind, generous nature. She'd never even considered kindness a sought-after quality. Suddenly, she realized, nothing was more important.

So she kissed him. She kissed in thanksgiving that the beam had not crushed him, in gratitude that he could continue to be her life, and in humility that this person cared for her.

The kiss was like no other she had ever experienced. Their mouths fit perfectly together. Their lips melded, and she adored the taste and texture of him.

He smelled of the oilcloth he wore, of the sweat of his struggle to save the man's life and of that which was uniquely him. He reminded her of leather and fresh air.

His whiskers were no deterrent. Their scratchiness told her that it was Breccan she kissed, good, strong-hearted Breccan.

He'd risen from the ground to stand on his two feet. His arms came around her. Their kiss deepened.

The world disappeared. In this moment, all that mattered to her was him—and she had no desire to let him go. Ever.

Had she been afraid of him?

What nonsense. One could never be afraid of a man as noble as this one.

His tongue stroked hers.

She'd never experienced that before. Her first inclination was to pull back, but then she couldn't . . . because she liked it. She liked it very much.

So, she returned the favor, her tongue brushing his.

His hips immediately met hers. His body embraced hers, and she was in danger of losing all reasoned thought.

Breccan broke the kiss, but he did not let go of

her. Instead, he rested his head against hers. The pins had fallen out of her hair. She did not have a care.

His breathing was ragged. Or was that hers?

"You both go on," Lachlan said, his voice helping to return her to the moment. "We'll clean everything up here."

"Aye," Jonas echoed.

Tara didn't know if they had smirks on their faces or disapproval. Her attention was on her husband.

Breccan took her hand. "Come," he said, sounding a bit shy. It made her smile.

They had only gone a step when a woman placed herself in front of Breccan. She took his free hand.

"Bless you," she whispered. "Bless you, bless you."

Her words seemed to release Breccan from a spell. "How is Ian, Mary?"

The man he had freed came over to stand by his wife. He limped, but he appeared fine. "My leg is sore but, miraculously, I don't seem hurt. Lucky I am that you were there, Laird. Very lucky."

"Rest," Breccan advised. "Take care of yourself and your family."

"Aye, Laird."

Breccan still held her hand. Together, they walked down the road, the dogs happily chasing after them.

When they were away from prying ears, Tara said, "We are going to our bedroom, yes?"

"Absolutely."

The desperate need in his voice summed up nicely what she was feeling.

"Are you worried?" he asked.

She thought of her fears, then pictured him lifting the beam off the man, and said, "No longer."

Tara thought about telling him what she was feeling, but it was all too new. Later, when her head wasn't dizzy with this insane desire to throw herself upon him and kiss him senseless in just the manner they had demonstrated, then maybe she would have the right words. Love was about trust.

Her pulse and her pace quickened as Wolfstone came into view. They were within twenty feet of the castle, when Breccan suddenly stopped. His whole manner changed.

"What is it?" she asked.

"We have a visitor."

Only then did she notice the high-perch phaeton on the front drive. A tiger, the name for the grooms who rode on the platform behind the vehicle's seat and attended the driver, was dressed in maroon-and-silver livery. He walked the horse with an air of self-importance.

"Who is it?" Tara asked.

"My cousin, Owen Campbell, the dirty bastard." He said the last under his breath as if, in spite of her presence, he could not stop himself. Nor did he apologize.

"What does he want?"

"We shall ask him." Still holding her hand, Breccan moved with the intent of a wolf guarding his lair toward the house.

Chapter Fourteen

*B*reccan could admire his cousin's rig. Before going into the house, he had to stop and look at it, and the jealousy he felt was palatable.

What man wouldn't want a phaeton with high yellow wheels and red spokes. The vehicle was so lightweight, it probably traveled on air. Of course, it would be a slow slog for a man as big as Breccan.

Owen's horseflesh was good, too. The animal was a flashy gray in fittings trimmed out in silver.

Ah, yes, any man would covet such a rig, but Breccan did not admire his cousin. They had a history. Some of Breccan's dislike stemmed from Owen's almost casual little cruelties. The man liked finding a weak spot and using it for his own gain.

Of course, what he really wanted was land. Every Campbell did. It was in their blood. They equated land to power.

Even Breccan understood this. Why else would he be sinking so much of himself into Wolfstone. He was building a legacy for his children, little beings he planned on creating the moment after he tossed Owen off his property.

He turned away from the rig and walked toward his front door. Owen stepped outside.

Owen was two years Breccan's senior and fancied himself part of the Corinthian set.

Some would think him handsome. He was lean and wore his graying hair in the windswept style, a silly affectation where the hair was combed forward over the brow and ears as if a great wind blew it from behind. The style also hid Owen's growing baldness.

Of course, to a man like Breccan, his cousin was a pretentious fool—especially when he was dressed as he was now in some sort of military-styled jacket. There was meaningless braid and brass buttons from the top of his head to the gold tassels on his boots. The outfit was an affectation like everything else about him.

Owen didn't have a title or position of his own.

He'd built his fortune with the East India Company, and Breccan had heard of the methods the nabobs had used. They abused the natives for what they wanted. Breccan had no doubt Owen wasn't at the head of the pack with his hand out.

His tenure in India had made Owen a wealthy man, but he was still a scoundrel. The worst of the lot.

"Hello, *cos,*" Owen drawled out in a voice that carried the flatness of London instead of the lilt of Scotland.

Breccan was about to growl that Owen could leave, but before he could speak, his cousin's eyes widened. His mouth dropped open, and for one rare moment in Breccan's acquaintance, Owen was speechless—and the reason was Tara.

When Owen had come out of the house, Breccan had instinctively put himself between his wife and his cousin. But Tara had stepped forward to stand beside Breccan.

Owen lifted a quizzing glass attached with gold ribbon to his jacket up to his eye. "Heavens," he said, breathing the word like a pray. "I have never laid eyes on such an exquisite creature."

"An exquisite creature who is *my* wife," Breccan said. He placed a possessive hand on Tara's arm.

"Well," Owen said, "some things can't be helped." He then moved forward as if Breccan weren't standing right there and made a pretty bow. "Let me present myself since my boor of a cousin is his usual clumsy self. I am Owen Campbell."

Tara didn't appear impressed, and Breccan was glad. He performed the introduction. "This is *my* lady Tara Campbell." He liked the way her name sounded. It was a good name.

"Tara?" Owen questioned. "Lady Tara Davidson, by chance?"

To her credit, Tara looked to Breccan. She had obviously divined the tension between the two men. He answered for her, "Yes, she is."

Owen actually rocked back on his highly polished boots with their silly little gold tassels. His brows stretched to his hairline before he said, "You are more lovely than any ever claimed."

He was sincere in his compliment. Breccan couldn't help but feel a bit of pride.

"Thank you," Tara said, a becoming blush to her cheek. However, there was a reserve about her. She must have heard this effusive praise all the time in London.

Breccan was conscious that while he would tell

his wife she was lovely, he didn't gush over her as if she were an object.

Owen shook his head in amazement. "I'd always heard of you. They told me your beauty was extraordinary, but isn't that a matter of taste?"

"I suppose so," Tara murmured.

"*You* are *my* taste," Owen answered, and moved forward as if he would jump into Tara's arms.

Breccan surged forward, ready to wrap his hand around Owen's neck. His cousin always pushed the boundaries.

Owen held up his gloved hands to ward him off. "I mean no offense, Breccan. She's exquisite. Perfect. It is rare to meet a woman who is all they say about her."

His words saved his neck.

Breccan tried not to be vain, but he wouldn't have been a man if he wasn't proud. He did have a lovely wife. Owen could have his fancy phaeton. Breccan was going to be taking Tara to bed. He would possess every square inch of her.

Who was the more fortunate cousin now?

"So what brings you here, Owen?" Breccan asked. He suspected Owen had driven over to flash himself around and see what he could learn about Taurus before the race. Owen was sneaky that way.

"We have a few details to discuss about the race," Owen said easily.

"I thought Ricks would be talking to your man?" Breccan answered. "Let them work out the details."

"It is a sizeable wager. Don't you think we should be the ones discussing it?" Owen countered with that air of superiority Breccan could not stand. He could hear what Owen wasn't saying, that Breccan was too provincial to know the ways of the world.

And then, because Breccan was busy fuming, Owen trumped him again by saying, "Should we not go inside? It could pour down rain at any moment, and I'm certain your lady would prefer to be under shelter if that happened."

Breccan should have thought of Tara's needs. He placed a hand on the small of her back. "Please, my dear," he said, opening the door for her.

She gave him a peculiar look, probably because of the endearment. It had sounded odd on his tongue to him as well. But this wasn't about talking to Tara. It was about ensuring that Owen knew she was his wife.

He would explain later about how his cousin always made him feel awkward and clumsy. Over the years, the two of them had been particularly hard on each other. Usually, Owen had started it. He had the ability to crawl under Breccan's skin.

But now, Breccan had the upper hand. He had Tara, and his horse Taurus would recover and be triumphant over any nag Owen could muster.

And then, well, then the other half of the Campbells would have some respect for Breccan and his ilk. It would be a victory . . . and never again could they look down on him.

Inside the castle, Owen said, "You've made changes since I was last here, cousin." He looked around the rooms with approval, and Breccan could see what he saw.

The arrangements of tables and chairs now filled rooms that had once been bare of comfort. The floors had been cleaned until they shone. Cobwebs and dust in the rafters had been swept away. There were other touches, too, women's touches—the candlesticks and rugs that gave the home warmth. All the hearths had been cleaned as well, and Breccan had overheard Agnes grumbling that the new mistress wanted them cleaned daily.

His chest swelled with pride.

"You are a miracle worker, my lady," Owen was saying.

Tara did not meet his eye. Breccan sensed she was uncomfortable. "Thank you, Mr. Campbell—"

"Owen, please. Call me Owen. We are cousins now."

She smiled, but did not use his name, and Breccan could have danced a jig.

This was what he had wanted. Respect, and it was sweet. Wait until Owen saw the children Breccan and Tara would have. They would be tall and brawny like himself but favor their mother's good looks. Every door would be open to them, and they would not have to tolerate an ass like Owen in their lives.

"Would you care for refreshment?" Tara asked with the good manners of the lady of the house.

"I would," Owen said. "Dougal makes a fine ale."

"Let me have him pour one for you," Tara said. She looked to Breccan. "Would you wish one?"

He shook his head no. He didn't want to drink with Owen or show good manners. He wanted the man gone from his house, and he wanted to take his wife to bed.

Something of what he was thinking must have shown on his face because a shy, secret smile appeared on hers. She excused herself and left.

Breccan wanted to follow her. He turned to see that his guest seemed to experience the same desire.

Owen met his eye and didn't even bother to disguise his admiration. "Extraordinary. I'd heard of her, of course . . . but I had not believed the gossip about her until just now."

Gossip? Breccan wondered what was said about his wife. He would not be human, or male, if he didn't. However, he wasn't about to ask Owen to explain.

Then again, he didn't need to do so. Owen said, "She is a heartbreaker. Do you know how many men begged her for her hand? Important men. *Wealthy* ones."

"What do you want to discuss about the race?" Breccan asked him.

Owen made a gesture with a wave of his hand. "Not anything in particular. Well, perhaps the rides. I was thinking that you and I should each ride our horses."

"I would think the same thing if you were as big as I," Breccan said. "We've already decided, the riders are of our choosing." And he'd chosen his lightest-weight exercise boy.

But Owen wasn't attending to anything he said. Instead, he craned his neck to look down the hall for Tara to return. "Beautiful," he whispered under his breath.

"I'm beginning to believe you didn't have any reason to pay this call other than to ogle my wife," Breccan said, letting a silky thread of threat linger in his words.

"I didn't even know you had married," Owen said, grinning. He had a sly cat of a smile. It was an expression no one would trust. "Does Breadalbane know?"

He referred to the earl of Breadalbane, Owen's first cousin and Breccan's second.

"Should he?"

"Oh, I would tell him. I would tell everyone. She is remarkable."

"She is," Breccan agreed. "And all is settled between us for the race. There are no loose details."

"The race?" Owen repeated as if needing to be reminded. "Of course, of course, all is settled." He had not let his eyes drift from watching down the hall for Tara.

"You know, Owen, I don't want you here—" Breccan started, disgusted by this farce of a call. All the man wanted to do was fish for information, and Breccan was not going to give it to him, and he'd tired of this fawning over his wife.

However, Owen interrupted him by saying, "Do you think your wife and the horse master were paramours?"

The question caught Breccan off guard. "My wife?"

"Aye, and Ruary Jamerson. You remember him, don't you? He worked for you."

"Of course I remember him," Breccan said.

"Your wife was his lover. I admit I am shocked to see that you have married her, but how else could you have captured such a lovely wife. Indeed, Breccan, I might have wanted to marry her myself. I don't know that I would have. What with the gossip, Tay was going to have a terrible time marrying her off, and everyone had heard he'd wanted the deed done quickly. Makes one wonder why. But she is good here, isn't she? After all, you aren't discerning. No one cares what happens in the wilds of Scotland, and you don't have a social position. Furthermore, Jamerson is a handsome man. If he has spawned a get off her, then you will be thought to be the father. Furthermore, you sleep with beauty every night."

Breccan barely registered most of what Owen was saying. His mind had caught on the word, "lover."

Jamerson and Tara had been lovers?

And who all knew this?

Suddenly, he realized why Owen was here. The bastard didn't want to talk about the race. He'd known Breccan had married the Davidson chit.

What he'd wanted to do was churn the waters. Owen had probably wondered if Breccan had known the truth of his wife and was taking gleeful delight in his speculations.

Now Breccan understood why Tara had not wanted to let him make love to her. He'd know once he'd bedded her that she'd been had. He would have realized it, and then what? He'd be trapped.

Jamerson had run away with the blacksmith's daughter. Everyone had said they'd been courting.

But what had Tara said just the day before, after someone had been around Mr. Jamerson as much as she had, they would have learned a thing or two about horses?

But he couldn't let Owen see that his words had found their mark.

Or let the man mock his marriage.

Breccan reached out and grabbed Owen by the gold-braided front of his jacket. He lifted his cousin into the air. In all their dealings together, Breccan had never used his superior strength against the rat.

He did so now.

Looking into Owen's piggish eyes, Breccan said, "You will not say a word against my wife."

Owen's face had gone pale, then red, as the collar Breccan held began to choke him. His feet moved in the air. Breccan didn't care. The man had been a thorn in his side for most of Breccan's life. Perhaps the time had come to remove it—

"Breccan, *what are you doing*?" Tara's alarmed voice penetrated his anger.

He turned his head toward her. She had carried the tankards of ale in herself and had set them on the table as she'd rushed up to him. "You are *killing* him," she warned. "Put him down. *Stop this.*"

Breccan released his hold, and Owen fell to the ground like one of her hard bannocks.

Tara leaned to help Owen up. His cousin was gasping for breath. Breccan surmised that his throat might hurt. A pity.

Fetching one of the tankards, Tara offered, "Here, have some ale."

Owen waved it away. He no longer eyed Tara but directed venomous rage at Breccan. He pushed himself to his feet, the silly tassels on his boots and jacket swaying from his effort. His eyes still bulged, but they did so now out of anger.

Breccan walked to the door and opened it.

His cousin reached for his hat, a silly, satin-covered thing, off the dining table and moved toward the door.

But before Owen left, he stopped in front of Breccan. In a voice intended for Breccan's ears alone, he said, "You attack me for your own failings? You think because she has a pretty face she's not a whore? You were cuckolded before you were married."

Breccan doubled his fists but Owen swiftly glided out the door. Outside, he made a mock bow. "Good day to you, cousin. Oh, and there is one bit of news that you may not have heard yet. Jamerson is back in Aberfeldy. Had you heard?" He raised his voice as if he were speaking to Tara. "His marriage is unhappy. Imagine that? The man was only married a month at the most. So unhappy. You should see him, Breccan. He's lonely." He drew out the syllables of the last word, then laughed.

Going out on the step, Breccan reached down and picked up a small rock.

Owen was climbing into his phaeton. The smug look had returned to his face. As Owen reached to pick up the reins, Breccan tossed the rock at the gray's rear. With a cry, the horse shot off down the road, ripping the reins out of Owen's hands. The tiger shouted and ran after the vehicle. Owen could do nothing but hold on and pray he wasn't killed.

Breccan hoped the horse ran him all the way into Loch Tay—

"What did you do?" Tara demanded. She had come out of the house and witnessed him throw the rock. "He could be killed."

"I wouldn't be that lucky." Breccan walked into the house, going straight for the tankard on the table. He did not look at his "wife." He couldn't.

Since he married her, he'd thought maidenly modesty had kept her from consummating their marriage. He'd not wanted to press her. He'd believed she was afraid.

And now?

Well, now, he realized he'd been the brunt of a cruel joke. He should have been more clever. He should have seen what was happening. Tay hadn't haggled much over his daughter. In fact, he'd appeared relieved with Breccan's offer.

If Breccan had asked a few questions, if he'd taken his time to consider marriage, well, he would not be in this place.

But her beauty had blinded him—no, it wasn't just the fact that she was lovely.

He downed the ale, trying to take ahold of himself.

There was more to his attraction to Tara than just her physical looks. The moment he'd set eyes on her, he'd felt a connection, a pull, something magnetic between them.

Of course, she hadn't felt it. He knew that then. He knew it now.

He remembered the day that they'd met; she had come looking for Ruary Jamerson. He'd believed she had been sent by her father. Jamerson worked for the earl of Tay, just as he had for a number of other stables in the area. He was the best trainer available and well trusted.

Jamerson was also a very handsome man. Many a lass had chased him. If he and Tara had married, there would be no doubt that their bairn would be as physically perfect as their parents.

Jealousy turned Breccan inside out. The world

that had moments ago been perfect now seemed a sham. He started to wonder why she would play such a trick on him.

Worse, what if she was carrying Jamerson's child? What if her being sweet to him today was a ruse. Many a woman had passed another's off in this manner.

Of course, he'd played the monk while lying beside her in his bed.

The insanity of jealousy is the tricks it played on the mind. Breccan could see her with Jamerson. He wondered if the reason Jamerson had returned was to claim her.

He took a step away. He wanted more ale, but he knew drinking wouldn't bring him peace.

Tara was watching him closely. "Breccan, have you taken sick? Here, let me help you up to bed."

He groaned aloud. Bed was the last place he should be with her. Because even knowing she'd been playing him for a fool, he wanted her. God save him, he wanted her, and if they did consummate this damnable marriage, then he would be lost. He'd be like any poor bastard led around by a woman.

"I'm fine." He moved to the door. "I need to see to the cottages."

"But the work is going well," she said, following him in confusion.

"I must see for myself." Work would give him time to think on this matter. Work helped him concentrate. It gave him pride, a purpose.

He walked out the door and didn't look back.

Of course, he took teasing when he appeared to help with the dismantling of the cottage walls. Jonas was the worst offender. He amused all with his jests about Breccan finally using what God gifted him with.

Breccan let him go on. To toss Jonas in the stable pond a second time would cause comment.

Instead, he wanted it to all fade away. Even himself. He wanted to disappear.

Chapter Fifteen

$\mathcal{S}$omething was wrong with Breccan, and Tara didn't know what to do.

It was as if he had been transformed into a different person.

She was puzzled when, after his cousin left, he had returned to the cottages. She had been eager to consummate their marriage. Yes, there was fear, but there was excitement as well. She trusted him. She now understood that Breccan would not do anything to hurt her. She was ready.

When he had abruptly announced that he was returning to work, she'd been disappointed but not worried. He was the sort of man who put his responsibilities ahead of his own desires. She was willing to practice those qualities as well. Breccan's example was helping her to become a better person and to think of others' needs before her own.

However, he did not return to join her for dinner.

And then, that night, he did not come to their bed.

She waited for him. After watching the candle burn down, she decided to go in search of him, thinking he might be at the stables. Perhaps something else was wrong with Taurus. He had staked too much on the race against his cousin. She sensed he thought himself a fool to have made the bet.

And yes, her sense of Breccan was just that strong. In a short time, she'd come to know him in a way she'd never known anyone else in her life. What concerned him, concerned her. What pleased him, pleased her.

Tara rose from the bed and took her cape off a peg in the wall. She picked up the candle, determined to find her husband.

However, when she opened the bedroom door, she discovered the dogs were not on the landing.

That was curious. They had taken up station

there every night, waiting for Breccan to return. That must mean the dogs were with him, wherever he was—and then she noticed that the door to the sitting room was open a crack.

Timidly, she pushed the door open and looked inside. Moonlight streamed in the bank of windows. She'd added furniture to this room. The desk now had a side table, and she'd found a very uncomfortable horsehair settee to go with the leather chair before the hearth.

No fire burned in the hearth, but there in the silver light Tara could see Breccan's big frame. He lay at an angle on the settee, his booted feet propped up on the seat of another chair. He didn't have a blanket or pillow. He appeared as if a moment's lapse of balance would tumble him to the floor.

The dogs wagged their tails in greeting, well, save for Daphne. She appeared miffed with Tara. Her eyes were shiny in the darkness.

Tara walked past Daphne, ignoring her low, "ruff." She stopped by the settee. "Breccan," she said, gently shaking his shoulder.

He came awake with the abruptness of a warrior who was always aware of duty. He glanced up at her and winced at the candle flame.

"Breccan, why did you not come to bed?" she asked, worried. Perhaps he had been afraid to wake her.

He stretched, frowned at her, and said, "I'm fine here." He lay back down, turning his head as if studying the floor.

"Fine here?" she repeated. "You appear so uncomfortable." She stepped closer, dropping her voice, coaxing him. She wore her hair loose from its braid, the way he liked it. "Come to bed, Breccan."

His frown deepened. "I can see your toes."

"That is because my feet are bare," she said, then, feeling bold, promised, "There is more of me that is bare as well."

If she thought that would entice him, she was wrong.

There was a beat of heavy silence, and then he said, "I don't want to look at your toes." He flipped onto his back and made a point of staring at the ceiling.

"Why not?"

"It is intimate," he grumbled.

Tara straightened. For the first time, she considered he was in this room because he was angry at her. But she didn't know why. She'd done nothing to deserve his scorn. She wanted him in her bed. Could he not understand that?

"Is this coming from the man who wanted to rip off my clothes?" she said.

He grunted like a sullen bear and gave her his back. He had trouble fitting his body on the settee that way. He had to be uncomfortable, but he would not admit it.

"Breccan, what is wrong? Why are you angry with me?"

"I don't want to see your toes."

That was it?

Tara took a step, feeling her temper start to rise. She had an easy disposition, but she'd never liked being given the Turkish treatment. If someone wished to discuss a perceived slight that she'd paid him, that was good. But she'd never appreciated being treated with silence or having her caring concern ignored.

"This is ridiculous," she said to his back. "What have I done to you? Tell me, and I will make it right. Breccan, I—" She caught herself. She'd been about to confess her love for him. She had almost blurted out the words that would lay bare her heart.

But such an action would call for a level of trust

Tara had never experienced before. What if she didn't know him as well as she believed?

And what if this moodiness was a defect in *his* character? Here she was, ready to offer that which she'd never given to another man, leaving herself wholly vulnerable, and he acted as if he could not abide her.

This sort of vacillating behavior made her uncomfortable because that was the way her father behaved. Tara never knew what to expect from the earl.

At the same time, she was surprised how edgy she felt. It was as if she had an itch that needed to be scratched and could not satisfy it. She wanted her husband in bed with her. She was *ready* for him. And she wanted him to be the man she'd come to think he was.

"Breccan, *please* join me in bed. *Please.*" She used her sweetest, most cajoling voice.

He didn't budge.

The temptress role had never sat well with Tara. She threw it aside for direct conversation. "Come to bed, Breccan."

Nothing.

She stood a moment. The dogs watched her, tails wagging.

"You don't like my toes," she repeated, the words themselves like tiny hammers on what control she could boast over herself. "You don't want to see them?"

No response.

"Well then here—" She raised the hem of her nightdress so that she could lift her leg and place her toes against the back of his neck. She wiggled them. "Do you feel that? Those are my toes." She lifted her foot so she could set it on his ear. She tried to trace the outline of his ear with her big toe. "Guess where my toes are now?" she dared him.

He had to respond to her now. If he hadn't, she probably would have climbed up onto the settee and stood on him.

As he started to rise, her foot was on his jaw. He batted it out of the way and fell back against the settee, appearing tired and irritable.

Tara put her foot on the ground, pleased she had commandeered his attention although he appeared as if he held himself back from mauling her, and not in a good way. His fists were clenched and his jaw hard.

"What have I done, Breccan? Why are you upset with me?"

For a long moment, he studied her. He was tired. He had dark circles under his eyes, and his shoulders stooped as if he carried a heavy weight. She wished to help relieve his burden.

She saw his dedication to his people. He was a true "noble" man, one who placed others before self.

"Please, Breccan, return to bed with me. How are we going to have children if we don't start doing what we must?"

For some reason, those words were the wrong ones to use. "Take yourself off, Tara. I'm tired. Leave me be." He settled back on the furniture, this time in the way most comfortable to him.

Disappointment churned in her stomach.

She toyed with asking him one more time why he was angry, then decided she would not. He was in a tiff. She had them herself from time to time.

Perhaps it would be best for both her and Breccan to be apart. Certainly, she didn't feel like cuddling with him, no matter how many stories he told.

She left the room. The dogs stayed with him. Of course.

It was a long time before she fell asleep, and

her last thought was a promise to herself that if he ever wanted to see her toes again, she'd make him beg on his knees.

*B*reccan's odd mood did not change the next day, or the next. Tara was glad he spent his time with his different projects around Wolfstone, because when he was around the castle, she found his presence disturbing.

He barely looked at her. He rarely talked to her.

After two nights of this, she tried to sleep in the main room with him. She'd made a bed on the floor and offered to tell him a story. She have one in mind about brownies and a bridge that couldn't be crossed without paying respect to the brownie who owned it . . . but Breccan fell asleep. He did not want to hear her story. He no longer wished to share.

She attempted to act as if nothing were wrong. She doubted if anyone beyond the dogs—who had also taken to following Breccan around the estate, they, too, giving her the cold shoulder, the ungrateful creatures—knew of the rift between husband and wife.

She was wrong.

Lachlan noticed.

They had finished dinner on the second night. Jonas had gone on to whatever diversions took his fancy. Usually, he rode into Kenmore and shared a drink with friends at the inn.

Tara had wrapped herself in a shawl and thought to pretend to read a book to while away the hours. Breccan was not home. She wasn't certain he had come home the night before because she had refused to check.

She sat at the table, sipping a glass of wine, wondering what to do, when Lachlan took the chair beside her.

"Are you all right, lass?"

She forced a smile. "I am." Since she didn't sound certain, she repeated, "*I am.*"

He seemed to think on this a moment. A weight formed in her chest. When she thought about the estrangement, she could become so angry she would shake. Earlier, she had wondered why and realized it was because she'd grown to trust Breccan. She'd opened to him in a way she hadn't with anyone else—

"I believe you are miserable," Lachlan said, interrupting the whirlwind of her thoughts. "I know my nephew is."

"Is he?" she challenged. "Has he said anything to you? He won't say a word to me."

Lachlan hummed his thoughts. "I hate silence."

"I do as well." The words rushed out of her, propelled by anger and fear.

"I admit it was an effective trick to pull on my wife. We men don't have as many words as you women do, so it comes natural to us."

"You did this to your wife?"

Lachlan actually laughed, the sound bitter. "Aye, a time or two. Apparently this is a method common to the Campbells."

"And then you stopped?"

"We Campbells have a stubborn pride. Time with my family, with her, was precious."

Tears stung Tara's eyes, both for her anger at the way Breccan was treating her, but also because of the pain she sensed in Lachlan's gently spoken words. "I'm sorry you lost everyone."

He nodded, growing silent himself. A moment later, he said, "I wasn't certain about you, lass. I'm male. I could see why Breccan wanted you . . . or I thought I did. But I feared you were spoiled and would make his life difficult. However, now, I believe there is more to you than meets the eye. My nephew is the man to bring it out in you."

"Why do you say that?"

He studied her a moment, assessing her. "You'll know. When the time is right, you'll know."

"How am I to know anything if he banishes me from his life?"

"Don't let him," Lachlan said.

"He refuses to come close to me," Tara protested. "Even his dogs ignore me."

"Then put yourself in his path."

"Chase him? I don't chase men," she said. She could have told him about the other night, how she had gone to Breccan. It wounded her pride that she had done so.

"He isn't just any other man. He is your husband. And I think you know as I do that he is a very special person. Not many are like Breccan." He stood, a sign that his offering of advice was over. "His mother did a good job with him. I can't say my bother was worth dung heap. However, together, they created an exceptional man."

Tara nodded agreement. Breccan was special. She'd recognized that fact. "How can I force him to pay attention to me?"

Lachlan grinned. "You don't have to force him, Tara. Just be a woman." He patted her shoulder and left the room.

She sat for a long time, thinking. *Be a woman.* All she'd had to do in the past was dress in pretty clothes and smile. When she wanted a kiss, she presented herself and received kisses. But Lachlan was suggesting something more.

More. The word beat like a drum through her being.

Yes, she wanted more from Breccan. She had finally been ready to offer herself freely, and now Breccan had created the wall between them.

Of course, Lachlan was implying that she had power over Breccan. She didn't know if he was correct. Her husband was a disciplined man, and yet, Tara could not continue this way much longer.

She thought of their earlier bargain, her desire to return to London. The city seemed far away now, and she felt as if she had become a different person.

Instead, she could see herself building a life here. She enjoyed making the rooms of Wolfstone more hospitable. She wanted to see the weavers' cottages finished and was interested in how the new machines would work. She admired Breccan's vision of a future and yearned to be part of it.

Thoughtfully, Tara rose from the table. Placing

herself in Breccan's path as Lachlan suggested might be outside where Tara felt comfortable, but wasn't that what a true marriage was?

In her mind, she examined the question. She'd never witnessed a marriage up close. Her father spent his time womanizing. There were couples in the *ton* whom people referred to as being very devoted to their spouses. They were treated as an oddity.

And yet, Tara found herself wishing for that sort of devotion—someone who accepted her, flaws and all.

She had thought Breccan was that caliber of man, that he was someone beyond those who only saw her face and figure.

The time had come to test him.

*B*reccan was in a private hell of his own making.

He missed Tara.

It was that simple. He'd liked having her company. And now he had her, but he didn't. Owen's words were a poison inside him. He did not trust his cousin . . . and yet, what if he was right?

Yes, Breccan had come to Tay with the marriage offer. He'd basically forced Tara to marry him to save her father from debtor's prison, but that knowledge made this whole situation worse. The idea that Tay may have wanted to be rid of his daughter, that Breccan's own lust had made him a laughingstock of those who knew of Jamerson and Tara's illicit romance sickened him.

And yet Tara did not strike him as someone capable of such duplicity. She had impressed him with her forthrightness. Still, she was a woman. Men throughout history, starting with Adam, had been played false by them. Why should Breccan think himself different?

The suspicion also crossed his mind that Tara could possibly be carrying the horse master's child, and once there, he could not shake it. What had she said the other night? *How are we going to have children if we don't start doing what we must?*

In his misery, he could imagine a scenario where his ogre of a self repulsed her. However, for the sake of her illegitimate child, she must consummate the marriage.

His saner mind would point out that, if such was the case, she would have let him have her on the wedding night or a dozen times after.

But doubt, once sown in a man's mind, always took root.

The only way that he could prove her innocent was to wait. She'd be showing soon if she were pregnant.

Of course, the rest of the world would assume that the child was his. This wouldn't be the first time one man's child had been foisted on another. He decided he would not take out his anger and sense of betrayal on a child.

But what of the mother?

He'd not touch her.

This would be the price he would pay for marrying a woman without first knowing her true character. And this way was safer for him.

He'd always been accused of having a soft heart. He'd always been the one to forgive easily, only to be played for a fool by others' dirty tricks.

However, Tara could hurt him in a way no one else could.

He'd fallen in love with her. He had only to look at her and his heart yearned for a world he feared did not exist.

But his dogs were poor company when compared to his wife.

He was thinking that one morning when he

woke. He did not like his makeshift bed of chairs or sleeping in his breeches for modesty's sake. After all, he didn't want to be caught naked by one of the maids. Yet his pride would not let him move to another bedroom. He knew his uncles and his clansmen. They would be in his business in no time at all.

Of course, pretending to be in the bedroom with his wife was not easy. It put him in close proximity to her every morning.

So far, he'd been able to steal into their room before she woke. He felt he was adept at it, so he had no reason to suspect that she realized what he was doing—until the next time he went in, reached for his clothes on a peg, and turned to find his wife awake and blocking his way out of the room.

"Good morning, Breccan," she said, her voice quiet. She wore her hair down. He ached to bury his hands in it.

"Morning," he answered. He started to move past her, but she stepped in his way.

"It is Sunday, Breccan. We need to go to church."

He frowned. "I don't go to church."

"You have before."

To see her. "I don't go to church."

She didn't budge from where she stood, and he

couldn't ease his way around her without touching her, a dangerous proposition. "We must set an example," she said. "Your clansmen, your tenants, they all need church. Besides, people will wonder what we are doing with our mornings if we don't appear in church."

He debated arguing with her. However, her hint that people would believe he spent his mornings rogering his wife, as desirable as that sounded, made him consider attending church this one Sunday. In fact, he might need the Reverend Kinnion's support if an annulment was required.

"We may go to church," he said.

"Good. Now sit in the chair over there by the basin and let me shave your face."

"I don't need a shave—" He'd raised a hand to his whiskers, feeling the roughness of his two days' growth of beard.

"You look like a goat," she interrupted him. "Now sit and don't argue with me."

There was a bite to her words. He could shave himself . . . and yet, a part of him wondered what she was about. A part of him appreciated and longed for her company.

Could he not indulge himself, just for a few minutes?

He sat in the chair next to the washbasin and

close to the window, so she could use the early-morning light. He noticed that she had found draperies and hung them. Every day she brought something new to his home, small touches that made it more welcoming.

She mixed his shaving soap in a cup with a brush.

"Have you done this before?" he asked.

"No." She turned to him, brush in hand. "But it can't be hard."

She started to lather his beard. He caught her wrist. Her bones were so fine, so elegant compared to his huge paws. "You wouldn't want to cut my throat," he cautioned.

Tara smiled. That lovely, lovely smile. A man could bask forever in the memory of it. "Be brave, Breccan. Live dangerously."

"I am. I'm married, aren't I?"

His response had come to his lips before he'd even thought of it. It was the sort of thing the men working with him would say a hundred times a day.

But it was not a wise thing to say now. Especially when a sadness came to Tara's expressive eyes. "Aye you are," she agreed, mimicking his brogue.

She picked up the straight-edge razor. "Hold still."

And Breccan did as she said, for many reasons. Perhaps because it was early in the morning and what harm could be done? He sat in a chair; she stood.

She placed the blade against his skin and pulled it. He could feel the whiskers being neatly sheared off. She must have sharpened the razor.

Her body leaned over him. She was soft, warm. Her scent reminded him of midsummer roses. Again, and again she drew the razor blade across his skin.

The tricky parts were the places around his nose and close to his ears. She tickled him, and he couldn't help but smile. He opened his eyes and saw she was smiling as well, as if she took great pleasure in her work.

"Tilt your head back," she ordered.

He did, closing his eyes. It felt good to be pampered.

But he also waited for the first nick, first burn of being sliced. It didn't come. She'd been careful—

She climbed onto his lap, her legs straddling his hips. Her lips brushed the sensitive skin beneath his jaw.

Breccan feared he dreamed.

He'd wanted this. *Dear God, how he'd wanted this.*

Her nightdress was hiked above her knees. He knew because he'd brought his hand down upon her thigh and felt bare skin. Her lips found his.

Breccan had been born to kiss this woman. He liked the taste of her. He adored her response to desire and willingness to take the kiss deeper, to make it meaningful.

Her body moved closer to him. Her sex was over his with only the material of his breeches separating them.

And she was hot, wet.

His errant manhood, which had always had a mind of its own and had been trying to rise to attention from the moment Breccan had first had a thought to enter the bedroom, now roared to life full force. The erection pressed against his breeches, a beast begging to be fulfilled.

Tara slid her arms around his neck, her kiss taking on urgency.

Did she know what she was doing to him?

Breccan couldn't tell. There was an earnestness about her as well as a woman's need. His hand rose to her breasts. Those sweet, sweet breasts that he'd only dreamed of touching. He'd yet to explore them. He wanted to taste them, to squeeze them, to celebrate them. Were her nipples pink or brown? Did she like his mouth upon them? All were questions he'd wondered.

She made the softest moue as his thumb circled the tip of her breast. They felt full, as if begging him to pleasure them.

Her hand came between them. He felt her trace the line of his breeches, searching for the button. She found it and twisted it free. First one, then a second.

Her head pushed toward him. The back of her fingers caressed him as they continued their quest to set him free.

Breccan wanted to help her. He wanted to pull the nightdress over her head and carry her naked to the bed. He wanted to lay her down upon the counterpane and plow into her over and over again—

And he realized what was happening.

He realized her hold over him. She bewitched him. She robbed of *reason*. Of *respect*. Of *honor*.

It took more strength than he ever thought he had to grab her hands by the wrists and push her away.

Aye, he lifted her up, but it wasn't to take her to the bed, but to set her aside. He was in such a hurry, he wasn't careful, and she fell to the floor.

He didn't offer to help her up, but ran from the room. God help him, he ran.

Chapter Sixteen

*B*reccan had rejected her.

Worse, he had run from her.

Tara pushed her hair back with a distracted hand. Hot tears ran down her cheeks. It had taken all her courage to be so bold. She'd been acting on instinct. She was surprised at how she'd seem to know what to do—and they had come very close to doing it. Even now, desire was heavy in the air.

She began shaking, whether from rage or some other emotion, she didn't know.

It wasn't right the way he was treating her. And she didn't have to tolerate it. She didn't.

A cold nose nudged her.

Tara looked over to see that Daphne had wandered into the room and sat on the floor with a worried look on her face.

"Why are you here?" Tara asked the dog. "You deserted me as well."

Daphne stood but did not leave. She placed a paw on Tara's thigh.

"I don't know what to do," Tara confessed. "And right now, I hate him. I don't understand him." A knot had formed in her stomach, one of fear and disappointment.

She placed her hand on Daphne. The dog moved closer as if apologizing for all that distressed Tara. "It's all right. It will be all right." She drew a breath, then confessed, "I never thought to fall in love. It is not what I thought it would be. I had believed love was where everything was perfect. But it isn't, Daphne. It is about knowing that someone is hurting. I've hurt Breccan, and I don't know what I've done."

The admission rang with truth.

And it made sense. Her husband was big and strong. He had a warrior's skill and courage . . . but he had a saint's heart. This was a man who thought of other people before himself.

"He is afraid of me," she told Daphne. "Does he believe I would hurt him?"

Daphne stared at her intently, as if trying to send a message to Tara. These dogs trusted Breccan. His people could trust him.

So why had he turned on Tara the way he had?

"Does he not trust me, Daphne?"

The dog didn't say anything, but in her heart, Tara heard the echo of truth.

Breccan's attitude toward her had switched dramatically. And yet, his response to her a moment ago had been very real.

So had hers. She'd been eager for them to consummate their union, but there had been something deeper driving her. She wanted to be as close as she could be to this man. And he'd wanted her. She'd never believe him if he denied it.

Indeed, from the moment they met on the road from Annefield, her awareness of him was far too keen for him to have just been a passing player in her life.

"He's the one." One life; one love . . . and if she wasn't careful, she would lose him.

Tara came to her feet. She caught sight of her reflection in the mirror. Her face appeared pinched, tight. Her eyes were sad, and the sight brought out her fighting spirit.

Before he'd married her, Tara had not known

what she wanted. She'd chosen to return to London because it was familiar.

But now she yearned for something more meaningful in her life.

Daphne sat on her haunches, watching Tara with anxious eyes, and that is when Tara had an insight.

"It was Owen Campbell. He said something." Yes, of course, it made sense. Breccan had been anxious for her company until after his cousin's visit. That is when Breccan changed. "I left them alone, and who knows what his cousin said against me."

Tara doubled her fists. "I should have seen this sooner. This is the sort of intrigue society thrives on. Breccan doesn't understand jealousy. Or mean-spiritedness." Or perhaps he did too well. After all, she thought him very mean to her.

"Well, I shall teach him a lesson," she vowed. She shook her finger at the dog. "He had better never shut me out again. I will let him have this one time, but he's going to learn." And with that vow, Tara began to dress. She wasn't certain what form her lesson would take, but she was determined to ensure he never treated her this way again.

*A*n idea had come to Breccan for an improvement to a bit of land that needed to be drained. It would not be a hard feat to perform.

The task also kept his mind off his wife.

She'd felt so good in his arms this morning. She'd filled them just right.

But he had to wonder at her change of heart. Before she had been shy about being with him. This morning, she was overeager, almost desperate. Perhaps because she needed his seed spilled to make him believe the baby was his—?

He threw down the pen he'd been using and pushed away from the desk. He was going mad.

The woman had him chasing himself with wild thoughts.

He didn't want to believe this of her.

Largo and the foxhounds were spread out across the floor sleeping. When he stood, they rose, tails wagging. They moved forward for a pat. "I don't want to feel this way about her," he confided. "I bloody hate it. And I don't know what I shall do if she is with child."

Would he live the rest of his life this way?

He picked up his drawing and stomped out of the room. He didn't know where Tara was. He'd not paid attention. He needed to work to release the impotent rage he felt.

A half hour later, he had a shovel in hand and was heading toward the land he needed to drain. His path crossed with Lachlan's

"Where are you going?" his uncle asked.

"I want to see what happens if I dig a ditch by that bit of marsh. I wouldn't mind having it dry."

"Breccan, it is Sunday, a day of rest. Why are you not with your wife?"

For a second, he thought of telling his uncle. He'd fling out the anger he felt, release the bitterness and the bile—but the words stuck in his throat.

Breccan found he could not hurt her. God help him, she had the power to sting with a hundred darts, and he could not raise a hand against her . . . because he loved her. He bloody loved her. Something about her connected with something inside himself.

"She had other plans," Breccan said, and would have moved on, except for his uncle's hand on his arm.

"Wait," Lachlan said. "I'll come do some digging with you. Let me change my clothes. Fetch a shovel for me."

Breccan could have said he would prefer to be

alone, but his own company was making him miserable. "I'll wait."

Lachlan did not take long. He met Breccan by the edge of the far field, and the two went down to the stretch of marsh together.

It did not take long for Breccan to tell Lachlan his plan for the ditch. The two men set to work, and in a little time, the task was accomplished.

"Were you expecting this to fill with water?" Lachlan asked when they were almost done.

"In time." Breccan climbed to the ground above the ditch to study it a moment. "There is a spring up there that has kept this ground wet. We'll see if the ditch will drain it in this direction. It may also provide us with water."

Lachlan shook his head. "All for a wee patch of land."

"We have to use all we have," Breccan assured him.

"You are always thinking. You are as far away in spirit from my brother as the moon is from the sun."

The compliment pleased Breccan. He did not want to be compared to his father.

"Well," Lachlan hedged, "except in one matter. Men can be selfish when they love."

For a second, Breccan didn't think he'd heard his uncle correctly. "I don't think anyone has ever accused me of being selfish."

Lachlan pushed some dirt with his shovel. "Aye, you are a good man, Breccan. A generous one . . . except to your wife."

Breccan straightened. "This is not a conversation I want."

"It is a conversation you are going to receive," his uncle said. "Your father is gone, not that he would have anything to say. Jonas is the next oldest, and we all know he has no common sense so, it comes down to me."

"And what do you have to say?"

"You aren't being good to your wife."

The accusation rankled.

"I don't know that that is your business," Breccan said.

"It has to be," his uncle returned. "You are being a fool."

"You don't understand." Breccan started to walk away. He did not have to listen to this.

"I know more than you think, lad," Lachlan answered. "You are not being fair to her. You are punishing her, and it is clear for anyone to see."

"I'm not—"

"Yes you are. And no one understands it, most of all your lady. You might as well beat those dogs." Lachlan nodded to Largo and Terrance.

Tidbit was rooting through the brush. Daphne had a mind and will of her own and had taken back up with Tara. Breccan was not pleased with her defection. It was as if the terrier disapproved of him as well.

"Tara and I are not a love match," Breccan heard himself admit. "We have an arrangement. A bargain. She's planning on leaving for London as soon as she is able."

"I did not have that impression of her," Lachlan said.

"Well, then, that's all you know." Breccan set off for the house, but his uncle stepped in front of him.

"Don't be a dunderhead, lad. Anyone with eyes can see the two of you are a match."

Breccan didn't want to hear this. He didn't want his thoughts directed this way. He would have walked off a second time, but Lachlan put a hand on his chest, a warning for him to halt.

"I will not let you be a fool, nephew. You are daft in love with your wife. From the moment you married, you have appeared like a man who has a priceless jewel and doesn't know what to do with it."

"I know what to do. I choose not."

"*Och*, the way you talk. What has she done to earn your disdain?"

"That is not a matter for you," Breccan answered.

"No, you are right. It is not my business. However, I used to have a rage with my wife. Something would set me off. Usually, it had to do with the fact I was leaving, and it hurt so much every time I walked away from them. Aye, I was doing my duty, but that didn't make it easier. Nursing some supposed slight or hurt, well, it made me feel justified for going off on one more voyage. I'd tell myself, she needed the time to do some thinking. Whenever I returned home, everything was forgiven. We would be at each other like rabbits." Lachlan laughed at memories. The years fell away from him.

He looked to Breccan. "I loved her, man. I loved my children. But my children would leave someday. That is what they are born to do. My wife, she was my rock. She was the only person who wasn't afraid to chastise me when I was wrong or laugh at me when I was foolish. It's good to have someone who loves you and who is that honest. Now, I'm left with Jonas. It is a sorry sight."

"I understand your sadness. I can't imagine losing all—"

"That's life, Breccan. None of us are meant to go on forever. What hurts, what weighs me down, is that I'd had one of these piques before I left on that last voyage. I thought I was teaching her a lesson by not talking to her, so she knew I was angry—"

The guilt of recognition whispered in Breccan's ear.

"—I don't know what we argued about. It no longer matters. I had hurt pride, and I was an ass. I looked at how she was behaving and didn't pay enough attention to my own manner. When I sailed into the harbor homeward bound, I couldn't wait to put my arms around her. I'd had an epiphany out at sea. I realized that I was causing pain to the most important person in my life. I was determined to change. I wanted to put my arms around her and promise I'd never behave that way again."

Lachlan drew a deep breath and slowly released it. He raised eyes shiny with tears to meet Breccan's gaze. "Don't be an ass. I had years with my woman. I think she understood me. I know she forgave me. You don't have that luxury, Breccan. You can destroy something good with your pride."

He handed his shovel over to Breccan. "There, that is all I wanted to say. You are a man. You make your own decisions. But I pray you are wiser than I." He turned and walked away.

Breccan watched his uncle cross the field. His shoulders were stooped. How many years had Lachlan kept that inside himself? It had to be almost twenty years since his family had died. And yet, the pain of losing his wife had been real and present.

It was a long time before Breccan left that place.

Tara had gone to church.

There were always women, mostly widows, who sat alone. Tara was not excited about attending without her husband, but she was thankful she was there. Church always gave her a place where she could think.

Her cousin Sabrina and uncle Richard were there, and she sat with them. Her father was not present. Sabrina murmured that no one had heard anything about him.

Sabrina and Tara were not close. Her cousin was more Aileen's confidante than Tara's. She also had an annoying habit of acting as if she thought Tara was a brat. The brat in Tara was highly offended.

Sabrina was a brunette of medium height. There was just enough red in her hair that people could claim to see the family resemblance.

But today, Sabrina's company provided a safe haven until her cousin said after services, "You are married?"

Tara could feel people around them pause in their conversations, waiting for her answer. She knew what to do. She put on her brightest smile. "Yes, I am, and happily so."

"But was this not sudden?"

"Sometimes matters work in that direction," Tara said.

"So, where is Laird Breccan?" Sabrina asked. "Why did he not accompany you to services?"

Tara vowed that the next time they were alone, she would scold her cousin on her lapse of manners. It was an awkward question. But then Tara realized the right answer was the truth. "The laird has many projects that will help the clan and the valley. He is working on one now." That was the truth. If Breccan wasn't seeing to the cottages, he would be with the horses or the mill or some new scheme hatching in his mind.

Her uncle looked down his nose at her. "Laird Breccan is an ugly man."

"He is not," Tara said. "He has strong features, but I find him the most remarkable of any man I know." And she spoke the truth. Looking around those milling about after the service, she thought Breccan far more handsome than any man here. His face had character.

"You might need eye spectacles," Uncle Richard replied.

"Perhaps my vision is better than yours," she returned evenly in a tone that would have made a duchess proud.

She was saved from more of this conversation by Reverend Kinnion's approach. "My lady," he said, "it is good to see you." He took the hand she offered and scrutinized her a moment. "Marriage agrees with you," he said.

Again, Tara plastered on her smile. "How nice of you to say so."

"Seriously," he emphasized, and took a step closer. "I had my doubts for you that night. I know the laird fairly well. I admire what he is doing."

"As I do myself," Tara agreed, hoping Sabrina and Uncle Richard were paying attention so that she would hear Breccan praised.

"But the largest difference is in yourself," the Reverend Kinnion said. "There is a new maturity about you. This is good. I look for this in the brides I marry. It is a sign that the marriage agrees with you."

It took all of Tara's willpower to not burst into tears. "Thank you, sir," she said, then excused herself. One of Wolfstone's stable lads waited with the pony cart she'd driven over. She now climbed into it, gave a jaunty wave of her hand to no one in particular, and drove home.

Sunday would be a day of rest for most people, except Breccan. She heard that he was doing some work in a far field. For a second, she was tempted to go after him, but then decided she could not do that. She'd gone to him. She'd humbled herself to him—and he had rejected her.

This was her third rejection by a man in the last two months, but this one wrenched her heart. The famed Helen of London seemed to be a Scottish crone in the valley.

Tara promised herself that she would not wallow in self-pity. If Breccan wanted her, he was going to have to crawl on his knees. And until then, she was done with men. They had become too difficult to understand. They were mercurial creatures prone to lunacy.

That evening, she escaped to her room as soon as possible.

The light of a full moon poured in through the bedroom window. She thought about closing the drapes but decided she liked the room filled with silvery light. She climbed into bed, then, needing company, went to the door to fetch Daphne from the pile of dogs on the landing. If Breccan didn't want to grace her bed, she would fill it one way or another.

But when she opened the door, she found Breccan there, preparing to knock.

For a long moment, they took each other's measure, then Tara slammed the door in his face as hard as she could.

And it felt good. It gave her a bit of her own back. How *dare* he knock at her door? How dare he appear now after she'd spent the day doing nothing but thinking of him?

But then the handle turned, and her husband walked into the bedroom.

Chapter Seventeen

$\mathscr{B}$reccan stepped into the room and held up his hands as if to show her he meant no harm. He shut the door with his shoulder.

But Tara wasn't feeling forgiving. "What? Do you need your clothes? Your shaving strop?" She crossed her arms tightly against her chest.

It was actually hard for her to speak. Her chest was tight with not just anger but also hurt, pain.

How did one overcome the sadness he'd brought to her?

And even though she tried to hold herself together, to keep her pride intact, what she was feeling must have shown on her face.

He raked his hair with one hand before saying, "Tara, I'm sorry."

She nodded. Anything she might have said would have been cruel, mean. Now that he was here, she wanted to strike out.

Instead, she pivoted on her heel and walked across the room, placing the bed between them. "Go about your business and leave," she said, sitting with her back to him. Indeed, it hurt to look at him. She wanted to detest him . . . but she didn't.

She loved him.

He'd won her heart. He was all that was noble and brave.

Breccan had also changed her. London no longer held any appeal. At Wolfstone, she could see her that life had meaning.

She could feel him watching her. She doubled the hands in her lap into fists, her nails biting the palms. She wished he'd say something, then immediately feared what he might say. What if he had come to tell her to leave?

"I have a story," he said.

To the devil with his stories.

"This one is about a troll. Do you know what trolls are?"

Tara didn't answer. Instead, she closed her eyes

as if she could make herself stop hearing him.

"Well, they are ugly creatures," he continued. "They come from the north. Some are small and some are tall. They aren't handsome. Each of them might have a good heart, but first you'd have to look past their big noses and awkward bodies. And being that way, well, it causes them to be a bit defensive."

"A bit?" The words just snapped out of her.

There was a beat of silence where Tara could see him smile. "More than a bit."

She nodded. That was better. She opened her eyes, focusing on the corner closest to her. When she'd first arrived here, there had been dog hair in the corner. She'd cleaned it with her bare hands. After all, this was their room. Their haven.

"This one troll," he continued, "he was conscious, perhaps more than the others, of being unhandsome. He felt slighted, and it colored the way he saw others. He also admired things that were lovely to behold. He thought that if he had children, he didn't want them to be trolls. He wanted to save them from being mocked."

"You can't save people from what others think," Tara said tartly. "Small minds can niggle on any detail."

"Aye, that is true. But the troll did not know that. Trolls aren't always wise. He looked at the world beyond his reach and wanted to be part of it. He wanted his children to feel as if they could go anywhere, do anything."

The mattress gave as he sat down upon it.

She tried not to think of his coming closer. Then she would have a decision to make—whether or not to trust him. She might be better off alone. Loneness would save her from living with someone judging her and constantly finding her lacking.

"So, this troll dreamed of winning the hand of a beautiful—" He paused as if searching for a word.

"Selkie?" she suggested.

"Yes, a beautiful selkie with blue eyes."

"What if her eyes were brown or green," Tara challenged.

"Or red," he acknowledged. "He just wanted her beauty. He also wanted everyone to see her on his arm; and then they wouldn't think him a troll. They might believe he was a man of merit."

Tara looked over her shoulder. Breccan was stretched out on his side, his hand propping his head up. "Shall I mention small minds again?" she asked.

Breccan waved a dismissive hand. "It wouldn't matter. Trolls don't think deeply."

"Some do."

"No, see that is where you are wrong," he assured her. "They fool you into believing that they consider their words, but trolls can act in capricious ways."

"This is unfortunate for them."

"Aye. But trolls are not perfect. Sometimes they don't think clearly."

Tara studied the pattern of the counterpane in the silver moonlight before ordering, "Go on."

"This troll tricked the selkie into marrying him. She had a father that did not take care of his debts, and the troll took advantage of that. He was willing to take advantage of many things because he wanted the selkie in a very bad way. Trolls can be selfish in that way. They can walk over anything for what they want. Even people."

She pulled her knees up, her heels on the bed. She wrapped her hands around her legs, listening.

"However, this troll discovered that selkies have minds of their own. A pretty face doesn't mean she can't think."

"Selkies aren't perfect," she pointed out.

"No," he agreed. "But it makes it difficult for a

troll when he realizes that what he married wasn't some mythical creature but a human one. And then, he starts thinking about his own faults, his own pride. Trolls have great pride."

"So do selkies."

Breccan smiled. "Perhaps trolls and selkies have more in common than what they thought."

"Perhaps." She unfolded her legs and faced him. "I'm not going to make this easy for you, Breccan. If this is an apology, I want to hear it."

The smile left his face. He sat up. She realized he was in his stocking feet. She wondered, distractedly, where his boots were. And then his hand tilted her chin up so she could meet his eye.

"You are right. This is one time a story can't help. I felt a disappointment, Tara, and I took it out on you. I realize I was unfair."

"What were you disappointed about?"

He searched her face, then said, "Nothing. It no longer matters."

"But it did at one time."

Breccan reached out and touched her hair. His hand rested on her shoulder. "Not really. The fear was in me."

Tara hesitated, uncertain, yet she had to ask, "And what do you fear?"

"Being hurt. I was born to love you, lass, and I had to learn that it was all right if you hurt me."

For a second, she couldn't speak. "You love me?" Gratitude overwhelmed her. He cared. He *loved* her. This remarkable man had just, in his own way, declared himself to her.

He took her choked silence for disagreement. He pulled his hand away. "I know men far better than I have declared themselves to you. I know that I'm not worthy—"

She cut him off by throwing her arms around his neck and kissing him with all she had.

Whatever words he was going to say, she swallowed, climbing into his lap.

The kiss broke only when she was forced to take a breath. Their noses were inches from each other. And was it her imagination, or were his eyes shiny with the same tears of joy that escaped from hers?

"I love you, Breccan Campbell. I love you with all the passion and depth of my being. You hurt me terribly when you wouldn't speak to me. You wouldn't even tell me what I'd done wrong, so that I could make it right."

"Tara, you didn't do anything wrong. I was a bumble-headed fool."

She nodded her agreement, but she wasn't going to let it go. Not yet.

"I would never treat you in that manner. You must promise me, you will never injure me with silence again. Shout at me, rail against me, hiss at me how angry I've made you—but no silence."

He gathered her in his arms. "No silence. Never again." He leaned to kiss her, but she pulled back.

"And trust between us? Please, Breccan. Trust me?"

She could see this request was more difficult for him, and then he said, "Aye, I trust you. You are my wife, Tara. You are my heart."

His words made her so happy, she felt she glowed with joy.

"Now," he said, a new huskiness in his tone, "where did we leave off this morning?"

She slid on his lap so that her legs straddled his hips. "We were here," she said.

He tilted back his head and laughed and she could feel that he was aroused. She was as well.

"You are such a brawny man," she said, her body moving against him with a will of its own.

His answer was to pull the hem of her night-dress, which was riding her thighs, up and over

her arms and head. He dropped it to the floor—
and she was gloriously naked.

Blushing wildly, she thought to cover herself
up but then caught herself. This was the man she
loved. She could be vulnerable with him.

"You are beautiful," he whispered. "More lovely
than any selkie, especially in the moonlight." He
cupped her breasts. His hands were warm on her
skin. "I have dreamed of these."

His touch felt good. She felt herself relax, trusting him and allowing herself to enjoy the feeling of his hands on this most sensitive of skin.
Deep within her, she experienced a tightening, a
hunger, a need.

Tara covered his hands with her own. Her nipples were tight and hard against his palm. He had
a man's hands, knowledgeable ones. She bent forward and kissed him.

He weighed her breasts, then traced the curve
of her waist to her hips. Her hair created a curtain
around their kiss. Their tongues brushed. The
kiss deepened, and suddenly they both tired of
waiting.

Breccan sat up and started undressing. Tara
helped him. It wasn't the most efficient method.
They managed to be in each other's way, and

the only negotiation was kisses . . . kisses and laughter.

*B*reccan had not thought of combining the act of love with humor. And yet, with Tara that seemed a natural combination.

She was sweetly shy and ticklish. There was also his determination to touch every inch of her body.

Unbuttoning his breeches was a challenge. First, he was ready to burst. He needed release. His body begged for it. But she almost unmanned him when she began helping with those pesky buttons. If he could have ripped his breeches off his body, he would have.

As it was, Tara would undo a button, then be too charmed by the velvety soft hardness of his erection and forget her task. It was as if she'd never seen such a thing before. She laughed when he was finally free and she could run a hand up the length of him.

Her soft laughter had the sound of joy in it.

Breccan was suddenly humbled that this lovely woman would honor him with her love. He no longer questioned her motives. He never would again. There was an honesty about Tara that no man could challenge.

He leaned her back on the bed, her glorious hair spread across the pillow. He raised himself up over her. She smiled and opened her arms to him. She was ready for him. It had not taken much, and Breccan was tired of denying himself. With one smooth thrust, he entered her—

He did not register the barrier he'd broken until she flinched in pain and tried to move away from him. He immediately understood what had happened and cursed himself a hundred times.

What a fool he had been to believe Owen.

Breccan rolled onto his back, wrapping his arms around her and carrying her with him. He held her tight so that she could not run. Her heart was racing like that of snared rabbit.

"It's all right," he whispered into her hair. He was still inside her. He could feel the tension in her body, yet she embraced him deeply. "Just relax. You are fine," he assured her.

She raised herself, her surprised eyes reflecting the moonlight from the window. "I don't like that," she said.

"I understand. It was a shock."

"Is that it? Is it over?"

Breccan tightened his hold on both her and himself. He wanted to thrust, to go deeper, but first he had to help her.

He rolled her back to the bed. He was settled between her legs. He braced his weight with his arms. "Can you trust me?" he asked.

That line of worry that marred her brow was there, but she nodded. Her hands rested on his shoulders, but they were doubled into fists.

"Will you trust me?" he repeated.

She looked into his eyes and nodded reluctantly.

"The worst is over," he promised.

"How do you know?"

His wife had the mind of a barrister. "I don't," he admitted. "But if it hurts, all you have to say is 'Breccan, stop,' and I will."

He hoped he could.

Even now it was hard to hold himself back, yet she nodded, offering the trust he had requested.

She was so tight, so deliciously hot. He could feel her deep muscles start to accommodate him as she relaxed. He prayed he knew what he was doing.

Breccan was well endowed, but his wife seemed to adjust for him. He began moving, tentatively.

He did not want to harm her again. He watched her eyes, those expressive eyes that mirrored every emotion she experienced.

Ah, but she felt good to him. People lauded his strength. Little would they know how much he had to use now to rein himself in.

Each movement took him a little deeper.

Her fists on his shoulders relaxed. She tilted her head back, changing the angle of her body to give him easier access. He kissed that neck. He lined it with kisses, then dared to bury himself to the hilt.

Tara gasped.

Breccan covered her lips with his, not wanting her to stop him. No woman had ever felt as good as Tara . . . and then she moaned softly, arching her hips, inviting him closer—and Breccan was lost.

He moved with intent now. Her precious body had no trouble accepting the length of him. It was as if she'd been made for him.

Too quickly, he reached the point where, if she'd said stop, he could not have, even if she'd shouted to the ceiling. He was driven to possess her. She was *his*. All of her.

And any child created this night would be his blood.

Tara responded to his thrusts, meeting him with a passion of her own.

Now it was Breccan who became the student. He wanted to learn how best to please her, to understand every nuance of her body and she was generous enough to teach him—

He felt her tighten. Her muscles grabbed him, pulled him.

She cried his name. Her arms were around his neck, and he held her as her body reached the pinnacle of desire. It ripped through her, tightening and moving in a way he'd never experienced from a woman before.

Breccan felt his own release. She drew out of him. And in that moment, he was completely hers. He would never let her go.

For the first time in his life, Breccan understood what it meant to "become one."

They were no longer two separate people but one joined in love.

His arms banded around her, and he gently rocked Tara, enjoying the completion of this moment. And then he whispered, "I love you. Tomorrow, I will love you more, and the next day and the next day and the next."

"Until we love each other ten thousand days

more," she suggested. She placed her hand along the side of his jaw. "So handsome," she murmured.

"I am a troll," he persisted, but she shook her head.

"You are the most handsome man I've ever known," she whispered, and he believed her.

*T*he next morning, Tara woke cradled in her husband's arms. She adored the experience and made him promise that from this day forward, she could always use him for her personal pillow.

He was happy to agree—and then they made love again.

Love. Her life now had purpose. She'd been born to love Breccan Campbell. In fact, she would happily climb to the top of any mountain and shout her love for him.

And he was not too big for her. This became a point of pride with her.

She delighted in discovering new ways to please him. In doing so, she pleased herself as well.

The first day, Breccan and Tara had not come out of the bedroom at all. They hadn't wanted to come out the second day, but the world could not be kept at bay. There was a horse race on the horizon, cottages to be repaired, and a hundred little daily chores that must be monitored.

But there was a difference now in Tara's attitude as she went about the tasks of being the Lady of Wolfstone. This estate would be her children's legacy. Indeed, she wasn't certain, but she sensed that the spark of life had taken hold within her, and she no longer had concerns for the future.

How could she have once thought that life ended when a woman married? She now saw that for those who loved, every day was a new adventure. Together, she and Breccan would build a home that would shelter not only their children but also their grandchildren's children.

Beyond their lovemaking, her favorite time of the day was becoming the aftermath, when she would lie on his chest, as satisfied and relaxed as a cat, and they would discuss their activities for the day.

They talked often of the upcoming race. Breccan confided that he had strained their finances by making the wager with Owen Campbell.

"Are you keeping Mr. Ricks away from Taurus?" she asked.

He frowned. "Why should I?"

"He is the one who put the hot nail in the shoe."

"I asked him about that. He said it was a mistake."

Tara lifted her head to look into her husband's eyes. "I do not have a good feeling for him."

"You have not been around him that often."

"Often enough." She wagged a finger at him. "And if you are going to have a canny wife, my laird," she said, broadening her accent, "then you should listen to her."

He promised her he would.

She knew he wouldn't. Breccan was loyal to the men he hired. He didn't understand that, in the horse world, men could be evil.

But she did. Ruary had told her of some of the tricks, and she endeavored to protect her husband.

Her first allies in the project were Jonas and Lachlan. They were not as trusting as Breccan. They understood Tara's concerns and lined up the right men to keep watch over the stallion.

The Thoroughbred seemed healed from the lameness. They started to exercise him again.

Tara prayed her husband's trust would not be betrayed. The horse looked good on the exercise field, but would he race? That was the question.

The race day was a clear one for November.

The route was to be from Moness House to the center of Aberfeldy. It was a wee bit over a mile, a distance Taurus should cover quickly.

Tara pinned a swatch of the Black Campbell tartan to her cape. She was proud to drive into the village beside her husband and accompanied by her kinsmen.

There was a good turnout for the race. Many people had come to witness the race between the two Campbells. Of course, whenever there has been talk and whenever money exchanged hands, well, there would always be a crowd.

Her father even put in an appearance. Tara was shocked at the condition of his clothing, and the man had obviously been tippling even though it was ten in the morning. Word had gone round that he had put a sizeable amount on Owen Campbell's horse.

She knew that Breccan was nervous. He had too much riding on this race.

Her prayer was a fervent one—please, God, let Taurus win. It would be good for the Black Campbells if they claimed victory. It would give a bit of their pride back.

Besides, as Breccan had said the night before,

no one wanted to lose to Owen Campbell. Tara could sense Breccan had a personal vendetta to beat Owen. She didn't know what it was, but she suspected it involved her.

Breccan parked the curricle in a spot with a clear view of the finish line. He was eager to see to his horse and his rider, a lad by the name of Willy. Jonas and Lachlan quickly decided to walk to the starting line where the horses and riders were gathered with him.

"You'll be all right here alone?" Breccan asked.

"I will be fine. My cousin Sabrina might come along. All will be well. Go see to Taurus."

The men walked off. Tara watched them, admiring her husband. He was such a fine and bonnie man. She felt herself lucky—

"Hello, my lady."

Tara recognized the voice immediately. She turned, and there was Ruary Jamerson, standing beside the coach.

He was a handsome man, but she found herself preferring Breccan's strong features to Ruary's perfection.

"You seem well," he said, and she sensed he was not.

"Is everything all right, Mr. Jamerson?" she

asked, trying to keep her interest formal. A crowd was growing around them. One never knew who could be listening.

"Well enough."

"I'm surprised you returned to the valley," she said. "I thought once you reached Newmarket, you would stay."

"My wife missed her family."

His wife. Jane. The woman with whom he'd eloped. The woman he had chosen over Tara.

"Well," she said, "it is good of you to think of her wishes. I'm certain you've been welcomed back to the valley."

He frowned, searched her face. They had been so close at one time. She knew there was something he wanted to say.

Tara kept her attention on her husband, talking to his rider and Mr. Ricks. But she was also aware of Ruary. She did not want him to be unhappy.

At the same time, she did want him to say, "I miss you. I should never have left you. I love you, Tara. I love you."

Chapter Eighteen

Tara experienced a moment of panic. What if people overheard him? And then she realized she had nothing to fear. Breccan knew she loved him.

In the distance, she could see her husband with his horse and his uncles . . . she adored Breccan with every breath of her being.

She looked to Ruary. "You made the right decision with me, and I thank you for it. I thought I ran away from marrying a man I had no feelings for because I loved you. And I do care for you, Ruary, but with the affection of a friend. You were kind to me at a time in my life when I needed it. And do you know, if we were both committed to each other, well, then you wouldn't have ever had Jane."

"I was confused—" he started, but Tara held up a hand to stop him.

"You were not confused. What we had was good at one time, but I love my husband."

"Breccan Campbell? The two of you are an odd couple," Ruary said in an incredulous voice.

"We are a troll and selkie," Tara agreed happily.

Ruary looked at her as if she were spouting gibberish. Her response was to let all the love she felt for Breccan shine in her smile.

Ruary took a step back and viewed her as if with new eyes. "He is a good man. I just thought he would not appeal to you."

"Perhaps he wouldn't to the woman I was in London, but then, I didn't know what I wanted. I'm happy, Ruary. Breccan and I are making a wonderful home."

At that moment, Breccan came striding back. He noticed Ruary but didn't acknowledge him. He climbed up on the curricle seat beside Tara. "Willy has Taurus in line with the others. Lachlan will stay with him. Jonas will be here on the finish line but on the other side."

"Good luck, Laird," Ruary said. "Taurus is a good horse."

"I wish you good luck working for Owen," Breccan said candidly. "You will need it."

Ruary nodded and backed off.

"He has been training Owen's horse?" Tara asked.

Breccan nodded.

"Owen will stoop at nothing," Tara said. "He probably believes Ruary knows all your tricks."

"He does. But I pray we beat the bastard's horse."

"I do as well," Tara said, slipping her glove hand in the crook of his arm.

Breccan nodded to two men passing by. "Do you feel anything for him?"

The question was not unexpected. He hadn't mentioned Ruary by name but Tara knew whom he meant. "Ruary was an important part of my life. Are you asking if I would run away to marry him again?"

"The answer is no," Breccan said. "He's a fine-looking man, but a woman such as yourself needs someone with character in your bed."

"You are right," Tara agreed. "You've spoiled me." She kissed him, right there in Aberfeldy, where all could see.

Breccan grinned his appreciation before admitting, "At one time, I believed that what was mine I kept. I would have fought any man for you. But now, I don't believe love is something you can cage and hold. I love you, my wife, too much to deny something you truly wanted."

"So you are not jealous?"

"I'm mad with it," he admitted. "But I trust you. Completely."

She leaned against him, savoring the spiciness of his shaving soap. He shaved regularly now, and someday, she would talk him into hiring a valet. But for now, she happily performed those services and more for him. They usually led to interesting outcomes.

"And I trust you," she whispered. "I always will." She sat up. "But I can't believe Ruary threw in his lot with your cousin. I've never heard anyone say a good word about him—"

A shout went up, a sign that the race was about to start. Owen Campbell's horse was a handsome dark bay. Tara was certain the horse could run.

Owen's men were also at the finish line, but a team of judges had been chosen. One of them was Tara's uncle Richard, who was also the local magistrate. He was an incorruptible man, even when family was involved—not that he approved of Tara. He'd made it clear on several occasions he thought his titled brother's daughters unruly, the worst label he could use on anyone.

There was a roar of encouragement from up the road. The race was on.

Breccan stood. The curricle rocked under his weight, and Tara said, "Go ahead. Go to the finish line."

She didn't have to suggest it twice. Like a child full of ambition, Breccan leaped out of the curricle and hurried to join Jonas.

The horses came into view. Willy and Taurus moved as one. Tara held her breath until she could see that Taurus was ahead. She stood and started yelling. She wasn't the only one. The noise was deafening.

Taurus pulled ahead even farther.

Tara had never been to a horse race before other than the early-morning exercise ones at Annefield. This was one of the most exciting events in her life. She shouted encouragement, expecting Taurus to win. He was a length ahead. What a mighty beast—!

And then he pulled up, tossing his head. He stumbled. Willy almost came off.

Owen Campbell's bay went sailing past, straight for the finish line.

Taurus limped, favoring the hoof that had suffered the injury from the hot nail.

They had pushed him too soon. Breccan had worried, and he had been right.

Tara looked for her husband in the crowd. There was much celebration. Many had won money on the race.

Breccan had run to Willy and Taurus. He was consoling the lad, who was unabashedly sobbing after losing. Even Taurus hung his head in shame.

Tara gave a boy a coin to watch the curricle, then climbed down and hurried to her husband's side.

"Willy, you rode a magnificent race," Tara said.

The lad nodded. "He was good and solid. I don't know what happened."

"It was that hot nail," Breccan said. "I knew I shouldn't have pushed him. It has thrown him off."

There was a noise by the finish line. Jonas was in a tussle with one of Owen Campbell's supporters. Lachlan had just come down the road to join them. He now sighed and moved past them to rescue Jonas from his own hot temper.

"Well," Breccan said, "let's take Taurus home." The defeat appeared to weigh heavy on his shoulders. A win would have meant a great deal to him. Tara knew that. It would have given her husband a touch of renown and acceptance he longed to have.

But something about Taurus's sudden injury didn't seem right to Tara. She'd seen the horse yesterday. He'd appeared sound. If his injury hadn't been healed, Breccan wouldn't have raced him.

"Breccan, remove the shoe."

Her husband looked at her. "I had someone other than Ricks shoe him," he said. "It is not the shoe."

"Then there is no harm in taking it off. Two hot nails, well that would mean someone deliberately sabotaged our horse. He had been running fine until he reached this point, even in practice. What happened in that race was sudden. A nail can do that."

"He started pulling shortly after the race began," Willy said. "He was running on heart most of the way."

Jonas and Lachlan approached. Jonas was muttering about "filthy Campbells." Lachlan kept a strong hand on Jonas's collar in case he decided to turn back and take up the fight again.

"Are we ready to leave?" Lachlan asked.

"Not yet," Breccan said. "Willy, run over to Sawyer the blacksmith. Ask him for a pair of shoe pullers."

The lad took off running.

People had noticed Breccan just standing with his horse. Some offered sympathy. Taurus had clearly been the better horse. Others had a few taunts to toss out, but they ran faster than Taurus when Breccan brought his icy gaze in their direction.

Willy returned. Sawyer the blacksmith came as well. He was the father of Jane, the woman who had married Ruary.

Sawyer gave a quick nod of respect to Tara, then addressed Breccan. "That was strange the way your horse pulled up hard that way. Thinking there is a problem?"

"I know he is lame," Breccan said. "I want the shoe removed."

The smithy was happy to oblige.

With the shoe off, Taurus was immediately more comfortable. "Here is your problem," Sawyer said, pointing to a nail hole in the hoof. "The nail is in wrong."

"These shoes were put on two days ago," Breccan said, "and I was there myself to watch it done."

"This nail is a new one." Sawyer held up the bent nail. It was shiny. "I'd say this nail went in today."

"But how—?" Breccan started, confused.

"*Och*, it doesn't take a moment to drive in a nail," Sawyer answered. "Someone played you dirty, Laird."

At that moment, Tara's uncle Richard Davidson, the magistrate, came walking up. He was accompanied by a party of people that included the other judges, Ruary, and a very smug Owen Campbell.

People in the crowd who had noticed the shoe being removed had sensed something was up. They moved close so that they could hear what was being said.

"Laird Breccan," Uncle Richard said. "We have a concern."

Breccan took the shoe from Sawyer and held it up. "I have a concern as well."

"Yes," Uncle Richard drawled, "but you'd be wise to hear from us first." He turned to Ruary. "We have both men here. Say your piece."

Ruary shot a glance at Owen. He frowned with distaste. "I was hired by Campbell to train his horse Bombay for this race. The horse is a good one. I have no quibble with the horse."

"Tell us with whom you do have a quibble," Uncle Richard said in his customary bored, judicial tone.

"After the race, I went to find my employer. He was over there by the Widow Bossley's house, away from everyone, with William Ricks, Laird Breccan's trainer. As I walked up, I heard Mr. Campbell tell Mr. Ricks he'd done a fine job. Ricks said he knew he had, and he wanted his payment. I saw Mr. Campbell give him money."

"I owed him money that had nothing to do with the race," Owen said. He started to walk away.

"Wait a minute," Uncle Richard ordered. "I am not done."

"I am," Owen replied belligerently, but before he could take another step, Breccan took hold of his arm. Breccan was so strong, he could have swung his cousin to the moon and Owen had no choice but to halt.

"*Take* your hands off me," Owen snapped.

"Not until you hear what the magistrate has to say, *cos*," Breccan answered. "You see, I believe you conspired with Ricks to have me default on the race."

His accusation set off an angry murmur through the crowd. The Scots enjoyed good sport, but cheaters were not to be tolerated.

"Talk to Ricks then," Mr. Campbell said. "Of course, he has left. He assumed you would give him the sack for losing the race. I saw him ride off."

"He hasn't left," Jonas said. "He's over there."

Everyone turned to see Mr. Ricks by the block, preparing to mount his horse. He hadn't noticed what was happening, but he did now. For whatever reason, he had lingered, and it would cost him dearly.

Both Jonas and Lachlan went running to stop him. However, it was Ian, the tenant who had been felled by the beam in the cottage who was close enough to grab Ricks's horse. The trainer could no longer escape.

Rough hands pulled the horse master from his mount. They practically carried him to stand before Uncle Richard.

"What is happening here?" Mr. Ricks asked.

"Breccan is a sorry loser," Owen bit out.

The blacksmith held up Taurus's shoe for all to see. "This shoe was tampered with. A bad nail was driven into the horse's hoof. He ran well because he has a good heart, but even the best of them would have to give up with this sort of pain."

Jonas whooped for joy. "What do you say now, Owen?" he demanded. "*You* rigged the race in your favor."

"I did nothing of the sort," Owen answered.

Uncle Richard addressed Sawyer. "Can you prove that nail was put in there today? Or that Mr. Ricks had a hand in mischief?"

"I can't," Sawyer said.

Uncle Richard spoke to Ruary. "Can you testify with complete certainty that the money you saw pass hands was because of any deed on Mr. Ricks's part?"

"No, sir."

A smile spread across Owen's face. "Then I win. I'll take my money."

"Not so quickly," Uncle Richard said. "We are the judges of this race. Give us a moment." He turned to confer with the other judges.

Owen proceeded to complain loudly about the unfairness of these accusations. Breccan stood quiet. Even Jonas kept his mouth shut.

Tara could have warned Owen that one did not push her uncle Richard.

At last, the judges reached a decision.

There was a huge crowd around them now. The fate of the wager rested on this decision.

"We have decided," Uncle Richard said, "that there is good cause to believe someone tampered with Laird Breccan's horse. The race is declared void. All money returns to the original owners."

Owen practically stamped his feet in fury. "This is unfair."

Uncle Richard was unmoved. "Then run the race again, but you'll need to wait until Laird Breccan's horse heals."

"And you will need another trainer," Ruary said. "I'll not work with the likes of you."

"Perhaps Mr. Ricks will work with you," Breccan suggested.

"I believe I'm going to leave," Mr. Ricks said, and marched purposefully to his waiting horse.

"I won the race," Owen Campbell said.

Breccan took his money, which one of the judges offered him, and said, "I don't care about the race any longer, Owen." He hooked his arm in Tara's. "If you have the better horse, fine. If you don't, that is fine as well. My sense of purpose is no longer wrapped around this nonsense." He started to lead Tara away, but then noticed Jamerson. "You are a good man. Do you want to work with me again, Jamerson?"

"I would like that," Ruary answered.

"See me on the morrow." Breccan guided Tara back to their vehicle, and, once there, they had to hug each other in relief. "It would have been nice to have taken Owen's money," he confessed, "but this is as good."

Tara laughingly agreed.

He helped her into the curricle and climbed in after her. With a snap of the reins, they started for home.

Home. The word filled her with warmth.

Tara placed her hand on her husband's thigh.

This was the life she wanted. *One life; one love.*

She'd never felt so at peace or complete . . . except for a still debated matter—

"You know, Breccan, if we did knock out that wall between our bedroom and the sitting room, we could have a nice nursery."

There was a beat of silence while laughter filled his eyes.

"Aye," he agreed. "Anything for you, love. Anything for you."

Don't miss the next book in the

Brides of Wishmore

series by *New York Times*
bestselling author

CATHY MAXWELL!

Read on for a sneak peek at

The Groom Says Yes

Available in print and
ebook from Avon Books
October 2014!

The Groom Says Yes

She wasn't alone.

Sabrina Davidson went still. The low-ceilinged shepherd's hut, or bothy, was eerily quiet. *Too* quiet.

The sound of her own breathing roared in her ears. She swallowed and held her breath, wanting to know why she sensed danger.

She should not be here. She should not have lost her temper and stormed off from the Women's Quarterly Meeting at the kirk. Of course, she didn't know if anyone had noticed her leaving. The ladies had all been too involved in exclaiming over the Widow Bossley's announcement that Sabrina's father, Mr. Richard Davidson, the local magistrate, had made her an offer of marriage, and Sabrina had known nothing about it. She hadn't even known her father was keeping company with *any* woman of his acquaintance let alone the most notorious widow in the valley.

What could he have been thinking? *And why*?

Her father didn't need a new wife. Sabrina's mother had just recently died—well, it had been over a year, but he still wore his black armband. He had declared to Sabrina he would never remarry and that, as his sole daughter, her role was to care for him in his old age as she had tended her mother in the long years of her illness.

While Sabrina's friends and cousins had attended valley socials and been courted, she had dutifully sat by her mother's bedside. As marriages were announced and children born, her only activities had involved her parents' wishes or charitable duties around the parish. She had performed her tasks humbly. She'd resigned herself to her spinsterhood. She had accepted that her lot in life was to be a helpmate to an important man like her father. She'd told herself she was happy.

And she'd thought she was—until the Widow Bossley had upended her life with her news, right there in front of everyone who was anyone in the valley.

Sabrina had charged away as soon as she could leave without drawing notice. She'd bypassed her pony cart, needing fresh air and exercise to quell the riot of her emotions. She'd walked up Kenmore Hill, heading out onto the moor, to a place where she could breath, where she could think, and rant, and yell, and even curse without prying eyes.

This was all so humiliating.

Her father was not a demonstrative person, but Sabrina had always believed he respected and valued her. Now she realized he thought of her as little more than a servant. She was only a daughter, a being inferior to his sons, who were out in the world *living full lives*.

And what could she do now? She was trapped. She was too old to marry. She'd never had a gentleman caller. They had all been interested in her beautiful cousins and other girls who didn't have a sick mother and an overbearing father. Girls who could flirt and dance and laugh and didn't have the weight of the world upon their shoulders.

Sabrina had ducked into the bothy before she'd started screaming her frustration and rage. Even here on the lonely hillside, one must be careful of appearances. The habit was deeply ingrained in her.

The hut was two small rooms practically built into the hillside. It was an unassuming building, one meant to offer only the most rudimentary shelter, and could have been easily overlooked from the road. She'd quickly marched right to the farthest corner of the second room, ready to unleash her fury over an unjust, uncaring world, when she'd had the first inkling she was not alone.

She slowly turned toward the doorway, her eyes scanning the close quarters of the room as if someone lingered in a corner ready to pounce upon her. In those tense seconds, every story she'd ever heard of robbery and murder ignited her imagination. As the magistrate's daughter, she'd heard more than her share.

However, all was still. She was alone.

A bird chirped from outside, and then there was the flapping of wings against a shabby thatched roof that appeared ready to cave in at any moment.

Sabrina released her breath. "A bird. How silly of me." She raised her hands to her head, resting the heels of her palms against her temples as she struggled with good sense. This was silly. She was must return to the kirk. She shouldn't have walked off. She'd been gone at least thirty minutes and her absence would be noted.

Besides, she had to return to collect her pony cart. And her coat. Her gloves. Her hat.

She'd probably meet the Widow Bossley when she went back. That was the way of such matters. One always ran into the person she'd most like to avoid. Sabrina did not want to talk to her.

However, she had more than a few choice words for her father, words she didn't know if she had the courage to speak. Anything that threatened to come out of her mouth right now would be very angry, and her father was not the sort to respond well to questions.

She lowered her hands. She didn't like scenes. She prided herself on being unflappable, but the members of the Women's Quarterly Meeting were shrewd. They never missed a trick, and many would know she'd been surprised by the Widow Bossley's news. Gossip would fly through the valley, and Sabrina's pride did not like the idea. Still, she needed to keep her chin up. Her pride demanded it.

With a resolute sigh, Sabrina started to walk

into the bothy's outer room when a strong hand reached out from the side of the door and clamped down on her wrist.

Sabrina's scream was cut short as her body was forcibly whirled around and slammed into the rough stone wall hard enough to knock the wind from her.

A man leaned against her, a huge man with broad shoulders and a jaw covered with several days' growth of beard. "What are you doing here?" he demanded, his voice a guttural sound. His eyes burned with menace. His breath was hot.

Sabrina stuttered, unable to make a word come out. His body weight was hot and heavy upon her.

The man studied her a moment as if trying to read her soul. His face was feverishly flush, his expression grim—and just when she expected him to put his hands around her neck, he stepped back. Sabrina was so surprised by his abrupt move, she started to slide down the wall to the ground, her knees almost too weak to hold her weight.

"*Go,*" he ground out. "But don't tell anyone you saw me. Do you understand? Not a word." He was Irish. She could hear it in his voice.

Sabrina shook her head, so thankfully relieved

he was offering her freedom she would have promised him anything. She pushed off the wall and stumbled toward the door.

The man watched her. She could feel his eyes, and then she heard him crash to the ground.

She should have kept running.

She didn't.

Sabrina turned. He was sprawled out, face down. Sweat dampened his dark hair into curls around his brow. He wore a soldier's uniform . . . and he was younger than her first impression. He was close to her age of eight and twenty.

He was also very ill. She realized that now. He had appeared feverish because he was.

A wise woman would have run out the door. Sabrina didn't. She had a gift for healing. Hours spent tending her mother had given her training. She sensed that if she left this man the way he was, he would die.

Sabrina took a step toward him, and then another.

He did not move.

She knelt beside him and felt his brow. His skin was on fire. "You need help, sir," she said. She glanced around the room and noticed a pallet in the room's dark corner. If she hadn't been so wrapped up in her own thoughts, she would have noticed it when she first entered the bothy.

"I need to take you to a doctor," she continued, weighing her options. He was too big a man for her to carry or drag. "I will go for help."

She started to rise but then his hand reached out and grabbed her leg around the ankle. He may have been ill but his grip was strong. She teetered.

He looked up at her. His eyes were blue, like two sharp pieces of stained glass. "No," he managed, his breathing heavy. "Can't let anyone know I'm here." There was a beat of silence and then he whispered, "Please." He dropped his head back to the stone floor and let go of her ankle.

Sabrina danced backwards. The man had closed those disconcerting eyes. They had a power about them. "You will die without help," she warned him.

He didn't answer. He'd lost consciousness.

She knew she should make her escape. She should tell Reverend Kinnion that the man was here. The reverend would know what to do. He'd probably organize a party of men from around the Kenmore Inn.

Or she could tell her father. Magistrates always knew what to do.

But the Irishman didn't want anyone to know he was here, and he might have a very good reason. She should fetch help . . . but she wouldn't. There had been desperation in that single word "Please."

Sabrina was not intuitive. She believed in what she could see, touch, and reason. Even her acceptance of the Almighty was sometimes challenged by those of a more superstitious nature.

However, in this moment, she made a decision to honor the Irishman's request, and she could not say why other than it was something she felt she must do.

Sabrina began coaxing him back to his pallet. His body was a dead weight so she gave up and picked up the heavy wool coat that served as his bed and placed it over him. A hat, a black leather tricorn favored by soldiers, was his pillow.

He needed good broth and a poultice of herbs, although it could be too late. He was very ill.

Sabrina spun on her heel and charged out the door, filled with a purpose that gave wings to her step. Her father would not approve of her tending a strange man. The gossip in the valley would fly if the Women's Quarterly Meeting had any idea what she planned, but she had no intention of sharing information about this man.

For the first time in her memory, Sabrina felt engaged in life. She had purpose.

Besides, her father had kept secrets about the Widow Bossley from her.

Well, now she had a secret to keep from him.